SLOW TURN

SLOW TURN

Mike Marqusee

LONDON
MICHAEL JOSEPH

First published in Great Britain by Michael Joseph Ltd
27 Wrights Lane, London W8

British Library Cataloguing in Publication Data

Marqusee, Mike
Slow turn.
I. Title
813'.54[F] PS3563.A7/

ISBN 0 7181 2734 X

Filmset in Great Britain by Alacrity Phototypesetters,
Banwell Castle, Weston-super-Mare
Printed and bound by
Billing & Sons, London and Worcester

It isn't the googly itself, it's the thought of it. No matter how well set the batsman – his eyes locked to the ball in flight, his feet moving rhythmically into place – if fear of the googly has taken root in his mind batting becomes an ordeal. Of course, facing up to a big fast bowler careering full tilt down the pitch bent on knocking over your stumps or your head can be pretty terrifying. And to the casual spectator, the slow, lazy arc of the leg-spinner, preceded by a gentle canter of four or five paces, might seem like child's play. But if a leg-spinner with a googly finds a pitch to his taste, and can strike that precisely tantalising length time after time, the batsman will need more than mere physical courage to withstand the torment.

In cricket parlance, a googly is an off-break disguised as a leg-break. Imagine a batsman standing at the crease to receive the leg-spinner's normal delivery. He sees the ball emerge from the back of the bowler's hand and follows it through the air until it lands in front of him and turns away. The turn may be slight, no more than a fractional deviation, but in itself it's more than enough to make the most experienced batsman think twice. More dreaded than the simple leg-break, however, is the leg-spinner's secret weapon, his rapier hidden but ready to strike at a moment's notice, the googly. Again the batsman follows the ball through the air. Again it lands in front of him, only this time, contrary to all expectations, contrary to all appearances, it turns the other way. No forewarning, no hint in the bowler's action, in the movement through the air, in the line or length – just that split-second turn into the right-hander's body, leaving him with bat outstretched, lunging, more often than not, at thin air. From then on there can be no security for the batsman, no peace of mind. He has seen the ball turn the wrong way, and the slower the turn the more painful it is to watch it roll onto your stumps.

The googly has been called a conjuror's trick, a rabbit drawn from a hat, an egg produced from behind an ear. And like magicians, the best leg-spinners with the most perfectly disguised googlies have carefully guarded the tricks of their trade. They have remained inscrutable. For one does not have to bowl the googly very often to use it effectively. The problem for the batsman is that it may happen at any time; and therefore appearances are not to be trusted and one must proceed with caution.

CHAPTER ONE

In Madras the umpire was murdered and it made us all uneasy. If this was the sort of place where umpires got murdered, then what chance had a handful of foreign cricketers? And without an umpire, who would enforce the rules? Who would give people out or let them stay in?

The real stars – the current England side – were in the West Indies, battling speed, skill, and an incredible run of injuries. Meanwhile fourteen of us had been flown to India to play a series of exhibition matches, courtesy of the Commercial Trust Bank of Southern India, our sponsors. We were a motley crew. Some were on their way up, or hoped to be, like Mark Kidleigh, the fast bowling sensation from the Home Counties, already a Test prospect to some eager journalists; others, ex-Test players and old county pros, like our wicket-keeper, Ernie Fairbanks, were on their way down, however they might try to deny it.

I was one of the latter. D T Stott – Dave, DTS in the dressing room – left-handed bat, ten years in county cricket, no Test appearances, once considered promising, as promising as young Kidleigh. In the blind eagerness of my first season I had knocked up a couple of quick tons and my photo appeared in more than one Fleet Street rag. Exactly how I made the transition from might-be to has-been remains a mystery. The big scores grew rare. Season after season I slipped down the order. Last summer I was in and out of the side, and when I did play I batted at number seven and the best I could do was a patchy twenty-eight. In the autumn my county club released me. I was thirty years old.

When Dougie Fraser, the tour manager, asked me to go to India, I said yes quickly enough. My divorce had come through. I had no other prospect of a winter job. Indeed I had no prospect of any job at all. I knew next to nothing about India, except that it was always considered the toughest overseas tour for any English cricketer. But it was a last chance to play cricket for money before venturing into the real world – the non-cricketing world – in pursuit of a means to live.

According to the Commercial Trust Bank the purpose of the tour was 'to encourage contact between English and Indian cricket in a convivial and uncompetitive atmosphere,' and while we were at it, to promote the Bank's new deal with one of the large English clearing houses. Goings-on in the sponsor's tent often attracted more attention than goings-on between the wickets. From the moment we landed in Delhi Indian businessmen swarmed around us. At receptions and dinners the conversation swung comfortably between cricket (and they knew a great deal more about the sport than their counterparts back home) and credits, loans, import and export licences, gross and net profits, all expressed in *lakhs* and *crores* (100,000 and 10,000,000, as I later discovered) instantly converted with the aid of pocket calculators (which seemed to have flooded the country in recent months) into sterling, dollars, Deutschmarks, even roubles. It was the kind of tour you read about in the back pages of cricket magazines, where they run two sentences on the cricket and twelve on the staggering mountain view from the pavilion and the sumptuous hospitality of the local supporters. For cricketers hard-pressed to find winter employment, it was a godsend.

For Dougie Fraser it was my last big chance. He had coached me at school and then brought me to the county second eleven he ran in the summer. He had emerged from twenty years of near anonymity on the county circuit with a seemingly limitless store of cricket nous and a power to mould young players. A restless character, much to the chagrin of his long-suffering wife, he had rarely stayed with one county for more than a few seasons. Still, wherever he had gone he had made his discoveries. Kidleigh was the latest. A genuine quickie, Dougie assured me, just what the England side had been looking for all these years. But still green, still just a damn fast kid, not yet a Test bowler. Dougie wanted to nurture him, to use the slow Indian wickets (and the absence of the English press) to prepare him for the arduous months of a full county season. He wanted me along, he said, as a 'steadying influence'.

I laughed. There was a time when that was the last thing he would have called me.

'But you've mellowed, lad.'

'You mean I've gone to rot.'

This annoyed him. My failure to fulfil my early promise was, I suspect, a greater frustration to him than to me. My making light of it showed a fundamentally unhealthy attitude towards the game. If I hit form on this tour, Dougie insisted, I might well pick up a contract for next summer. He was already making enquiries on my behalf.

I said I appreciated the favour.

'It's no favour. We need all the talent and experience we can get. Anyway, you were one of the few players Robin and I could agree on.'

I was surprised that Robin Barnett, the tour captain, even knew who I was. We'd played against each other often enough (once I caught him, fast and low, at point) but we'd never spoken. Of course, like everyone else, I knew about Robin. One of the masters of modern batsmanship, the nearly-man of the English Test captaincy, aloof and patrician, he had toured India with England sides in the past and enjoyed immense success on and off the field. In fact he had been born in India and received his early schooling there before his parents returned to England in the years after Independence in 1947. From a public school in the West Country he went on to Cambridge, where he became one of the most successful Varsity batsmen of all time. He ended up captain for his last two years and was already touted as a future leader of England.

He established himself early as a Test player, scoring a meticulous century on his debut, and was rarely out of the side after that. He was a complete strokemaker with a straight bat and an erect stance that came to seem old-fashioned in his time on the county circuit. He stood statue-still at the wicket, tall and lean, almost gaunt in his later years. His footwork was deliberate and his demeanour unnaturally calm. He was one of the few stars who could lure people away from their television sets into the grounds. He had a habit of matching the big crowd or big occasion with a big innings, though some complained he spoiled these feats with his air of *noblesse oblige*. Hardly a cricketer in the counties would begrudge his tactical acumen and few would have cared to compare it to that displayed by any of the various England captains he had served in his fifteen years of Test cricket.

He was seen early on as the natural successor to the captaincy and conducted himself as heir apparent. The problem was that there was no longer any natural succession and the vagaries of cricket politics being what they are he never succeeded to what he – and many others – felt was his entitlement. Every time there was a vacancy he would be mentioned, and every time passed over. There was always someone in line ahead of him. At first it was unlucky injuries or temporary loss of form which denied him. Gradually it became clear he was disliked, and not just by the old guard of the Test and County Cricket Board. He was a lonely figure, apparently indifferent to affection or friendship, determinedly unmarried. To some, his deliberation was condescension and his confidence arrogance. His finicky cricket lectures reminded people that he had started off at Cambridge as a theology student, before switching to law. Besides cricket his only interests seemed to be his golf handicap (minimal) and his stocks and shares. It was rumoured that his shrewd investments had made him a rich man. He was less ostentatious about it than some younger stars, but it came out in his hand-tailored clothes, detailed knowledge of wines and spirits, and his fastidious and costly diet. In India he paid for a private weekly shipment of smoked oysters from England.

He was said to pack a copy of the *FT* in his cricket bag and players often sought his advice on how best to invest their hard-earned benefit-year lucre. (And after a summer slog of exhibition matches, wine and cheese parties, discos, croquet, and country fêtes, you want to make damn sure you reap a full return on capital.) People in the game came to respect him as a class cricketer, a top mind, and not a bad bloke, if a bit on the strange side; but they were disinclined to be led by him. Year after year the captaincy slipped from his grasp. Among the young Test players he was regarded as a master from a former era. Isolated, he staked out a corner in the England dressing room and kept himself to himself.

He kept making centuries in his text-book manner, battling bad pitches and staring down hesitating, incompetent umpires. On several overseas tours he alone emerged with any credit. Throughout he maintained a flawless self-control, whatever his disappointments.

Until three years ago.

It was the last England tour of India. They were getting nowhere on slow pitches and a varied if uninspired attack was having no luck against a solid batting line-up. Barnett made a long, slow, chanceless hundred-and-fifty. After the match he indicated to journalists that there was little point in making a good score when 'tactical naivety' and poor field placings meant the runs would be cancelled out in two sessions of play. The story caused a storm. One does not criticise an England captain in the middle of a Test series – especially if one is playing under him. Robin's seniority and undeniable talent – plus the uncomfortable consensus that what he said was true – only made it worse. He was publicly reprimanded by the tour management and received a telegram from Lord's, contents undisclosed but easy to guess. Whatever he thought then he kept to himself.

In the next Test England worked their way from a solid start to an irretrievable losing position. Throughout the match Robin appeared to be offering the captain advice, though it was impossible to tell whether it was being followed or not. Suddenly, in a fit of pique, Robin turned away from the proceedings with a look of disgust and marched off the field. The crowd was stunned. The captain called for a substitute. Next day the photo was in all the papers: one of those brilliant sports photos that sums up a whole complex of events. Low angle, from the side of the field, Robin staring icily ahead, while behind him the England players, Indian batsmen, and umpires stand helpless with open mouths.

He was suspended from the series and flown home in disgrace. He refused to comment in India, he refused to comment at Heathrow, and had kept his silence ever since. Even after the suspension was served and the fine paid he was not selected. No captain or prospective captain could tolerate his presence in the dressing room. His Test career was over.

Securing his services as captain was a coup for the Commercial Trust Bank. His presence gave the squad a status that the combined credentials of the rest of us, for all our years on the county circuit, could never match. And Robin had a following of his own in India. His early years there and his interest in Indian history and what they called his 'pukkah sahib' bearing: it was all fodder for the Indian press. In the past he had played some of his best innings in the country, and despite the incident on his last visit, he was regarded as charming and affable – something which baffled his critics in England, to whom he had always appeared remorselessly dour and distant.

He had his first argument with Dougie somewhere over Iran on the flight to Delhi. Dougie, a fussy, stammering northerner who could be as stubborn as Robin in his own way, whispered in my ear that he would arrange for me to room with young Kidleigh, presumably in order for me to exercise my 'steadying influence'. I made no argument. Dougie was clearly my sponsor on this tour and I had resolved to place myself in his hands. It was the least I owed him. But Robin vetoed the scheme. I watched the two of them standing in front of the aeroplane, obstructing the stewardesses, heatedly disagreeing. Both were used to being listened to and neither was used to being told what to do. Robin had a good six inches on Dougie and stared implacably over his bald head, ignoring his fierce gesticulations. Eventually Dougie gave up and slumped wearily in the seat next to mine.

'He won't have it, Davey. Says as the youngest member of the touring party with the least experience, Kidleigh should room with the senior professional, and that's him. I don't like it but there it is. You'll have to share with me.'

I was relieved. I had been watching Kidleigh since we left Heathrow and didn't like the look of him at all. He might be quick of arm but he was definitely slow of brain. He had been harassing the youngest and prettiest of the stewardesses non-stop.

Dougie was unhappy. 'If he thinks the whole tour is going to be his little show he's much mistaken, I don't mind telling you. I've not come to India to take orders from Robin Barnett.'

I had my doubts. Hadn't he already lost the first tussle?

'Why's he so keen on sharing with Kidleigh, anyway? Doesn't seem much of an honour to me,' I said.

'Wants to impose his authority, show who's boss. He knows Kidleigh's a good prospect and wants him for himself.' He sat hunched over in his seat, muttering. I had to laugh.

'You're jealous!'

'Get off with you!' He wriggled uncomfortably. 'And I want no nonsense from you on this tour. Any shenanigans and you're out of the side. We didn't bring the extra batsman for nought. And you'll get to bed of a decent hour at night.'

'I promise, Dougie,' I swore sincerely, suppressing my mirth.

We climbed down the stairway at Delhi airport to an official reception on the tarmac. The heat hit me like a mallet. The air smelt like a stale greengrocer's and it was heavy to breathe. I had heard about Indian cricket mania, but this was my first experience of it. Photographers, journalists, television cameras jostled to get near us and were only restrained by well-built turbanned Sikhs in airport security uniforms. It was a dizzying scene. I hung at the back of the touring party with Dougie while Robin took the limelight.

We were welcomed to India by an official of the Commercial Trust Bank, a Mr Narayan, who, in a florid speech worthy of an old-fashioned public school valedictory, assured us of the goodwill of all Indian cricketers and indeed all Indian people, who he knew would receive us into their hearts and who of course would recognise the enormous contribution of the Bank to the welfare of Indian and indeed world cricket. As he reeled off the phrases – the international fellowship of sport, the special relationship between India and England, the honour of receiving a team led by the illustrious Robin Barnett – I could feel the heat from the black, sticky runway burning through my trainers and warming the soles of my feet.

Narayan was a man of medium height whose large stomach and thick neck and shoulders gave him a dominating air. He was dressed in a grey western-style suit, heavily bejewelled with rings and bracelets, and he spread his arms about generously as he spoke. A few cursory photos were snapped, but the real barage came when Robin stepped forward. The throng leapt and shoved against one another, angling for the best set-up and urging Robin to move this way or that, stand closer to Narayan, then closer to the players, then somewhere off on his own. I knew Robin was news here, but surely this was a bit out of hand? Dougie shook his head in disapproval. Robin managed to comply with the photographers' requests while giving the impression of not hearing them at all. He shook hands with Narayan and the other be-suited members of the welcoming committee. He made a brief speech thanking all the appropriate people, expressing the team's excitement at the prospects for the tour, and of course, on a personal note, his own delight in returning to India, the land of his birth. He ended, surprisingly, by introducing the tour manager, 'Mr Doug Fraser,' whom he was sure was well known to them all for his many contributions to English cricket. Nonplussed, Dougie stepped gingerly forward, nodded his head once, then hid himself again among the players.

I think it was the heat and my impatience for a cup of tea that made me miss the first few questions. It soon became apparent, however, that something was bothering the sweaty, eager reporters. I tuned into the exchange, trying to forget the temperature and the glare off the runway.

'But Mr Barnett, surely you have other plans in mind, other counties?'

'I can't answer any questions on this matter, gentlemen. The whole affair is under negotiation.'

'But reports from England . . .'

'How big a rise are you seeking?'

'Is it true you're considering retirement?'

'Will you play for another county?'

'Will you play abroad?'

Robin demurred like impatient but ever polite royalty.

'I'm sorry, but you know perfectly well it would be most inappropriate for me to comment at this stage.'

'Mr Barnett, what value do you place on loyalty?'

Robin shot an angry glance at the questioner.

'A great deal of value, sir. And I can assure your readers, and most important of all those who pay to watch cricket and thereby keep the game alive, that my loyalty is to them first and foremost. Any decisions I might make in the future will be on that basis and that basis alone.'

'Did I miss something?' I asked Dougie as he paced the runway and looked at his watch.

'No more than the rest of us,' he snarled.

It turned out that while we were dozing on the plane the morning editions of the British press had carried a small report: BARNETT IN CONTRACT DISPUTE WITH COUNTY CLUB, etc. It was just a rumour at the moment, but it had the makings of a big story. Robin had served his one and only county club for over twenty years, the last ten of them as captain. He earned considerably more from them than most county cricketers could ever hope to make, and it was said he had the committee in the palm of his hand. It was a puzzling development, especially on the first day of a seven-week tour of India.

On the coach that took us from the airport to the hotel in Delhi, Robin said nothing. But as he reclined in the high-backed seat and opened his *Financial Times* he wore the air of a man highly satisfied with his morning's work.

CHAPTER TWO

Soon after we landed in Delhi we began to see reports in the Indian press of disturbances in Madras. An 'unofficial strike' in a car assembly plant had led to rioting in the streets, injuries, and a curfew. Police action was tough, but central government condemned local politicians for failing to maintain 'productivity and discipline' in the state. We only noticed the articles because Madras was the final stop on our tour, our last and most important match. The Bank was sponsoring a specially selected South Indian XI to play us over five days in Chepauk Stadium. Perhaps it was the prospect of facing Chaughiri, the deadly leg-spinner, on a made-to-measure wicket that frightened the players as much as the stories of barricades in the streets and the hellfire rhetoric of politicians. Nonetheless, Robin took it upon himself to reassure us.

'These things happen in India,' he said in that professorial voice which was so well known and so widely mimicked. 'Sometimes they just need a release. Violence in a society like this is inevitable. But I have received assurances from the sponsors that the situation will be well under control by the time we reach Madras.'

Mr Narayan was at pains to set us at ease. The reports in the Delhi and Bombay press were much exaggerated. The state administration was more than capable of guaranteeing law and order, and our safety in particular.

Robin took me aside early in the tour.

'It's a marvellous country, David. Marvellous people. Only a fool would miss the chance to see it.'

To begin with we saw most of it from the tinted windows of our hired, air-conditioned coach. On both flanks red, white, and blue letters spelt out: 'Commercial Trust Bank of Southern India English Cricket XI.' The coach came complete with a remarkable driver, a Sikh in purple turban (or rather *patka*, as Robin corrected me) named Kushwant. He was a cricket fanatic who claimed to bowl leg-cutters at will, and certainly a resourceful, if unnerving, driver. Any impediment to our coach's progress – bullock cart, broken down lorry, old beggars or little children –

he regarded as an insult to his illustrious passengers and acted accordingly. Our trip was punctuated with shouting matches, and in more than one town near riots as Kushwant leaned on his hooter and tried to blast his way through dense crowds.

Our hotels were westernised but hardly luxurious. The players said you could always trust a bank to pinch pennies, or in this case rupees. Whenever and wherever we arrived there was chaos and delay, but invariably we were treated as honoured guests. Some of the players moaned, as cricketers will, about sheets or ceiling fans or food. But Robin was a model of patience. Not that he didn't ask for and get precisely what he wanted. But he rarely raised his voice and never sank into the frustrated whine which ran like a motif through most of our dealings with Indian clerks, porters and waiters. Our social life had been entirely organised by the sponsors. There was an endless round of receptions, tea parties and promotional events, at which Mr Narayan tended to pop up with a display of back-slapping and effusive concern for our comfort and health.

'You must attend to diet while you are in India,' he advised Dougie. 'Eat peanuts for protein and bananas for potassium.'

He was clearly pleased with the publicity arising from Robin's protracted negotiations with his county club. It was, in fact, generating a lot more interest than the quality of our cricket. We played one-day and three-day matches at a bewildering succession of venues against variable opponents: North Indian Railways XI, Madhya Pradesh President's Select, Ranji Trophy sides in Nagpur and Vijayawada, Indian Universities in Allahabad. The pitches were dry, brown and nearly grassless. The nets might have football-sized holes and divots popping out on a length, but young Indians surrounded them and vied fiercely for the honour of bowling long hops and half volleys at us. Often we were asked to act as arbiters in angry debates over who was or was not the fastest bowler, the quickest cover, the sharpest keeper. The crowds at the matches were staggering. Twenty thousand people might turn up for a mid-week exhibition match that would draw two hundred in England. For middle-rank cricketers like us it was a strange sensation. You couldn't help feeling a bit of a fraud.

For Alan Cowper, an aspiring opening bat who had joined the tour after barely missing out on a cricket scholarship to Australia, his first exposure to an Indian crowd was simply too daunting. He palpably froze at the crease, hardly daring a stroke of any kind for forty minutes. Eventually he was talked out of it by his fellow opener, Paul Walker, a slim, slow-scoring veteran whose single Test appearance ten years ago had left him sour and sardonic. I asked Paul how he'd loosened the youngster up and he replied with a lopsided grin that made him look almost malicious, 'I told him all the crowd wanted was for one of us to get out so they could see the great Robin Barnett do his stuff and that if he didn't play a few shots soon I'd have to sacrifice my wicket in the interests of public relations.'

Young Cowper, who stayed in until he had compiled a respectable thirty, later denied the story.

'It was the noise,' he said. 'I couldn't hear myself think.'

'A blessing for some, I should say,' chipped in Ernie Fairbanks, and proceeded to grip Cowper's close-cropped head in a powerful armlock. Walker said Ernie should have been a professional wrestler, not a cricketer.

'Just the right mentality,' he added, then dodged out of the way of the wicket-keeper's enraged charge across the dressing room.

Our form was poor. Even our lowliest opponents knocked over at least half our wickets. Of course the motivation was all on their side. An ambitious teenager took sixty-five off us one morning in Nandad, and the next day in the local press he was a Test prospect. There was a dull, desultory mood in the dressing room. Complaints about the food (which I liked) and the accommodation, obsession with bowels, fascination with Indian women and how they wore their saris, English cricket gossip – the same topics came round and round again and nothing seemed to change and no one seemed to care. We were trounced by a second-rate side somewhere in central India and at tea that evening no one said a word.

Robin seemed determined to lead by example and nothing else. His own form was the magic exception. He hit a century in Allahabad before the vast crowd and took fifties in both innings off the best attack we faced in Nagpur. His performance seemed to be fuelled by the running battle with his county back home. Meanwhile, in the dressing room he was winning few friends. He barked out the batting order and fielding positions with clipped precision and brooked no dissent. He could wither with a glance. If he was dissatisfied he would adopt the professional athlete's argot – obscenities, mockery, derision – with weirdly pedantic exactitude. A blast of his 'You've fucked that up now, haven't you?' would send a shiver down your spine.

Kidleigh took ill shortly after we left Delhi and missed match after match as we made our way south. His groans as he raced for the toilet would shake hotel corridors. Personally I found it hard to work up much sympathy for the child prodigy, but Dougie was beside himself. He hinted darkly that Robin was responsible. 'Feeding the lad on that quack diet of his.' He was no happier with me. I was giving my wicket away with bad shots and my timing was pathetic. I had quickly slipped from the rigours of Dougie's training schedule and was chronically late for nets. All my good resolutions had evaporated in the Indian sun.

At least out here no one besides Dougie seemed to mind whether I made one or one hundred. For years my guilty secret was that I just didn't seem to care enough. My increasingly frequent bad patches depressed me, but not as much as I thought they should, and the commiseration and advice offered by players and coaches only made me feel more guilty about it. My indifference, I knew, had driven my wife to distraction and ultimately to divorce.

My biggest sin in Dougie's eyes was not my bad net habits or low scores but my sightseeing with Robin. He had taken me aside and suggested a visit to Fatehpur Sikhri, an abandoned Mogul city outside Agra. Of course he had seen all the famous sights many times already, but going with me gave him a chance to display his knowledge of Indian history and his mastery of the strange nomenclature of Indian architecture. *Diwan-i-am, diwan-i-khas, hawa mahal, grand durbar, stupa, torana, gopuram* – he ran through them with ease. It was a chance for me to observe him at close quarters: his military firmness with taxi drivers and wayward guides, his spotless garb no matter how dirty or dusty the surroundings, his love of an audience (me), and his nostalgia for the days of the British Raj.

'You know, David,' he confided to me during an expedition to the great fort at Gwalior, 'Churchill said that the loss of India would reduce England to a minor power, and how right he was. Still, remarkable that a little nation like England could come to rule an entire sub-continent.'

He was an admirer of the Moguls, their splendid open-air palaces with cool streams channelled through marble halls, their warrior's courage and command.

'Strange, don't you think, that all India's great rulers have come from without – the Aryans, the Moguls, the British.'

Our sightseeing was a joke with the other players, who laughed and nudged each other when we returned, weary and dry-throated, from another excursion to yet another fort, temple, or palace.

'It's the tourists, is it?' said Ernie, grinning from ear to ear. 'See any dancing girls?' His hands made the rapid, phantom stumping motions which they seemed to perform of their own accord whenever his mind was elsewhere.

'I know what DTS is after,' said Geoff Robinson, our much-travelled off-spinner. 'It's those erotic sculptures they've got hidden away.'

'No, it's never that,' Paul Walker threw in, then winked at me. 'He's buttering up the skipper.'

Robin was not amused. 'It would do none of you any harm to absorb a little of the culture of the land you are being paid to visit. It is precisely this sort of opportunity which is one of the few compensations of professional cricket.'

Every morning he took a long session in whatever nets were available. After Dougie he was the oldest man on tour and undoubtedly the fittest. While Kidleigh lay in bed in agony he would perform his morning ritual – a mixed regimen of yoga and air force manual. Everywhere he was asked about his county contract and his plans for the future. His replies were polite yet utterly evasive. In England his county committee was getting desperate. They claimed they had made every possible effort to comply with his demands. Robin, for his part, insisted all negotiations were being handled by his agent in London. In the evening he would often spend up to an hour in private phone conversation. Behind his back, speculation was rife. How much was he asking for? How many more years did he want? What perks? Was he holding out for another benefit? (He'd enjoyed a record success with his last one five years ago.) Despite the general conviction among us that it was the duty of every cricketer to squeeze as much as possible out of his committee, it was felt that this time Robin had gone too far.

'When he was a Test player he was the super-patriot,' Paul Walker observed. 'Now all he cares about is money.'

Dougie disagreed. 'It's not money he's after. He does it just to string them along. Likes to feel his power over them. Even out here. Likes to feel it at a distance.'

While we followed Robin's battles on the sports pages, we kept an eye firmly on the front page and developments in Madras. The 'unofficial strike' had turned into a lock-out by management. Workers were accused of intimidating managers by what the newspapers referred to as a *gherao*, the precise meaning of which I couldn't determine. Fits of alarm would run through the squad, always firmly suppressed by the captain.

'They know how to deal with this sort of thing here,' he insisted, with a palpable contempt for their anxieties.

I took to reading the Indian papers. (And what papers!) Unfathomable (to me) analyses of labyrinthine political faction-fights, features on astrology, urinology, cow protection, holy men, movie stars, endless rumours of defection, old alliances broken, new ones formed, and a steady stream of reports of corruption in both high places and low. Cricket coverage was thorough, to say the least, and usually the part of the paper I could best understand. The other players thought me a strange sight as I ignored Kushwant's capers behind the wheel and buried myself in *The Statesman*, *The Indian Express*, *The Hindustani Times*, or any of a dozen other English language papers which are certainly a better bargain for the reader than what we get back home. Their teasing didn't bother me. In my old county dressing room I had been a notorious newspaper reader and as a result it was assumed I was well informed on world affairs. I suppose compared to most cricketers I was. But really I liked the papers because they were an escape, a refuge from the repetitive slog of professional cricket.

'What's to become of you, Davey?' Dougie appealed to me one night in our hotel room. 'Gallivanting round a load of ruins with his lordship won't get you a contract next year.'

I tried to soothe him. I promised to re-apply myself. But my batting grew even more indifferent and I was dropped from the side for a one-day match in Hyderabad. While the others were sweating out a narrow victory I wandered off on my own, exploring India for the first time without Robin's guidance.

Hyderabad is the Muslim capital of central India. My first stop was an enormous mosque, which my guide assured me could accommodate over ten thousand worshippers. Next to it was a magnificant triumphal arch. On Robin's recommendation I climbed to the top to enjoy the view. The city was laid out beneath me like a multi-coloured Persian carpet, only here the patterns were alive, made up of moving streams of humanity. I descended the arch and on an impulse plunged into the bazaar. I passed row upon row of stalls selling fruits and vegetables and silks and spices. The thoroughfares were choked with cabs, rickshaws, horse-drawn carts, cows, people. I looked into narrow lanes packed with stark, hungry-looking people, young and old, who jostled me, crying for rupees, rupees, rupees. How did Robin cope with these people? I couldn't remember.

Further on I walked along the outskirts of what appeared to be a huge tent city. God knows how many families had made their homes there under scraps of plastic, matted reeds, tattered canvas. Children ran up to me, eyes streaming, red with sores, limbs so slight you thought you could break them like twigs. Everyone knows about poverty in India. Everyone's heard of the beggars and untouchables and people sleeping in the streets. But it's surprising how easy it is in an air-conditioned coach, driven by an amiable Sikh, meeting Indians only at pre-scheduled engagements, how easy it is not really to see it, not really to feel it.

I took the first cab I could find out of there, out of sight of the tent city and its miserable inhabitants. On my return to the hotel Robin asked me what I'd made of the mosque and the view from the arch. I told him about the tent city and the sick children.

'Ah, but this is India,' he told me. 'All that is accepted here. It's part of their tradition. It's been that way for thousands of years. We couldn't change it and as far as I can see neither can they.'

The next day the paper ran yet another story on the crisis in Madras. The headline ran: PRESIDENT'S RULE FOR TAMIL NADU? It began, 'The Central Government in Delhi today warned that any further deterioration in the public order situation in Madras would force them to actively consider the removal of the State Ministry and the imposition of direct rule from Delhi . . .'

CHAPTER THREE

My first glimpse of Madras was a dark, dusty square at two in the morning. I had dozed off somewhere east of Bangalore and despite numerous jolting halts for animals or train crossings I had slept soundly enough. Tomorrow was a rest day before our big match at Chepauk and the players were lured from the coach by the prospect of a long lie-in the next morning. Dougie ushered us off, one by one, like sleepy children. Buses and coaches were parked every which way in the square and threaded among them were tea and snack stalls, each with a noisy little knot of customers. Because of a traffic problem which Kushwant vainly tried to explain we had to walk to our hotel. It was only a few minutes away but the players grumbled as they followed the two cartloads overflowing with luggage pulled by a team of waif-like young boys. They wore white cotton cloths tied round the waist which exposed their legs from the thigh down.

'Lungis,' Robin explained as we walked side by side through the streets, which even at this hour were busy with people carrying and loading things. 'It's a different world down here, David. Different dress, different food, different language, different culture. Very ancient. Dravidian. The original Indian culture, before even the Aryans came. We must hire a car and drive to Madurai while we're here. See the temples. Tremendous things, tall as skyscrapers and painted in the most lurid colours.'

We reached our hotel. It looked more like the Brighton Metropole than anything to do with 'Dravidian culture'. Despite the hour a small circle of reporters awaited our arrival in the hotel lobby. Kidleigh, deathly pale and unrecognisable as the speed merchant with the 'whip-like' action, trudged past muttering about 'bleeding useless foreign roads'. I made to follow him towards the lift, an old-fashioned one encaged in an iron grille, when without warning Robin pulled me to his side. For whatever reason, I did not resist.

Before I knew it he had introduced me to the reporters as 'one of England's many under-rated batsmen'. They showed little interest and persisted in their habitual litany: would Robin sign the new contract, why was he delaying, would he consider playing under another captain? He raised a hand – his large but refined slip-catcher's hand – and signalled for silence.

'Good professionals like Dave Stott are the backbone of the game, whatever committee-men back home like to think.'

Paul and Ernie walked by giving me mock salutes. The bemused reporters seemed stricken dumb. Was it as embarrassing for them as it was for me?

'Mr Stott,' one of them ventured at last, 'you will be playing in the match at Chepauk?'

'That's up to Mr Fraser,' I answered.

Now it was Dougie's turn to be eulogised. 'One of the unsung brains of cricket . . . a back-room genius . . . should have been a selector long ago.'

I slipped from Robin's grasp and took the lift to the room I was sharing with Dougie. He was already busy unpacking and hadn't heard a word of the praise Robin had lavished on him downstairs. It was just as well: he would have been furious. Whatever neglect Dougie might have suffered, whatever resentments he harboured, he maintained a perfect loyalty to the powers-that-be and a stubborn belief in holding one's tongue in public.

He stood in his underwear scrubbing himself at the basin and griping about the lack of hot water.

'And what am I going to do about Kidleigh?' he asked himself aloud, addressing the craggy, sunburnt face in the mirror. 'Hardly touched his food in days.'

I was suddenly very weary of Dougie's complaints. And it annoyed me that he still kept himself awake at night worrying about a minor match at the end of a long, fruitless tour.

'I'll just see if I can't get something to drink downstairs,' I said. 'I'll come straight back, promise.'

'If you want to play at Chepauk you damn well better.'

The reporters had abandoned the lobby by now. With its old chandeliers, ceiling fans, darkened woodwork, and cracking plaster it took on an empty look of faded elegance. I opened a door only to find a vacant lounge with a snooker table in the middle. Retreating to the lobby I asked the clerk at the desk if I could get a cup of tea.

'Cup of tea,' he said brightly. 'This way.'

He showed me into a large, dark room. After a moment's grappling he found the switch and when the lights came on I was standing amidst round tables covered with starched white linen.

'Sit down, sit down, sir. I will get the boy.'

He disappeared into the kitchen and after some angry shouting a young boy of no more than twelve wearing a baggy white shirt and patched trousers arrived to take my order. In a slow, deliberate voice that reminded me, disconcertingly, of Robin's, I demanded tea, toast, and jam (I had found this a good antidote to excesses of spicy food). When the toast arrived (the tea came later, for no apparent reason), I spread the butter and jam from the plastic pots (the same rubbish we have in England) and chewed my first mouthful with care, savouring the bland melting butter and textureless toast.

Two westerners entered noisily, Robin and another man, a stranger. He was middle-aged and stout, with a bright sunburnt nose carrying all before him. A tweed hunting cap perched on the back of his head.

'Ah, David, we'll join you.'

This was the last thing I wanted. I had been annoyed with Robin before, and his unwanted intrusion on a rare moment of privacy made me snap.

'Whatever game you're playing with the press I'd appreciate it if you left me out.'

'I'm sorry I offended you,' he said, the corners of his mouth forming just a hint of a smile. 'I'm sure you're right. It is just a game. But don't fool yourself. It's your game as much as mine. And you won't get far unless you're prepared to play it.'

'I think I'll stick to cricket.'

'Well, you haven't got very far with that, have you?' His face was static. It had the weird effect of blunting the immediate impact of the cutting remark while making it slice that much deeper.

Before I could respond he introduced me to his companion.

'David, this is Roy Cuthbert,' he paused meaningfully. 'A name you'll know.'

It rang a bell but it wasn't until Robin mentioned a famous first-division football club that I could place it. Roy Cuthbert: press baron from the East Midlands, self-made millionaire, who a few years ago had waged a desperate campaign to buy a controlling interest in one of the nation's oldest footballing institutions. For a while the papers were full of it: ROY TO BUY HIS ROVERS... CUTHBERT COUGHS UP. In the end the football league closed ranks and backed off. There was something about Cuthbert that made him unacceptable as an owner of what was described as part of our national heritage, like Blenheim Palace or the Boat Race. Apart from that, his chief notoriety had been won by his success in breaking a printers' strike by bussing in non-union workers under the protection of armed security guards.

'I've already told you about David,' Robin said to Cuthbert, who gave me a friendly nod.

What had he told him? What was there to tell?

'I thought you were a football fan, Mr Cuthbert,' I said.

He smiled benignly and took off his cap, laying it gently in front of him on the table. 'I'll tell you what, I'm a bloke who loves sport. Cricket. Football. Tennis. Golf. Never a player, mind you, wasn't cut out for that. But a fan, certainly.'

'And one with the interests of the game at heart,' Robin added.

'You're not going to tell me you've come all the way to India to watch this pathetic little tour on its last legs?' I tried to laugh.

Robin adopted his listening pose, hands laid before him, head held high and back. It made me think of a split personality – half passive, neutral, observant, the other half incisive, calculating, hidden.

'It's lucky us meeting this way, when it's quiet,' Cuthbert said, 'because Robin and I have been discussing something we want to share with you.' He talked as if we were old friends. 'I don't know how you'll react to it and of course that is completely up to you. But I would very much like to take you into confidence for a moment.'

I stared blankly.

'In other words,' Robin clarified, 'if we're to talk about certain things it will have to be strictly between ourselves.'

'Of course.' It came out spontaneously. Why of course? What were they on about? The boy waiter brought my tea and Robin ordered two more.

Cuthbert began. 'I'm an outsider, I know, but it seems to me one of the things people say about cricket these days is that it's in a state of crisis. It's a commonplace and like a lot of commonplaces it's more true than people realise. I don't want to go into all the reasons for it but I think you'll agree – every other cricketer I've spoken to has – the game today has more than its share of problems. But on the other hand it also seems to me people love cricket as much as they ever did, maybe more. Maybe they need it more now than they ever did. They love their football, I know, and they love their football heroes, but cricket is closest to their hearts. And through one thing and another they don't get to see as much of it as they want – or when they want it and where they want it. Above all they don't get to see the players doing what they want them to do. People want style, originality. It's the individuals that thrill the punters, believe me. That's why they'll always pay to see Robin bat, whatever Lord's may think.'

I nodded neutrally and sneaked a look at Robin. He stared over my head and far away and yet I felt him closer to me than ever before, not an entirely pleasant sensation.

'It's my belief,' Cuthbert began again, as if rehearsing an appeal, 'that there are many people – cricketers of all descriptions – frustrated, stymied, pissed off. Fed up with their personal lives, because they can't earn the kind of money they deserve, and fed up with their cricket lives, because they can't play the kind of cricket they want to play, the game the fans are crying out for them to play. An open, exciting, freewheeling cricket that would pack the grounds time and again. And why do you think that is?'

The question was rhetorical. I knew I only had to sit back and wait for the answer.

'Monopoly,' he pronounced, decisively. 'British Telecom, the Post Office, the BBC, you name it – bureaucratic, inefficient, conservative monopolies that can't and won't deliver what the public wants. The TCCB, the ICC, the MCC, the whole incestuous Lord's set-up – they're a monopoly, and they're worse than the others because they've got an international franchise and they reach out and strangle the game not just in England but all over the world.'

I looked again at Robin and this time he returned my gaze. 'Yes, David, it's true,' he said softly. 'When you've travelled like I have you see it clearly. The same faces. The same control. The same deadly hand.'

'But how do you challenge it?' Cuthbert resumed, leaning forward, his stomach pressing and folding over the edge of the table. 'How do you break a monopoly? How do you make it act in the public interest? There's only one way. There's always been one way: competition. Reform from within is a waste of time. Believe me, I've tried it.'

There was silence as the tea was served. The boy set before us a perfect, matching tea set, the like of which you'd expect to find in Fortnum's. Deftly, Robin poured each of us a cup, then refilled the pot with hot water from the jug.

The boy sat on a high stool in the corner and let his head fall on to his narrow chest. In a moment he was asleep.

'Is this all right to drink?' Cuthbert looked anxiously at Robin, who was calmly stirring his tea.

'Not to worry, Roy, the water in Madras is chemically treated. Anyway, it's all been boiled up for so long it must be safe. Of course I don't touch the milk, but then I never do. Not even in New Zealand.'

Cuthbert decided he too would do without milk. I slopped an extra drop in mine just for the contrast.

'If you're thinking of doing a Kerry Packer in England, Mr Cuthbert, with all due respect, you're mad.'

Cuthbert laughed. It was a laugh of self-confidence. It was the laugh of a man who'd made a million before he was forty.

'No, Dave, not a Packer deal – at least not in Packer's style. Packer was after his television rights and nothing more. Once he'd settled that, his series collapsed and his players returned to the fold, cap in hand. But he showed what could be done. He showed that traditional cricket was vulnerable. The old monopoly is on its last legs. And since Packer everything is different.'

Robin himself had never gone over to Packer, though many thought he would. It was said he'd turned down an astronomical offer when Packer refused to guarantee him the captaincy of his rebel 'England' side. Greig had been Packer's recruiting officer then, just as Boycott had been for South African Breweries. Was Robin set to do the same for Cuthbert?

'My intention is to take up where Packer left off. Only this time there'll be a commitment behind it. I've made it to Robin and to all the other players and I'm making it to you. I intend to see this thing through. Next summer there'll be a new cricket league in England, and I'll back it – financially, politically, legally – for as long as it takes. We're going to call it "Grand Prix Cricket".'

Cuthbert beamed like a proud, middle-aged father. Robin sipped his tea, staring over the rim of his cup into the blank space behind me.

'That's why you haven't signed yet?' I said to him. 'That's the reason for all the phony delay?'

'You have a choice.' Robin set his cup down, pulled in his chair and pushed his face close to mine. 'All cricketers have a choice. You can remain a serf, like the rest, serving the county gentry, playing out your time waiting for your benefit. Or you can exploit your talent, which is the only asset you've got, and seize the opportunities which come your way.'

Without waiting for a reply Robin outlined their plan for 'Grand Prix Cricket'. They would set up teams based in each major English city. Each team would consist of half local and half foreign players. They would stage matches on converted football pitches, as the TCCB were certain to ban them from the old grounds. There were, in any case, plenty of football clubs eager for the extra revenue. They would hold a one-day knockout cup and a simplified four-day league, with each side playing once against every other side. With time they hoped to establish a two-division structure, with the added drama of promotion and relegation to spice up the season.

'You see,' Cuthbert interrupted, 'the punters get what they want: a local team to support and identify with that's still packed with stars. And half-way through the summer we'll organise an old-fashioned north versus south match, like the all-star games in American baseball.'

A stranger might have taken Cuthbert, with his down-to-earth enthusiasm, for the professional athlete, and Robin, with his frozen logic, for the successful businessman.

They had all the details at their fingertips – the teams, the league, the grounds. I was taken aback. Was it really possible for all this to be plotted in secret? And divulged over tea in a hotel restaurant in Madras? Then I remembered the secrecy that had surrounded other attempts to out manoeuvre the cricket authorities, and how often people had been caught on the hop in the past.

'And television?' I asked, determined to fire the probing question.

'That's no problem,' Robin assured me.

But Cuthbert wasn't so definite. 'I've received promises. Once the cricket monopoly is blown the television monopoly will follow. I can't go into specifics, but I've had discussions and there's more than sufficient interest, I can say that. When did you ever know the telly not to cover an event if there are enough big names involved, no matter who's boycotting it? If we get the players we'll get the coverage, and the extra sponsorship money that comes with it. At Lord's they take the sponsors' cash and expect them to be grateful for the privilege of financing the great game. We'll offer more. Each local team will seek sponsorship and be encouraged to promote it when their matches are televised.'

'And there'll be no problem with coverage in the local press,' I offered.

'As you say.' Cuthbert was not in the least ashamed of his power. Robin, I thought, might have been more delicate.

'And players?' I asked. Surely that was the key. With bans and suspensions and fines hanging over their heads, most players would think twice before committing themselves to an experiment like this.

But this too, they insisted, was no obstacle. The counties were seething with disquieted players worried about their futures, as I had reason to know. As for the big stars, it was simply a question of money. This, they assured me, would be available in quantity.

'And not just from me,' Cuthbert explained, 'though of course my own pockets are open as far as Grand Prix Cricket is concerned. But there are others who prefer a back-seat role, but when the time comes they will be just as supportive. What's important is that the whole venture is properly capitalised from the start and I've been making arrangements to ensure this.'

I had a vision of the two of them caught in a press photo and the captions that would be devised for it . . . ROY TO BUY ROBIN HIS NEST . . . NEW MONEY BUYS OLD BOY . . . SVENGALI AND TRILBY . . . Only which was which? The scheme was crazy, it seemed to me, and yet here were Robin and Cuthbert, two men of experience who should know better, backing it to the hilt. What disturbed me was how easy it was for them to counter my every objection. Grounds, sponsors, even umpires – it was all arranged. Robin reeled off a list of top cricketers whom he claimed were already committed to Grand Prix Cricket. I could hardly believe it. Yet I knew Robin was no daydreamer. He was a man to consider all the options with great care and caution. And Cuthbert? Could it be mere folly on his part, like those gothic castles built by nineteenth-century tycoons to give themselves the semblance of an ancient patrimony? There are certainly plenty of businessmen around prepared to take some heady risks in pursuit of sporting immortality. (I've met more than one wealthy fan who swore he'd trade it all in for a single line in Wisden.) But it struck me that this kind of fantasy was not in Cuthbert's line. As an investment, he would take Grand Prix Cricket as seriously as any other.

'We have the capital. We have the market. We have the labour,' he said, with pointed sobriety, despite the late hour.

I felt the need to counter-attack. 'What about Lord's, Test matches, old county loyalties, all the traditions that tie people to cricket? You don't expect people to forget all that?'

And soaring county deficits? Players on the dole half the year? Empty stands on Monday afternoons? Disappearing sponsors? Grounds turned into leisure centres? Competition from tennis, athletics, snooker? And politics, politics, politics, disrupting, interfering, suspending play more often than the rain?

Their answers hailed down on me. Suddenly the old cricket structure seemed ready to crumble around my ears.

'It's vulnerable,' Cuthbert repeated, stabbing the table-cloth with a pudgy index finger. 'It just needs a last push, and it'll fall apart at the seams. Where money can be made, money will be made. That's why I know Grand Prix Cricket will work. You can't turn the clock back, not in history or economics or cricket. It's all a question of eliminating the interference. There'll be cricket – more cricket and better cricket. A better deal all around.'

'And Test matches?' I asked weakly.

'We can provide them.'

Cuthbert made the last point with an even greater display of confidence than before. I sat in silence. It was now very late, or rather early. There were sounds of morning outside: bullock carts creaking and clopping, whips and shouts; a rattling and clanking of metal pots from the kitchen. The boy slumbered, perched precariously on his stool. The remains of the tea were cold. I knew they had more to say to me. I only had to wait for it.

'Of course some vestiges of the old game will survive,' Cuthbert ruminated. It was not his intention, and certainly not Robin's, to destroy; only to revive, to spur, to develop. Of course he wanted to make money. He didn't deny it and didn't see why anyone else should be embarrassed by it.

'Least of all you, Dave.'

I stared at the coarse black leaves soaking in the bottom of my cup. It was true. Everything they said was true. Why should I deny it? What interest could possibly make me stand shoulder to shoulder with the Moguls of the cricket establishment, safely ensconced in their clubhouses while the rest of us faced cold economic reality for the meagre reward of earning a living doing 'something you enjoy'. And there's a limit to how much you can enjoy a weekday afternoon spent chasing balls round an enormous field under the blank gaze of pensioners, dogs and little kids.

They made me an offer. During our conversation I had gradually become aware of it, lurking behind all their words. When they spelled it out I wasn't surprised. A one-year contract with an option for two more and an assurance that if Grand Prix Cricket was the kind of success they expected there would always be a job for me in it. They were choosing their pioneers with great care and intended to reward them handsomely.

And then there was the money. The figure they quoted was far in excess of anything I could ever earn in county cricket. It only increased the weird sense of unreality hovering over the scene.

'Why me?' I had to ask. 'I know I'm an easy target with no other prospects, but I'm not the only one. Why me?'

'Because,' answered Cuthbert, 'you're precisely what we're talking about. I know your potential. Robin's told me. What happened to it all? We need players like you just as much as we need big names. You're nobody's stooge and you owe Lord's nothing.'

'And you know Siva Ramachandran,' Robin added languidly.

I looked at Cuthbert. 'Yes,' he said, 'you know Siva.'

It was true. Ten years ago we'd played together. As beginners at the same county club, we had become good friends, different as we were. That was before he became a superstar. He was an all-rounder of terrific power and flair who'd vied for the captaincy of his country only to be denied it, like Robin, but for other reasons. In India he was more than a cricketer. He was a pin-up, a playboy, a cavalier adored by his compatriots. And now, according to the paper, he was also an aspiring politician.

'We need Siva,' Robin said. 'We need his talent. We need his charisma. We need his authority.'

'If Siva comes in, others will follow,' Cuthbert added.

I hadn't seen Siva in several years, not since the Indian Test side last toured England. And I had been in two minds about whether to call him on this visit. Yet Cuthbert and Robin were right. To get to Siva I was probably their best bet. Despite everything, I still regarded him as a good friend, and I was pretty sure he felt the same about me. A strange friend for a lowly county batsman? Yes and no. Siva wasn't always famous, and our lives back then, in a basement flat in a provincial English market town, had been less than glamorous. That was a memory we had always shared, and laughed about when we met in years afterwards. We didn't meet often, true. But whenever our paths crossed we made a point of getting together, out of earshot of the press and other cricketers, and reviewing what had happened to us and where we thought we were going next. As it became more apparent that our career trajectories were quite opposite – his rising, and mine falling – our meetings did become a little embarrassing, though more for him than me. I had always known he was talented, and more important, because of all our late-night talks and hours stuck in traffic driving from one ground to another, I knew he had something more than talent. He had this wild ambition, this quiet pride that brooked no obstacles. Others saw just the politeness, the educated charm, the modesty. I saw the fire, and I think Siva always felt close to me because of that. He knew I didn't resent his success.

I was half-pleased now that Robin and Cuthbert had offered me an excuse to call him. Had the two of them somehow known that I wanted this excuse, like they seemed to know about so many other things? I felt like a fish wriggling in a net. Somehow I'd agreed to this whole scheme without ever saying yes. Was this how deals were made in Cuthbert's world? Did they lure you into the house and then shut the doors and windows one by one?

I shook myself. Of course I had a choice. It was the lateness of the hour, the strangeness of the surroundings that made me feel trapped.

'Why don't you approach him yourself?'

'I think you'd be more effective,' Robin replied. 'You're rather convincing, David. No one could imagine you putting undue pressure on anyone.'

'And if the press were to get wind of a meeting between Robin and Siva, well, you can imagine the stories. At the moment secrecy is paramount.'

Cuthbert looked at me with small, round, baby's eyes that gave away nothing.

'I know we can rely on you.'

How could he be so sure?

The two of them persisted for a while with their arguments,

their certainties, leading me gently down the golden path of Grand Prix Cricket. I did not resist. Why should I? This tour of India had been the last throw of the dice. Perhaps what had always been in store for me was not a return to county cricket but an entirely new departure. Dougie would not approve, but did that really matter? I was risking nothing. If Grand Prix Cricket ended up the biggest flop in sporting history, well, it would only be one more duck to add into my average. Without ever saying yes, though certainly without saying no, or anything like it, I found I had agreed to take on their mission. I would talk to Siva. I would sign up for the new league that would revolutionise modern cricket. Perhaps that had been obvious to Cuthbert and Robin all along. They had correctly assessed my options even before I knew them. In the early morning light I left the two conspirators and made my way wearily to the ancient, ornate lift.

'Any chance of breakfast in this flea-trap?' I heard Cuthbert ask. 'I've had nothing but airline food today.'

As the lift carried me away I heard Robin's voice barking orders to kitchen staff.

It was some time during my conversation with Robin and Cuthbert, I later learned, that the umpire was murdered. He was attacked in his home in a street not far from our hotel, his skull speared with an old cricket stump.

CHAPTER FOUR

I woke to the sound of Dougie gargling with green mouthwash. I pretended to sleep but that didn't stop him warning me that I'd better be in the nets on time. When he left I went downstairs and asked the desk clerk for a telephone. There were none in the rooms. He shook his head from side to side, meaning yes, of course I could use the phone (Robin had already explained this South Indian mannerism to me). I called the *Madras Banner* and asked for the cricket correspondent, Gopal Srikkanth. He was a friendly character I'd run into a few times on our way south, knowledgeable and mildly amused by the antics of his fellow journalists. He was delighted to receive my call and only too pleased to provide me with Siva's phone number.

'I know you're old friends,' he said. 'Did you know that I may ghost his autobiography? Negotiations are in progress.'

I said I was sure it would sell and thanked him for the number. Then, after a deep breath, I dialled. There was shouting and mayhem on the other end of the line. Then silence for what seemed an eternity. And then, quite clearly, and somehow surprisingly, it was his voice, just as I remembered it.

'David! When did you get in? I've been waiting for your call!'

He'd been following our tour in the press and planned to attend the first day's play at Chepauk, a ground he'd graced many times with superb performances.

'I've been watching you, you know,' he said. 'Every day I look in the paper to see where they've got you playing next. My lord, what a tour!'

I said I hadn't stopped reading about him for ten years.

'As long as you don't believe everything you read!' he laughed.

In no time at all a visit was arranged. I would come and see him in his house that afternoon.

'You'll like it – very English, very colonial. And quite cool, even at midday.'

He gave me directions and advised me to let the hotel order a cab. I hung up, slightly breathless. There was a haze in my head from lack of sleep. I had taken the first step on the path Robin had laid out for me, and it had been painless.

I dashed from the hotel to the practice ground at a school not far from the ocean. It was my first daylight view of Madras and it seemed unreal. Maybe it was talking to Siva, or a hangover from my conference with Robin and Cuthbert, but the city looked broad and airy, suspended in a medium of dusty hot air. It was just as chaotic as the other cities we had seen, but somehow the chaos was less concentrated. I barely had time to take it in before the taxi let me off at the school. The driver charged me a fortune for the five-minute ride, but I had no time to argue. Dougie noticed my late arrival and gave me a dark look.

'Watch out,' Geoff Robinson warned me, flicking an old ball from hand to hand with a snap of the fingers. 'The old boy's in a temper.'

Robin stood tall in the nets, belting the ball as if he'd enjoyed the soundest of eight-hour sleeps. I padded up and took my turn after him. Speaking to Siva had left my giddy. But I found my reflexes soon enough and hit the ball cleanly all around the wicket.

The field was surrounded by an old brick wall, crumbling in places and overgrown with yellow flowering vines. Despite a few grassless patches it was as good a place as any to practise, though some players feel honour-bound to complain about facilities when abroad. As always in India, a crowd gathered to watch us. Whether they bribe the attendants or know secret entrances or just wander in, I don't know, but they're always there, and always cheerful, and always keen to bowl at the white-skinned batsmen smelling of sun-tan oil. With a few brisk commands and a wave of his long arm, Robin organised them into a queue and was soon stroking their innumerable varieties of spin and seam back down the nets at high speed.

At the far end of the field Dougie put Kidleigh through his paces, trying to correct a flaw he had detected in the young demon's action. The old man stood behind the young one, his hands shaping Kidleigh's stance, like photographer and model.

I took some practice fielding slip catches, leaping to left and right and spearing the ball one-handed. I was soon soaked with sweat. The sun stood high in the sky and the intense heat made it pointless to continue. On the way back to the hotel Dougie told me I was in the side for the big match tomorrow. He and Robin had agreed it this morning.

'I seem to be the only thing you two ever agree on.'

On Dougie's insistence Kidleigh would also be included in the side, though he hadn't been well enough to play for several weeks. For once Robin hadn't put up a fight.

Back in the hotel the morning papers carried the first news of the umpire's death. *The Banner* ran a brief front-page article. A man named Bharat Pannedimbi, who had been chosen to umpire the forthcoming match at Chepauk against the English tourists, had been found murdered in his home in the early hours of the morning. He had hoped to be elevated to the Test panel for next year's series against the Australians. His employers, the Commercial Trust Bank of Southern India, expressed sincerest condolences to his family. A new umpire would be appointed today. No motive or explanation for the killing was offered and no suspects detained.

Really it had nothing to do with us, and yet it did touch us, if only remotely, and there was nervous laughter when someone said Indians had the right idea about umpires. The news was unsettling. Why on earth would anyone kill an umpire?

'Maybe he refused to fix the match and they had him bumped off,' suggested Alan Cowper, our young opener. It got a laugh from Kidleigh but no one else.

Donald Blackburn, our token all-rounder (actually a medium pacer with few pretensions as a bat), studied the article and passed it on with a frown. 'Maybe it's got something to do with this strike business.' He thought for a moment, in the slow, serious way of his that always invited ridicule from other players. 'Or maybe it's one of those religious squabbles they have.' He scratched the day-old growth of stubble on his chin.

'And maybe it's a Russian plot to take over cricket?' Paul Walker chimed in, and this time everybody laughed.

Donald didn't mind. That was one of his values to the tour: he was a willing figure of fun. The unease left by the report of the umpire's murder – *our* umpire's murder – was soon dispelled in pulling Donald's leg. Meanwhile, I made my way casually through the lobby and into the street. I didn't want any of them to know where I was going. My visit to Siva would instantly displace the umpire's death as the talk of the dressing room and any hope of conducting my business in private would be lost.

I told myself that my real mission was to see an old friend and not simply to ferry Robin's proposal across town. After all, I hadn't yet made up my own mind about Grand Prix Cricket. And hadn't Siva said, in those bygone days in the Second XI, that I should come to his country so he could show me what he always called 'the real India'? Hadn't we imagined it all together, the two of us meeting as Test cricketers in Eden Gardens in Calcutta or Ferozeshah Kotla in Delhi? Well, I was in India now, if under somewhat different circumstances than we used to imagine, and I was paying my old mate a call.

I told myself all this, but I couldn't help feeling anxious, as if some unpleasant business was hanging over my head, this business of Robin and Cuthbert and Grand Prix Cricket.

Despite my attempts to follow the little plan of the city placed by the sponsors in our hotel rooms, I was soon hopelessly lost. The people, blacker and thinner than in the north, seemed bewildered when I asked directions. Frantically I searched for a taxi, but there were none in sight.

A bicycle ricksha driver, a young man in a T-shirt and lungi, followed me doggedly from one end of a narrow street to the other, despite my repeated insistence that I was looking for a cab. He took this as an affirmation of my need for transport in general and smilingly offered me the tatty, cloth-covered seat bouncing along behind his bicycle. People moved slowly in the midday heat, clinging to the small margins of shade provided by the plaster walls of the low buildings. I alone zigzagged back and forth until reaching a corner where, instead of the main thoroughfare I had convinced myself would be there, I found only another identical narrow street and no other landmark in sight. I turned to the ricksha driver, who smiled again and, with a wave of his hand, seemed to be urging me to accept the inevitable. I clambered on to the hard seat and read out the address Siva had given me. The driver spoke no English, not even the few useful phrases common in India, and I couldn't be sure he understood where I wanted to go. I had also neglected to agree the price before getting on, as Robin had instructed me to do before dealing with any kind of Indian transport. You get tired before you know it in that sun, and I was relieved to be off my feet and to have placed my destiny in someone else's hands.

The driver pedalled off, lurching from side to side, swinging round animals and children and exchanging curt utterances with the owner of a mule that stood in his way. He turned at last into a broad avenue lined with big shops on either side and began winding his way through the dense traffic. It was Mount Road,

Madras's elegant high street. Dust rose up and seemed to spread a silvery light over the scene. The buildings were low and fronted with light, airy arcades. There were shops with names like Piccadilly, Mayfair and Cheltenham, neatly painted in Victorian letters. In and around these relics of empire, throngs of Indians jostled among cars, lorries, rickshas and animals.

The driver encountered a slope and laboured mightily to surmount it. I could see his back muscles strain and ripple through the holes in his shirt. He stood up and leaned heavily first on one pedal and then, shifting his weight, on the other. He had long, slim calves, small knees, and strong thighs. I guessed he was twenty years old and thought of the young Siva, not unlike the ricksha driver, except that he, like all Indian cricketers, was born to a caste that would never engage in menial work.

After much bumping and boring through traffic we crossed a bridge and left the city centre behind. Shockingly, a church steeple loomed into view. Not a temple *gopuram* or a minaret or a *stupa*, but a gothic spire with a cross on top. We passed through leafy residential streets lined with grand wooden houses. Except for the dust in the air and the sight of barefoot Indians going about mysterious tasks it might have been suburban Surrey.

As we approached Siva's house the driver pointed out a group of people loitering in front of its whitewashed walls and spoke to me excitedly in Tamil. Though I didn't understand a word I involuntarily nodded in agreement. The driver couldn't have known that the great Siva lived behind these walls, but the crowd outside provoked his curiosity. He stopped and quoted me a price which I also couldn't understand. I dug into my pocket and handed over a crumpled note. It must have been more than he was expecting because he waggled his head gratefully and shouted a farewell several times as he pedalled away.

The group outside the house eyed me with interest but stood aside as I rang the bell suspended over the wrought-iron gate. They were all well dressed and two of them carried large cameras and shoulder bags bulging with lenses. Assiduous Indian journalists, I surmised, lurking here in hope of entrapping the famous cricketer in the company of a woman, preferably beautiful, rich and unmarried.

I was admitted by a small, elderly, bare-footed woman in an orange sari. She guided me through a dense garden down a curling flagstone path. There were fruit trees (I recognised mangoes, bananas, guavas), flowers and thick green shrubs. Giant purple orchids nestled in bunches of spiky yellow leaves. At the end of the path steps led to a vast wooden veranda, over which hung a red tile roof, with carved wooden insets forming arches between slender pillars.

From out of the shadows, shielding his eyes with one hand, Siva stepped forwards to greet me. He was dressed in snug white trousers with a crisp crease and a gold-embroidered, open-necked shirt. His feet were sandalled in pale new leather (buffalo and not cow, I knew, as he was a practising Hindu). His thick black hair was swept back from his forehead and between his narrow jaw and high cheekbones he flashed a cool white smile. He looked blacker than I remembered.

He embraced me warmly, asked whether I'd had any trouble finding the place, and urged me to sit down. I fell into one of the cushioned wicker armchairs on the veranda and began telling about my ricksha ride.

'How much did you pay?' he asked with concern.

I told him and he gave a yelp of horror.

'That is too much.' He shouted into the house and the old woman trotted out. They conversed rapidly in Tamil. She gestured towards the road and made an angry sound. He dismissed her with a flick of the fingers.

'Manni,' he informed me. 'She's been with me for years. She says you paid twice the going rate.'

'It doesn't matter.' The transaction appeared to have cost me all of one pound sterling extra.

'But you set a bad example for others,' Siva said.

He sank into a chair and faced me across a low table elaborately inlaid with woods of varying colours and grains. Slipping his feet out of his sandals, he folded one leg under the opposite thigh.

'I am coming to the match tomorrow. I will be sitting in the pavilion.'

'Substitute umpire and all.'

'Ah, that business.' Siva frowned. 'I knew him, vaguely.'

'Sorry, I didn't mean to . . .'

'No, no,' he grinned broadly, 'it's not important at all. What's important is seeing you again! And seeing you play, I assume.' He paused. 'You will be playing tomorrow?'

'It seems to be the only thing Robin and Dougie can agree on.'

We laughed together, the old conspiratorial laugh we hadn't

shared in years. It felt strange to share it here, in Madras, shaded from the afternoon heat by the tiled roof.

'And how is Mr Fraser?' Siva enquired with deference.

'Still trying to keep me on the straight and narrow, cricket-wise.'

'I can imagine. And Robin?' A glimmer of gentle amusement appeared in his eyes.

'Same as ever.' I was cautious.

'But in the doghouse – and out of Tests?'

'Afraid so. And this time it's for good.'

'It was inevitable. Though many here could not understand it. Robin is much admired in India despite his maddening eccentricities.'

The subject reminded me of my ulterior motive in paying this visit and I changed it. I wanted a chance to share his company again, to watch him, and to let him watch me. We talked about old times and mutual acquaintances. Siva had always been genial, but over the years he had grown more confident and comfortable with himself. When I first played with him he'd just completed two years as a boarder at an English public school and the experience had left its mark. He was scrupulously polite, but diffident, shy and easily wounded. His father, a Madras textile merchant, had dreamed of his son one day claiming a place in the Test side and even captaining his country. He had been prodded along the cricket path from an early age. But his own ambition was as strong as his father's. Those years in England were hard for Siva. Only later, after his return to India, were his ambitions fulfilled – and then spectacularly. From the moment he walked into our dressing room his talent was obvious, but somehow in those days it wasn't always there on the field. He spent long periods – often in my company – in the second eleven and found it hard to raise his game in front of the proverbial three men and a dog. I remember batting with Siva one day at a deserted ground somewhere in the West Country. One well pitched-up ball he cut with a mixture of ease and power the like of which I've never seen before or since. I could play first-class cricket for twenty years and not make a stroke like that. But there was no one there to see it, no crowd to applaud. And for Siva the emptiness was deflating. For the rest of the afternoon he struggled and played and missed like any ordinary cricketer trying to build a respectable innings and win a place in the first team.

We used to share digs then. We were both young and lonely and a bit out of place in the sweating, swearing world of county cricket. We talked to each other because, for different reasons, we both found it hard to talk to the others. He liked to talk about India, about his family, and about his plans to break into the Indian Test side and to one day rid the whole Indian cricket scene of what he called its 'dead wood'. He could be fiercely serious in those days and I liked to tease him and make him giggle, something I think he used to feel was beneath his dignity. He knew that I sensed his frustration with county cricket and this made him trust me. He tried to encourage me – he accused me of downgrading my own talent – and would happily bowl at me in the nets for hours. As for me, I admired him from the first. Not just his cricket – though that spectacle was startling enough sometimes – I admired his bearing, his idealism, his seriousness. I suddenly felt very wrong sitting on his veranda in Madras, drinking in his coffee and his affection, and waiting for an opportune moment to put Robin's proposal. Was this where my cricket career had taken me, seeking personal advantage from an old acquaintance with the rich and famous? I felt low and mean. And by contrast, Siva, with his openness and relaxed confidence, installed magnificently in his English-style mansion, looked high – well beyond my reach.

Manni trundled out with a tray loaded with coffee in a silver pot and delicate ceramic cups. She poured the coffee, stirred in two spoonfuls of sugar (which I hadn't asked for), then scurried off. Siva disregarded her entirely. The coffee was hot, rich and thick. It was from the Thekkady Hills in Kerala, he explained, and was surprisingly expensive considering it was domestically grown.

'Like all Englishmen who visit India you've been making the mistake of trying to cool yourself down with those awful fizzy concoctions. Hot and sweet, that's the secret,' he advised. 'One cup of strong coffee will quench your thirst better than five Colas.'

He asked about my wife and was genuinely sorry – though too well brought up to enquire closely – when I told him about our divorce. I didn't have to ask about his marital status, as it was a favourite subject with the Indian press.

Instead I asked him about the reporters outside.

'An occupational hazard,' he said. 'In Madras I'm followed everywhere. I expect it.'

'And they're here every day?'

'No, not always. Today they are expecting an announcement.'

'What kind of announcement?'

'You haven't heard the rumours, then?' He seemed disappointed. 'About my running for office?' He smiled with unashamed pride. 'I believe it's called going into politics.'

Siva smiled his toothy, photogenic smile, so innocent, so disarming. We both laughed. It was partly the laugh of cricketers at the outside world, at the daftness of a cricketer in politics. But it was also a nervous laugh, as if neither of us was quite sure what to say about such a strange turn of events. Still, maybe it wasn't all that strange. In India, as in America, it's not at all uncommon for film stars to enter politics. Only they and a few other celebrities can actually build up a sufficiently large following in such a huge and still mostly illiterate country. Everywhere, Siva left adoring fans in his wake. His picture hung above thousands of street stalls. Magazines never tired of featuring him in yet another dashing pose on their covers. He spoke on behalf of worthy causes, and most recently had been raising funds for Tamils in Sri Lanka, which only strengthened the devotion of his following in his native south, among his own Tamil people. They were convinced that only gross Hindi bias had prevented the selectors from naming Siva Test captain long ago. Siva himself always played down that factor.

'It's just the Bombay clique, you know. It's not a calculated thing. They've never been mad about me. I suppose they think I don't back them as I should. You heard about the Bangalore affair? It's not being Tamil really, it's just . . . my style!'

No doubt his style did set him apart. He wasn't muscle-bound, but his hard, compact frame concealed unexpected strength. He had wrists like steel ratchets. A push through mid-off could race to the boundary in a flash. When he bowled his run-up finished perfectly side-on, so that his arm came down at the batsman like a bullwhip. It looked even better in slow motion and made him a darling with TV crews wherever he played. And with Siva there was always the spice of drama. He blew hot and cold inexplicably. After a fast fifty he might get bogged down for ages in the sixties and seventies. He was lucky, I thought, to have left county cricket when he did. It would have defeated him in the end. The moments of glory were just too few and far between.

I'd never really thought of Siva as political, in the sense of party political, though he'd always had an interest in world affairs and in his days with me on the circuit had been a passionate Indian patriot – quick to correct the many misconceptions about India in the English mind, and eager to advance claims on behalf of its history, civilisation and people. He had felt strongly about stopping the planned South African tours of the early seventies. His calm manner of explaining the issues to pros ten and fifteen years his senior had impressed me. He was more like a statesman, I thought, than a politician.

Still, it wasn't hard to imagine him running for office in Madras, and easy to imagine him winning. He had a kind of innocence that carried all before him, an authority with others that Robin Barnett, for all his striving, would never possess.

The Bangalore affair was a good example. It was a zonal match. Decisions had been going against Siva's side for most of the day. In the midst of a sizzling stint of fast bowling, Siva let out a thunderous appeal. The batsman stood his ground and the umpire's finger remained in his pocket. Siva's face clouded over. The crowd grew restive. Oranges were thrown from the stands. A riot was brewing, by no means an unheard of occurrence at an Indian ground. Siva's team-mates let the crowd see their dismay and raised the temperature still higher. Siva, who later admitted he'd been furious with the umpire, spread his arms wide to the spectators and called for silence. It was described in the papers the next day variously as a 'gesture of supplication' and an 'attitude of command'. Whatever it was, it worked. The orange throwing stopped. The umpire looked relieved. In the next over Siva clean-bowled the offending batsman.

The Indian authorities, though grateful to their star for cooling things down, were alarmed. A man with the power to control a mob might someday use it to incite one. His team-mates were no more pleased. They felt that he should have let the crowd have its say and that by his gesture he had set himself above them. His hopes for the captaincy had taken a beating, but his standing with the people had increased.

We talked of English cricket; and the tour; and my prospects, or lack of them. Like every other professional cricketer I had talked to, Siva endeavoured to assure me that somehow I would get a contract for the next season. Of course no one wanted to see me unemployed. But behind their wishful thinking lay more than friendly concern. Underlying every cricketer's love of cricket and brightest hopes for the future is the disturbing thought: What can I do if I can't play or coach or promote or commentate on cricket? What else am I fit for? The insecurity of the professional athlete's life is such that he doesn't even want to think that a career could be over as suddenly as mine seemed to be. I knew my plight made people uncomfortable and it was clearly having this effect on Siva, who was promising all manner of things: counties in England, coaching schemes in New Zealand, promotions in Australia.

The more he went on in his earnest way, the more I felt I had to come clean with him. I put my head back and drained the last sweet drops of coffee. Looking away from my old friend into the green and yellow depths of his garden, I began.

'Actually, I do have one prospect for next year. It may be completely off the rails. I don't know. It's partly the reason I rang you. Robin wants me to pass it on to you.'

He looked puzzled. His head drew back and his neck went taut. 'Robin?'

'He's got a plan. Or rather a friend of his, a businessman named Cuthbert, has a plan. They want you in on it. And my job is to get you in.'

I couldn't bring myself to look at him. Sensing my discomfort he shouted into the dark entrance of the house and shortly Manni emerged with more coffee and a plate of pale, doughy balls floating in clear syrup and topped with rose petals.

'Come, David, you'll like these. Cricketers from England are too protected. What do you know of the real India? You eat tinned corned beef and drink Fanta and sit in hotels.'

I tasted the doughy balls. They were phenomenally sweet but I praised them to the skies. The old woman, pleased with my accolade, waggled her head.

'So tell me, David,' he said when she had left, 'tell me about this plan. They say Robin's a shrewd businessman. What does he want? Money to invest?'

I laughed. 'No, they have all the money they need. It's you they want. You and your influence.'

Then I told him everything I could remember about Grand Prix Cricket. He listened carefully. To my relief, he was not in the least annoyed with me for using him in this way. The rich and famous can be like that. At times thin-skinned in the extreme and universally suspicious, they also like to display their power and enjoy hearing people appeal to them to use it. With supplicants at their feet, most behave with the utmost tact and courtesy.

Siva asked me many of the same questions I had asked Robin and Cuthbert. I tried to repeat their answers.

'Basically I think they're both mad,' I concluded. 'It'll never work.' I wanted to apologise, not only for coming to him in self-interest, but for coming with such an outlandish proposal.

'Not at all, David, they're both quite sane, I assure you.' He moved to the edge of his chair and leaned forwards. I saw his strong, sculpted face in the deep shade of the veranda, with the heat lifting and insects buzzing in the foliage. 'You may think I see things only from the top, but there are things I see from there which may not be so clear from where you sit. In the last few years I've travelled everywhere.' He spread his palms to indicate the breadth of his voyages. 'I've talked to players and administrators and sponsors and politicians. Believe me, this sort of thing is in the air. The moment is right. This Cuthbert will find plenty of friends – inside and outside the game – willing to put their money where his mouth is. Remember, investing in cricket is still cheap at the price. A rich man can buy large pieces of the game for a song. And there's plenty on sale. In Australia last year the players were barely on speaking terms with their board. None would sign a contract for more than a year. They can't afford to, not with people like Cuthbert knocking about. No, no, whatever you do, David, do not dismiss this Grand Prix Cricket. It can work. And what's more, though you mustn't tell anyone, I hope it does.'

'You do?'

'Yes. The game needs shaking up. The rewards should go to the players, not the hangers-on. Too many English cricketers still have the forelock-touching mentality. Strangely enough in India, with all its other feudal aspects, we often provide more security for our players than you do.'

'They can even go in for politics?'

'And why not?' He sat up straight in his chair as if to dispel any doubts on this score. 'The Party wants me. It respects my contribution. The people want me. I can help them. Why should I spend my life autographing bats?'

I couldn't argue with him.

'Take Cuthbert's money,' Siva said. 'What do you owe Lord's or the TCCB or any of them?'

'You sound like Robin.'

'And why not? How many years did you play for these gentlemen?'

'Ten.'

'And what do you have to show for it?' He said it sadly, gently. 'You know people talk about all the corruption and favouritism in Indian cricket and this is all true, indeed, it is worse than you will ever know. But is it so much better in England? You are slaves to business and politics more than we because you don't realise it. What is this conspiracy in England that keeps money out of the game, drives spectators from the grounds and throws good players onto the streets?'

'It's cricket,' I said and we both laughed.

'Not any more, David. It's open season now. Everything else in the world changes. Why not cricket? Of course, I keep these opinions to myself. They do not sit well on an aspiring politician.'

He told me of his plans to stand for the State Legislative Assembly, a body that met in Madras to govern the great southern state of Tamil Nadu. The ruling party in the state would certainly endorse his candidature. Indeed, they had eagerly sought him out. His constituency would cover the vast working-class slums of outer Madras, where much of the trouble of the last few weeks had taken place.

'You saw nothing on your way here?' he asked, a hint of anxiety in his voice. 'It was quiet?'

'As far as I could see.' But what, I asked him, was it all about? And what was all this talk of President's Rule?

'Toppling state ministries. It's an old habit of theirs. They look for any excuse to remove their opponents from power. They want to show that Tamils are unfit to govern themselves. But the Party has their measure. We have the matter well under control.'

He spoke of his desire to give leadership, to renew and revitalise the Party, to make it once again the Tamil Party of the Tamil people, owing nothing to outside interests of any kind. In everything he said the Party's name rang out like a slogan. For the central party ruling in Delhi, Siva had nothing but contempt. They were 'parasites' who deeply resented the Party's hold over the people of Tamil Nadu.

'But our people are loyal to the Party,' he said. 'They know it has served them well in the past, whatever problems there are now.'

'The strike?'

He sighed wearily. 'It's a terrible situation. Both sides must come to their senses. Management have perhaps acted high-handedly, but this street-brawling must be stopped. These extremists only want to hurt the Party.'

He stood up, stretched his legs, and led me on a tour of the house. There were, he informed me, fourteen rooms in all. Each was elegantly furnished in a mixture of traditional Indian and modern western fittings. Many of the rooms were in pristine condition. The house had a dark, cool atmosphere. Walking through it you might think you were anywhere but in the middle of a hot, south Indian city. Sounds of children arguing and shouting floated in through open windows.

'It sounds like a row but really they're just having a laugh,' he giggled softly, the shy, private Siva I remembered.

Out at the back, in a dusty patch cleared beside the rear entrance, three children played in bare feet.

'Manni's children. They have a room in the back. They're very decent.'

Decent, I recalled, was one of Siva's public school words. He always said it gravely.

He showed me his stereo and extensive record collection, mostly Indian music but some western pop and jazz. With pride he demonstrated his new home computer, complete with dozens of video game programmes. He challenged me to a game of video cricket, but I convinced him it would be a mismatch.

We sat down at last in a spacious living room with a high ceiling and large windows screened by venetian blinds. How strange it was to see the one-time retiring novice transformed into the lord of all he surveyed.

'It's a fabulous place, Siva,' I congratulated him. 'You deserve it all.'

He grinned shyly. In the years since we'd shared digs he'd come to seem to me a remote figure, only tenuously related to the Siva I had once known so well. Now the old Siva was restored to me and I was pleased.

'I'll make a good legislator, don't you think?' he asked brightly.

I told him he would make an excellent legislator. I told him I would vote for him if I could. I didn't understand the strike or

President's Rule or the Party, but I felt Siva's grand innocence would carry him through.

We talked again of Robin and his plans for Grand Prix Cricket.

'I wish him well in this,' Siva said. 'But honestly I've never been able to understand the man. Such talent, such intelligence, and yet he behaves as he does – storming off the field in the middle of a Test match. You know, arrogance is unbecoming in a cricketer. A certain humility is required. And yet I've learned things from Robin Barnett. I've learned that a man can be a big star and still a prisoner. And I intend to avoid that.'

Did he feel a prisoner in this mansion? Encaged by his adoring countrymen?

'Tell Robin I am very sorry, but I cannot join this new cricket circus of his. There are plenty of others, don't worry, but I can't be one of them. And David, please be careful. It would hurt me if it were to come out that I was in any way associated with this scheme.'

I assured him I would be careful and that I quite understood his reasons for rejecting the offer. Anyway, I'd done my bit. I'd asked him the question.

'Oh I'm sure they'll find some other errand to send you on. It's the way it works. But by all means do it. Do what they ask. This is a chance for you and it would be foolish to throw it away.'

It was time, Siva announced, for his late afternoon nap. He tried to keep regular hours these days and had become completely teetotal.

'But you must come to my party tomorrow night – a big party after the first day's play. Everyone who is anyone will be there. Not just cricket people, either. Friends from the Party. And beautiful women!' He laughed. 'You must come. I can show you off.'

I was glad to accept. It would be a relief to avoid yet another dreary team function, however Dougie might grumble.

'Remember, I owe you,' Siva said as we shook hands on the majestic veranda. The twilight had sapped the colour from the gaudy little jungle and left it a darkened, humming glade.

'You were good to me in England.'

And with that he called for Manni, who escorted me down the curling path and let me out through the wrought-iron gate.

CHAPTER FIVE

The little knot of reporters had vanished when I stepped outside. I found myself alone in the street. The evening had relieved the dusty air of its oppressive heat and tinted the high, whitewashed walls with a rosy glow. There were sounds, intermixed human and animal sounds, coming from behind the walls, but no shadows of movement outside them. There were no cabs, not even any rickshas in sight, and I knew Dougie would be expecting me for the team dinner and the team talk before the match the next day. I was about to ring the bell and ask Siva to call a cab when I heard a brief hiss, like a jet of steam turned suddenly on and off. I looked across the road towards the noise; a man waved anxiously to me from the shade of a large willow tree. I could see a smile on his face and walked over to him, thinking here was yet another friendly Indian offering to help me out. I smiled back at him. Perhaps he was a ricksha man and could take me back to the hotel.

As I crossed the street the expression on the man's face seemed to change. It grew less helpful and more urgent, even hostile. I dropped my smile and began to turn away. The man darted out of the shadow and with an almost silent step reached me in the middle of the road and grabbed my arm. He was a young man, no more than twenty, thin and gangly, with round eyes that looked as if they'd been sleepless for days. I tried to pull my arm gently away, but the hand held fast and pinched my skin.

A torrent of Tamil came from him, soft, as if he wanted no one to overhear him, and yet angry, as if he bore me a personal grudge. He wore cheap black cotton trousers and a grimy T-shirt that said 'University of Illinois' across the front. I pulled my arm hard and loosened his grip, at the same time raising myself to my full height and adopting a stern demeanour (I remembered seeing Robin use this technique to discourage beggars).

The words poured out of him, regardless of my incomprehension, serious, at times almost inaudible. All I could make out were the repeated syllables 'Siva, Siva.' The *s*'s hissed and sang drily like a knife being sharpened.

'Go away. Leave me alone,' I snapped and continued to walk away.

He lunged again, but I dodged him and shot back the most threatening look I could manage. He let out an angry red-hot scream, as if he'd been seared by fire. 'Siva, Siva,' he repeated. Then he looked up. His eyes widened. He went still, his body wound in a tense crouch.

'Can I help you?'

The voice came from behind me – a woman's voice with a clear, English accent. Turning round I saw a young Indian woman in western dress, long black hair held in a silver clasp, gold bangles rattling on both arms. She looked familiar.

She spoke to the young man in Tamil. It sounded brisk but patient. He growled back at her. Again I heard Siva's name, invoked like some powerful mantra, or perhaps a curse which takes effect only when repeated often enough.

The woman questioned him tersely, holding her head at an arrogant angle, but looking increasingly puzzled. The man pointed at me, repeated the imprecation – 'Siva!' – one last time and then ran, his sandals scuffling along the dry road. He disappeared beyond the next corner.

'What was that about?' I wondered aloud.

'You don't know him?' she asked cautiously.

'No,' I stared at her. 'What did he want?'

She gazed at me for a moment then shrugged. 'Something about Siva. I didn't understand, really.' She kept looking at me, as if something the man had said made me very interesting indeed.

'You were with the others,' I said, laughing nervously. 'Waiting out here, I mean. Before, when I arrived.' I had just become conscious that she was a very attractive woman, with a fine oval face and sharp, clear eyes.

'That's right.' She eased into a smile. 'We abandon the vigil at sunset. But we'll all be back tomorrow. If the editor says there's a new Siva story, we wait till we have a new Siva story.'

'Or you make one up?' It came out sharper than I meant it, but her breezy manner, after my encounter with the young man, had caught me off guard.

Luckily she thought it was funny. 'Sometimes we do,' she admitted with a laugh. 'You look lost. Maybe I can help.'

I told her I wanted to return to my hotel but couldn't find a taxi.

'You're one of the English cricketers, aren't you? The Commercial Trust lot?'

'That's my excuse, yes.'

'You were visiting Siva on business or . . .' she could not quite hide her curiosity. I was touched.

'No, he's an old friend, from county cricket days.'

'Ah, I see. Well, we can't have you wandering around Madras till all hours, can we? My car's over there. I'll give you a lift.'

I was relieved. Apart from the problems I had already encountered getting from one end of Madras to another, I felt a new sense of unease brought on by the episode with the strange young man and his insistent repetition of Siva's name. I also couldn't help thinking what the other players would say when they saw me dropped off at the hotel by an attractive young woman – and an Indian woman at that.

Her car was an old but perfectly preserved Morris Oxford, a model ubiquitous in India where it is manufactured under the name of the Ambassador. I complimented her on its fine condition.

'I make an effort. I had one like it when I lived in England. They're not very fashionable here, as you can imagine. Anyone with the money would prefer a new German or Italian model, especially since they eased the import restrictions.'

We took our seats. Before she started the engine she turned to me and said, with a gay glint in her eyes, 'I must warn you. I have an ulterior motive in picking you up this way.'

I looked straight back at her.

'You must tell me all about your friend the famous Siva. My editor will love it. An insider's view, so to speak; better yet, an Englishman's view!'

She said she would buy me a coffee then drop me off at my hotel. The prospect of postponing my return and lingering a while longer outside the closed world of touring cricketers was a pleasant one.

We headed down the broad lanes with their curious, English-style mansions and glimpses of scurrying servants. The church spire loomed into view and I asked her about it.

'The Church of San Thomé,' she explained, like a patient tour guide. 'The old story is that Saint Thomas came here to preach the gospel and was martyred out on Saint Thomas's Mount, near where the airport is. His relics are still kept in the church – some horrible bit of bone or something. You can see it if you like. The church itself is quite old, seventeenth century, I think.'

'That goes back a bit.'

'Not really. Tamils traded with the Romans two thousand years ago. You lot are upstarts compared to us.'

'I must tell Robin about that. It's his sort of thing.'

'Robin Barnett?' she brightened. 'I see I really will be getting the inside story.'

'He's a history buff. Relics, churches, temples, forts, you name it. He's mad about the Raj. It's a kind of a speciality of his.'

'Now that would make an interesting story.'

I glanced at her. What kind of story was she looking for? And thinking of Grand Prix Cricket and Siva and his Party, I wondered if I wasn't getting into something I should stay clear of.

'Don't worry,' she said, as if reading my mind. 'I won't write anything you don't want me to. No quotes, no attributions, just an off-the-record chat.'

She worked, she said, for a Tamil-language magazine, one of the glossy pictorial periodicals popular in India, featuring photos, gossip, and interviews with celebrities, mostly film stars, but also people like Siva and a few politicians. Her name was Lakshmi Kumbaikonam. I relaxed and watched the scenery go by. We left the relative quiet of Siva's neighbourhood – which, according to Lakshmi, had been known since the days of the British as the poshest in town – and entered the centre of the city, where traffic was heavy.

'It builds up at this time of day. Workers coming home from the factories, clerks from the offices. The buses are packed. Absolute murder.'

She might have been moaning about rush hour in London. Maybe it was just her relative restraint with the horn in that dense, angry traffic churning the dust, but there seemed something comfortingly English and familiar in her bearing, her speech, her manner. And at the moment she seemed as pleased to be with me as I was to be with her.

She told me she'd spent two years in London at a drama school and had once entertained hopes of a career in the theatre.

'I found out soon enough there were virtually no parts for Indian actresses in England. And I certainly didn't intend to spend my life playing shopkeepers' wives.'

'So you came back to the family?'

She laughed with a deep, quiet heave of the chest, her chin rising to reveal a delicate golden throat. 'No. My family are quite tolerant by Indian standards but by that time I'd crossed too many bridges. I came back to act in films. You know, Madras is quite a film capital – far more lively than London.'

But no acting career materialised. Gradually, through her contacts with actors and actresses, she drifted into writing about films, found she had a talent for it and, more important to her, she enjoyed it.

'Besides, I like Madras.'

'Doesn't everyone?'

I wasn't just being polite. Looking out of the car window at the sprawling streets choked with people and cars and animals, I'd decided I too liked this jumbled, spacious, friendly town, despite some of the odd people who might approach a stranger in the street.

'Some people spend their whole lives trying to leave here.'

'What makes you different then?'

'Ah, now who's supposed to be interviewing who?'

'I'll tell you what,' I teased her, 'if you answer my questions, I'll answer yours.'

'It's a deal.' Again the silent laugh, the upraised head.

'Good. First question then: Shall we have dinner instead of coffee?'

I surprised myself. No one in England would ever have accused me of forwardness. But out here my grip had loosened on so many things – my career, my colleagues, my future – it seemed easy.

'What about your team meeting?'

'I've sat through enough of them already.'

'It's your funeral.'

Lakshmi knew a wonderful place, she said, near the city centre, not far from our hotel – in case I got cold feet.

'But there's one condition,' she added, 'you must allow me to pay – or rather my employers. After all, they owe you something for all the good quotes you're going to give me!'

I wondered aloud whether journalists and cricketers wouldn't both starve without their expense-account meals.

'It's a cardinal rule here. Never pay your own way if someone else is willing to.'

'The same applies at home.' I thought of the countless team meals, benefit dinners, free drinks I'd been bought, summer after summer, for ten years. I also thought of dingy cafés, motorway snacks, microwave meals in provincial hotels. Perhaps I wouldn't miss county cricket much after all.

The restaurant was on the roof of one of the big hotels on Mount Road. It was an old style imperial palace with an inner courtyard and an iron-railed stairway crossing from one level to another. We reached a terrace spread with potted palms and lamplit tables. Lakshmi glided among them with complete assurance as I trailed in her wake. Driving in her Morris and listening to her BBC English she had seemed so un-Indian, yet here she was utterly at home. We sat down and were approached by a waiter wearing a neat black tunic with buttoned-up collar. He ignored me and was soon engaged in lengthy conversation with Lakshmi. I didn't understand a word but watched fascinated. It was like a pantomime. She: enquiring, cautious, sceptical, indecisive. He: complacent, cajoling, reassuring, and at last delighted when our order had been agreed. I revelled in the scene. For six weeks I'd been in India and this was the first meal I'd been able to enjoy without another cricketer at my elbow. And I'd never dined in a place like this, and certainly not with a woman like this.

'I hadn't stopped to ask, but you do eat our food, don't you?'

'Of course. I love it!'

'Touring cricketers are notoriously hopeless about these things, you know.'

Siva had made the same point. Was our reputation that bad? 'Not all cricketers are the same,' I said, sounding dismally defensive.

'Oh, I know that,' she waved a wrist at me and it jangled with jewellery, 'and a good deal more about cricket besides!' she added.

'You're a fan, then?'

'Not really,' she replied, and – refreshingly – didn't bother to apologise for it. 'But I take a professional interest. I have to.'

'I can imagine.' I told her I'd never seen such a cricket-mad country as India. The game seemed to take place on a whole different level out here.

'In England people treat the game with reverence,' she said. 'There's none of that here. I know you have your die-hard fans and little boys with autograph books and old colonels guarding their shrines like Brahmins. But in India it's more than that, it's . . .' she groped for the word. 'It's symbolic.'

'Of what?' I asked, puzzled.

She leaned forwards and talked across the table in a low voice, intense and penetrating.

'You see, we're a big, divided country. Anyone who takes on representing this country, in any way, like the Test side does, takes on all kinds of burdens, all kinds of feelings. Only a few people can actually play cricket. Mostly rich people, upper-caste people like Siva, or clerks and professionals. But our people know and care about their cricket more than the English. So I have to know about it. It's more than sport. It's politics.'

I told her I wouldn't argue with her. The more I'd seen on this tour the more I'd realised how little I knew about the game I'd been earning my living at for all these years.

'And now there's this poor bloke, this umpire who's been done in. What the hell is that all about?'

'It could be anything,' she said. 'No one seems to know, though everyone guesses. The police have been cautious, some people say too cautious.'

She changed the subject (not a pleasant one when dinner was being served) and asked me who I played for and how I had got into the game. I gave her my usual story about slipping into the first-class game from school and never having really intended to spend so much of my life in it. I mentioned the fact, which I usually suppressed, that I had turned down a university place in the hope of playing a full season in the First XI at the age of nineteen – hopes which materialised only two years later. I told her about the early excitements and the recent disappointments and ended with the sad truth about my release from county cricket.

'Any regrets?' she asked.

'It's hard to have regrets when you're not sure exactly what you've missed.'

She nodded, in the western style, head bobbing gently up and down.

'Yes, I can imagine,' she leaned back and away from me, as if to take a broader view of the specimen in front of her. 'It's difficult for cricketers. For every Siva Ramachandran and Robin Barnett there's dozens of . . .'

'Of Dave Stotts!' I helped her out.

She leaned forwards again, and touched my arm, ever so lightly. Her bangles rattled against the white table-cloth. The candles on the terrace flickered in the warm evening air. Waiters hurried to and fro, arms laden with oval steel dishes trailing pungent herbal scents. At the other tables sat middle-aged couples, businessmen, family parties, talking volubly, gesticulating extravagantly, or so it seemed to me, barking orders to the waiters pitilessly. By contrast, Lakshmi and I seemed clandestine, conspiratorial, shielding our faces and voices in conclave around our dim candle. It lit up her face beautifully: the long, straight nose, the high, expressive lines of the black brows, the wide mouth, by turns tight-lipped and serious, then open and laughing.

'And what about the future, then?' she asked, beaming encouragement to her interviewee.

Grand Prix Cricket flashed in my mind in giant neon letters, accompanied by a cacophony of television and radio jingles. I tried to block it out, but it was only supplanted by the red nose of Roy Cuthbert, glowing with self-assurance, a self-assurance mysterious to me because I so utterly lacked it.

I told Lakshmi I had various possibilities for next year. They might work out and they might not. I would have to wait and see. In the meantime, I was loving India.

'Excellent,' she said, 'you pass the test.'

The meal was staggering. Dish after dish arrived at the table, all vegetarian, which is the rule in south India, each one subtly different in smell and taste and colour. There were soft, silky dumplings in a yoghurt sauce flecked with black mustard seeds and fresh coriander; rice cakes in spicy, sour gravy; strange vegetables I'd never seen before, let alone eaten; hot, fluffy poori – flat discs of rice flour that puff up golden brown in clean, sizzling peanut oil; bright yellow 'lemon rice' with hot green chillies. We drank yoghurt lassi made with rose water and poured into chilled glasses. A little crusty skin of curd was dropped on top. Others around us ate delicately with the right hand (or rather two poised fingers of the right hand). We started off with fork and spoon. In my case, it was necessity; in Lakshmi's, courtesy. Soon, however, we dispensed with implements and set to with relish.

As we ate Lakshmi told me about herself. Though her family were well-off professionals who had enjoyed an English-style education, they had objected strongly to their daughter's independence. When she first went to England she'd stayed with remote relations and written home – literally – every day.

'But I was always different. My mother said I was strange. After a while my wanting to be an actress or a journalist was just one more strange thing about me. None of it would matter if I were married.'

I said Indian women seemed much more restricted than women back home.

'Are they so free in England?' she replied sharply, in her abrupt, serious manner. Then she told me about something called the Widow's Remarriage Movement which had swept across south India in the nineteenth century . . .

'Now that I must tell, Robin,' I joked.

She was frustrated by her job. She wanted to write serious stories, about real events.

'So much in India is under the surface,' she said. 'Most of the so-called stories are just shadow play.'

I thought of the strike reports in the papers, Siva's political prospects, the press handling of Robin's wrangle with his county.

Gaily she asked me if I had a wife or girlfriend. Carried away with the food and lamplight and the warmth, I told her about my divorce and the pitiful excuse for a marriage that had preceded it. I had met my wife on the cricket circuit (a fatal mistake) and ended up working for her father, an estate agent, selling expensive properties in London during the winter. I suppose he felt a promising young cricketer would be an appropriate ornament for the company. To tell the truth, I never liked the job and certainly had no talent for it. Eventually, I was sacked, though in the politest possible manner. My father-in-law broke the news just like the chairman of my county committee – amidst assurances of friendship and respect and deepest regret. What neither of them realised was that I had been expecting the blow for so long I was relieved to receive it at last. My father-in-law said he was sure I'd be wiser to concentrate my talents on the cricket pitch. By then my wife had given up on that, and soon after gave up on me in general. It wasn't a process I'd ever resisted.

I tried to make the story amusing and Lakshmi tried to take it in that vein. But again I was uncomfortable, and changed the subject.

She told me about her father, a solicitor, who as a young man had been active in politics in the years leading up to Independence.

'For him, 1947 was the beginning of a new era. Not that he hated the British – at least not all of them – but he believed in India. Most of all he believed in the Tamil people and what they could offer India. He has been bitterly disappointed.'

At one time he had been active in the Party, Siva's Party. Then it had stood for something: popular change, land reform, clean government, Tamil rights in a federal India. They were affluent people, businessmen and professionals, and they came to power as champions of the poor and downtrodden. But those days, she said, were long gone. In a low voice she called them the new *Cholas*, the new Raj, and she didn't mean it kindly, as Robin would have done. The Party traded on the loyalty of its lower-caste supporters and made deals with anyone who could help it retain power. Corruption was rife.

'And now your friend Siva,' she added, 'is poised to become the new leader. The latest in a long line of Tamil messiahs claiming to speak for the people.'

'You're sceptical?' It was the first time I had heard anyone in India openly disparage Siva.

She shrugged, as if reluctant to reveal herself to someone who was, despite the intimacy of our talk, still a stranger and a foreigner.

'Why did you visit him this afternoon?'

She had already asked me this question and I had already answered it. I resented her apparent refusal to believe me and simply repeated coolly that he was an old friend and I was just paying a call.

'Yes, yes, so you said. But Siva is in the middle of some delicate political dealings – a sort of reshuffle in the Party. Narayan, you know, your tour organiser, is also a figure in the Party. Though of course he never runs for office himself.'

'I don't know anything about all that,' I assured her.

'Someone certainly thinks you do.' Suddenly she had gone cold on me. Her face had closed down.

'That young man who spoke to you in the street, outside Siva's, do you know what he was saying?'

'I thought he was asking for money or something.' It was a stupid thing to say. I could have kicked myself.

'He was asking you,' she leaned forward to make sure no one could hear our words, 'to talk to Siva for him.'

I looked blank.

'He said "Tell Siva." He kept repeating it. "Tell Siva I cannot wait forever. Tell him. Warn him. They will get me. They will get him too." He kept saying it, over and over.'

She looked hard at me as if to see whether these mysterious words carried any deeper meaning.

'Maybe it loses something in translation,' I said lightly, though somewhat disturbed at the strange message. 'I can't make anything out of it.'

'He said to warn you, too. He said they would get you as well.'

'What does it mean?' I asked. The stifled alarm in my voice seemed to appease her. Her face softened.

'You've got no idea?'

I shook my head. 'I'm a foreigner here, you know . . .'

'But a foreigner who visits Siva . . .' she said. 'And just now, Madras, you know . . .'

'The riots?'

'Yes,' she looked cautiously around, 'the so-called riots.'

'It's seemed perfectly quiet while I've been here.'

'Quiet? You've just been threatened by a stranger in the street and you think it's quiet?'

It was not the last time she was to make me feel stupid.

'Well, explain it to me,' I demanded, keeping my voice as low as hers. 'No one else will.'

She couldn't resist. In a hushed but steady murmur she described the factory where the trouble had started. It was British-owned, though of course through an Indian subsidiary. According to Lakshmi it served as a dumping ground for obsolescent and surplus machinery from Europe. Wages for the largely semi-skilled workforce, many of them immigrants from the impoverished countryside, were a fraction of those paid to their counterparts in England. Nonetheless, they had risen in recent years and with the recession hitting the parent company economies were required. A wage cut was imposed by management, with the agreement of the official union, which was linked politically to the Party leaders in Madras. The workers rebelled, formed their own union, and went on strike. The police and hired thugs intervened and the whole affair was used as an excuse to harass dissidents of all kinds. The management closed down the plant and prepared to sit it out. Small groups of workers took to following the English manager wherever he went. When they encircled his house they were met with physical attack and arrest.

Meanwhile, the Party made attempts – or at least appeared to make attempts – to pressurise the company into concessions. It appealed for calm among the people.

'But the people are confused. They don't know who to blame. They have looked to the Party for leadership for so long.'

Their loyalty, Lakshmi insisted, was wearing thin. That's why the Party was looking to Siva. They needed a new image – and what an image!

'And while all this is going on I'm standing outside his house waiting for titbits. Gossip!' she moaned. 'The political angle will go to someone else – a man, of course.'

I tried to console her. 'Maybe I can give you something interesting for your profile. The personal angle's not always unimportant.

'No,' she perked up, 'you're right. Maybe I could do something comparing Siva and Robin Barnett: the two greatest players never to captain their countries.' She frowned as she weighed the article in her mind.

Robin kept popping up in all my conversations. He was the last person I wanted to talk about. He made me think of Cuthbert, and then of Dougie, back at the hotel, fuming.

'But they're completely different,' I protested, overcome with an urge to do justice to the friend of my youth. Siva, I insisted, believed in fairness, believed in his people. I told her about his role in the South African ruck back home. There wasn't a stroke of artifice in him, I said. He was an innocent.

'Which is the last thing you could say about Robin,' I added.

'Then perhaps he's the one who should go into politics.'

'That's pretty cynical.'

'It comes with the job,' she said, stretching her arms in the air like a cat satisfied with its dinner. 'Don't think I begrudge Siva his ambitions. Madras is full of aspiring politicans. There are worse around than him. Much worse.'

We were nearly alone in the restaurant. Loitering waiters loosened tunic buttons and extinguished lamps. The night was mild. We finished our meal with strong coffee and an ice cream tasting of cardamum and burnt milk. We talked about the match the next day and agreed that my anxieties about Chaughiri were well-founded. Last year on the same strip he had bamboozled the Pakistanis.

'And Robin Barnett. Did you know him before?'

He seemed inescapable. 'No, but we've been seeing the sights together.'

'You don't want to talk about him?'

'No, it's just . . .'

'I'm not listening as a journalist.'

If not as a journalist then as what? My hopes soared.

'Why don't you come to the match tomorrow. I'll leave you a ticket.'

She thought for a moment. 'I'd be delighted,' she said.

Then, to the waiter's astonishment, she paid the bill and left a tip.

CHAPTER SIX

Outside we ambled slowly in the evening air. On the street Lakshmi walked easily, observantly, and I felt it was a different world that caught her eye from the one that caught mine. A woman with two children bundled under a grey cloak approached us and whimpered for rupees. Did Lakshmi ignore her? Did she see and feel her in a way I couldn't? I felt once again what a stranger I was in India.

But strangers do meet and things do happen between them.

'There's a party at Siva's tomorrow night,' I said, hands thrust deep in my pockets. 'Would you like to go with me?'

She stopped and looked at me. I looked back sheepishly.

'He says everyone who is anyone will be there.'

'I'm sure!' she laughed. 'But do you really think he wants a journalist there?'

'I won't tell on you.'

She hesitated. 'All right,' she answered finally, 'I'll pick you up at your hotel after the match.'

I felt a huge grin spreading across my face and did my best to suppress it. We reached her Ambassador. She unlocked the door and slipped into the driver's seat. I went round the side and just as I put my hand on the door I heard a noise behind me and a hand grabbed my shirt.

Whirling around I saw the young man in the T-shirt, eyes more haunted than before, lips protruding angrily. A hot burst of Tamil issued from them. He twisted my shirt in his hand and tried to pull me towards him. He was smaller than me and I had no trouble freeing my arm and pushing him away.

Lakshmi shouted from inside the car. I let myself in, slamming the door with a crunch.

'The little bastard . . .' I started to say.

A fist came through the window, shattering glass and finding its way to my left ear. Lakshmi said, 'Oh my god!' and tried to start the engine.

But I was already swinging the door open and knocking my attacker across the broken, rocky pavement. Blindly I charged at him, only to be met square in the face by a flying concrete shard the size of a cricket ball. I stumbled and swore. My hands went up to my face and covered my eyes. When I took them down I blinked through a mist that I later realised was blood, and dimly saw the youngster legging it down the street and disappearing down an alleyway.

Lakshmi helped me rest against the car bonnet. 'He's gone,' she said. 'You'll never catch him in those little streets.'

I had no intention of chasing him. My left ear burned like a bee sting and on my forehead there was a soft, tender ridge.

People crowded around us. There was a bilingual babble in Tamil and English.

'The thief!'

'The police! When you need them . . .'

'He is Englishman?'

'Attacked in the open street!'

'It's a disgrace!'

'A doctor! Please, the man needs a doctor!'

Over the years I've had my share of injuries playing cricket. Once a West Indian quickie cracked a rib and believe me it hurt, and it went on hurting for days. I've been hit on the elbow and once had a glancing blow on the head. But this was different. It wasn't just the pain, though that was bad enough. It was being assaulted out of nowhere. It was the furious look on the young man's face. It was being an outsider in India, conspicuous, vulnerable, endangered. My stomach churned and my legs wobbled.

But then I felt Lakshmi close to me. Her face was next to mine, staring into my wounded ear. Then she held my head in her hands and examined my face. I was groggy but tried not to show any pain. She looked down from my battered forehead and fixed her eyes on mine.

'You still say you don't know what he was on about?'

Such a lovely, friendly face – and such a sharp question!

Two policemen approached us and made great play of protecting me from any further assault by despatching the ring of onlookers with stern professionalism. Lakshmi summarised what had happened and told them abruptly, 'He needs a doctor, for goodness sake. You can ask your questions later.'

They looked away from her with bored indifference.

'You will tell us please what has happened?'

I confirmed Lakshmi's story.

'So this man has already approached you once today?'

I said yes. They seemed surprised.

'But why did he follow you?'

I said I didn't know. They seemed even more surprised.

I was ushered into a police car. A first-aid kit was produced and the blood was cleansed from my face. One of them started the motor and before I could ask about Lakshmi they had driven me off.

'Wait a minute . . .'

'It's no problem,' said the driver, 'we make reports at the hotel.'

The journey was brief. They accompanied me through the doors and into the lobby. One stood on either side of me, as if they were afraid I might keel over at any moment, even though I was feeling stronger now and quite capable of standing on my own two feet. The desk clerk looked up with a ready smile which instantly dropped into a shocked open mouth. Paul Walker, Ernie Fairbanks and Donald Blackburn sat round a table playing cards.

'Holy Christ,' said Ernie, 'what the hell happened to you?'

Donald leapt up, came over to me, and peered at my injuries. 'Looks nasty that does.'

'Run into a riot, did you?' Paul said, shaking his head as if I should have known better.

The police talked with the desk clerk. In no time word spread through the hotel and I found myself surrounded by Dougie, Kidleigh, and the others, who gazed in wonder at the sight of a man wounded off the cricket pitch. Even the little boy from the kitchen popped out to have a stare.

'But why should anyone hit you?' asked Donald in his befuddled manner, after I'd attempted to explain the evening's events. 'I mean, they don't even know who you are.'

'You daft twit,' said Ernie. 'You mean if they did know who he was they'd have a reason to hit him?'

'Why should anyone have a go at DTS?' wondered Kidleigh.

'He's harmless enough, all right,' said Paul, staring at me suspiciously.

Dougie, furious with me for missing the team meeting, nevertheless fussed over my wounds and even looked in my ear with a small torch.

'Any damage?' asked Paul.

'No,' drawled Dougie. 'He'll be no more deaf than before.' He gave me a sour look.

At that moment Robin appeared, gliding down the stairway with a look of schoolmasterly severity.

'They've got DTS, Skip,' said Donald.

'Who's got him?' Robin frowned.

'I don't know,' I said, and repeated my tale.

I'd mentioned Lakshmi. She was my excuse for missing the team meeting. But it had also come out that she was a journalist, and I caught the momentary widening of Robin's eyes as he heard the word.

'It's 'cause they think we're all bloody millionaires,' said Kidleigh. Everyone looked at him.

'Yeah, compared to them I suppose we are,' said Donald after a pause.

'Funny then this geezer didn't try to pinch anything from Dave,' snapped Paul Walker. The others fell silent.

'The man was clearly insane,' pronounced Robin, as if this was the final word on the subject. 'I'm sorry it should happen to you, David. But we do have a match tomorrow and it's time we all got some sleep. Am I right, Dougie?'

Dougie, reluctant as ever to agree about anything with Robin, simply turned on his heels and headed for the lift. He was followed by Paul and Donald and a few others. Ernie, never one to take orders from a captain of any calibre, said he fancied another game of cards. He invited Kidleigh to share a hand with him. The young demon, freshly recovered from his latest stomach bug, seemed eager to agree. Robin dismissed him with a sharp monosyllable: 'Bed.'

While I sat and sipped a cup of Robin's 'special' tea ('It'll quieten your nerves'), the captain dealt with the police, who reported back to him as a matter of right. They had informed the British Consul of the incident and he would be calling in a moment.

'Let me handle this, David,' Robin said gently. 'You go up. Get some sleep. If I win the toss I shall bat. You'll have to be ready.' He smiled stiffly and I obeyed.

The phone rang. Robin spoke to the Consul. The last I heard of their talk was Robin assuring him that of course he remembered the last time they'd met.

Back in the room Dougie stood over the sink, stark naked, soaping his face, chest, armpits.

'What the bloody hell were you doing wandering about the town in the first place is what I'd like to know.'

'I told you, I . . .' I looked down at my feet, the way I used to when he told me off at school.

'Look at the state of you!'

In the mirror I saw for the first time a brown, lumpy-looking wound with spreading purple edges. My ear was swollen and red. Dougie bandaged me up. He cut strips of elastoplast and placed them tenderly over the injured areas.

'You'll never bloody learn.'

'Siva asked after you' I said in a monotone. I knew I would simply have to weather Dougie's vitriol. I thought of the young man in the T-shirt. In my memory he seemed no more than a boy. Strangely I found myself feeling sorrier for him than for myself.

'Siva's going into politics,' I murmured as Dougie applied a fluffy cotton gauze to my ear and delicately taped it in place.

'I don't hold with that. Politics and cricket don't mix.'

He lay down on his bed and was snoring rhythmically in no time. My head was full of images: Siva's mansion; Lakshmi and the restaurant; the young man's face more desperate than angry. My ear hurt when I lay on it and periodically I woke to change position.

CHAPTER SEVEN

Chepauk Stadium, one of India's great Test grounds, is on the banks of the Chepauk River not far from the Bay of Bengal. It is now a modern concrete oval surrounding a perfectly flat, grey-green pitch, with high wire fences separating the spectators from the playing field. It is owned and managed by the Madras Cricket Club, an institution founded by the British and as exclusive as ever, though the guiding hands are no longer white.

It's been a good ground for Indian sides against foreigners, with memorable victories scored against English, West Indian and Australian sides. The crowds, though appreciative of good cricket whoever plays it, are also notoriously partisan. A few years ago, after the local side had suffered a defeat in a Ranji Trophy match, a temporary stand of bamboo scaffolding and thatched roofing was burnt to the ground by dismayed supporters. With the disturbances of the last few weeks we weren't surprised to find a heavy police presence on our arrival. Men in pale green uniforms and peaked military caps guarded the entrances, occasionally searching a shoulder bag or cooling box, and stood in little groups around the edges of the playing field. They were armed not only with guns in holsters but with more menacing-looking lathis, long bamboo coshes with which they are said to whip through disorderly crowds in shoulder-to-shoulder phalanxes.

Kushwant, our driver, shook his head anxiously and muttered, 'Big crowd, big trouble.' The players made an effort to ignore the whole scene, as is their habit, and Dougie prodded us into the dressing room with injunctions to 'Never mind that.'

I'd been surprised to find my name on the front page of the morning edition of *The Banner*. ENGLISH CRICKETER ASSAULTED ran the headline. Robin was quoted ('An unfortunate incident which we will put behind us for today's match.'), then the Consul ('The police have assured us that everything is being done to apprehend the culprit.'). I was described as a middle-order batsman and my injuries as 'superficial'. 'It is thought the attack may have been an attempted robbery,' was the last line of the brief article.

More attention was paid to another article in the paper, though its prominence was restricted to the sports page. The chairman of Robin's County Committee had announced, regretfully, that the club would be seeking a new captain and batsman. They could wait no longer for a decision on their improved – and final – offer. Robin had been sacked.

He must have known about it last night, though he'd given no hint. In the dressing room no one dared mention the story or even offer any consoling words to the captain. Robin assumed the sullen air of a victim of injustice. Knowing what I did, I couldn't bring myself to look him in the face. But I marvelled at the way he played it, the control, the discipline, the disguised daring of such a big lie. He had manipulated his county into dismissing him. He had made it look like it was the old hacks at the club and not Robin himself who had provoked the whole affair. It would make a fine launching pad for Grand Prix Cricket.

Robin had said nothing yet of my interview with Siva. I knew that he would. It was only a matter of time.

We gazed out from the dressing room at the sun-soaked crowd, a crowd of brilliant colours and, wafting up to the players' balcony perched over the members' enclosure, heady smells. Men with steel trays packed with samosas or bhel pooris or ice creams or crisps or cucumber slices spread with lemon and chilli hawked their wares with vigorous repeated cries. Spectators filled not only all available seats but shimmied up poles and rafters and clung to the scoreboard. Tickets, of course, had multiplied several times in value as they were sold and resold. There were also a few thousand 'extra' spectators admitted on tickets that had never been placed on public sale and were in excess of the official capacity. Somehow, through administrators, players and officials, these 'extras' find their way into various hands in payment of outstanding debts, bribes, favours of all kinds. Cricket tickets are a special currency in India and there is not much you can't buy with them.

'When I first played here the rollers were drawn by elephants in harness,' Robin told me as we unpacked our kit.

I looked at the square. There was no elephant today but a modern roller being painfully dragged up and down by two men in lungis.

Robin went out for the toss and was greeted by loud applause, which he acknowledged in his usual manner – a touch of the cap, an upraised palm. We watched as he examined the pitch, squatting on his haunches and rapping the earth with his knuckles like a careworn geologist. He won the toss and elected to bat. There was, as usual, no debate in the dressing room. Dougie and the others had learned that Robin's word was holy writ in such matters. Ernie joked that if they cut any more grass off the top they'd hit the sand underneath. Robin said nothing but his thoughts were clear. The pitch was hard – bone-dry, nearly white in colour, making the yellow grass around it lush by contrast. It might not help the bowlers much to begin with, but if it started to break up – and pitches in India have a habit of doing that – it could turn into a killer. Robin sent out the openers with strict instructions to get their heads down and take their time. This was our only five-day match of the tour and he wanted to take home at least one big victory.

Our opponents were the best side we'd faced on the tour. It was said that the Indian selectors were using the match as something of a trial for the series against the Australians later in the year. Among the crowd hopes were high that some of their young stars would seize the chance to shine on the big stage. In the side were four capped Test players, prominent among them the leg-spinner Chaughiri, their captain. The hubbub among the spectators was constant. Above the continuous din of talk and cheering were the sounds of ringing bells, blowing horns, piping whistles. Police patrolled the boundary languidly, stopping in their tracks to watch play, apparently unconcerned by the huge assembly they were supposed to chaperone. Dougie and I took seats on the balcony and settled in for a long, slow morning session. After ten minutes' play a roar from the crowd distinct from the general noise swelled up and distracted people on field as well as off. Below us, in the members' enclosure (where reserved seats with cushions rather than concrete benches or folding chairs are the rule), Siva came into view. He was surrounded by an entourage of older men in suits and younger men in casual western dress: sweatshirts with lettering, plimsolls, creased denims. The crowd hailed him. He stood and returned their warmth, his smile visible throughout the ground as he turned and applauded his admirers, hands reaching high over his head.

'Silly fuss over a cricketer,' Dougie said. 'You'd think he was the crown prince.'

'In a way he is,' I replied, but Dougie paid no attention.

The opening bowler approached from the far end, switching the ball from one hand to the other, and sent down a straight, medium-paced ball that died when it hit the ground and lobbed up in front of Paul Walker, who gazed at it with his habitual mistrust and tapped it gently back down the pitch.

'It's going to be one of those days,' Dougie said.

He was right. For the first hour the ball did nothing, the bowlers did nothing with it and still our openers – Walker and Cowper – crept along at a snail's pace. Of course there were five days to fill and no need to hurry. And a dead, slow pitch like this one can inhibit the batsmen just as much as a moist, green seamer. It seems to sap something from the ball. Your bat never quite meets it solidly. You worry about getting yourself out to a nothing delivery, an easy half-volley that looks ripe for driving and ends up popping harmlessly into mid-off's waiting hands.

Chaughiri brought himself on. You could feel the crowd's anticipation. He set his field meticulously, threateningly, with close catchers on either side of the wicket, back and front, symbols of his uncanny ability to turn the ball either way without warning. That was his mystery. He combined probing control of length with one of the most well-disguised googlies the game has ever seen – or not seen, as was more often the case. The long arm swung over from behind the back and with a flick of the wrist he sent the ball spinning like a top through the air. It was enough to set the nerves on edge. And on opening day, in front of fifty thousand people, they were already frayed.

Soon enough he had Walker trapped lbw. Ironically it was to a ball that did nothing, just landed on middle stump and kept going straight through. But the batsman, circumspect as ever, was playing for all kinds of turn that never came, and finished with bat flailing humiliatingly toward midwicket.

The difficulty of 'reading' Chaughiri was one of the game's shibboleths. And he had an even, unchanging, neutral demeanour to match. Watching him bowl, I was reminded of things I'd already seen in India – apparently passive, static on the surface, while underneath . . .

Robin, our number three, strode to the crease. He marched with bat on shoulder like a soldier on parade. The crowd greeted him with applause, though only a fraction of the tumult that had greeted the fall of the first wicket to their favourite son.

They had read the papers. They knew Robin's position. They were torn. They wanted a Robin Barnett innings, a classic to remember. But equally they wanted him out. They wanted to see the would-be English captain decisively humiliated by one of their own.

Dougie retired from the balcony. It was his little protest. He took an interest in everyone else's form, but not Robin's.

Kidleigh, who had been sitting in a half-naked stupor on the dressing room table, rose and ambled toward the balcony.

'Think the old man'll clobber a few. Bowling doesn't look much.'

Walker, newly returned from the wicket, looked up from the stool where he was removing his pads.

'That's a valuable opinion,' he scowled. 'I'll remember when I go out in the second innings.'

Kidleigh smiled awkwardly. He was dimly aware he had said the wrong thing. Tall and gawky, black hair falling over blank eyes, he appealed to the rest of us with an innocent look.

'Kiddo,' said Geoff Robinson, putting a fatherly hand on the pace bowler's bony shoulder, 'one of these days you'll just have to learn to shut your gob.'

Kidleigh shrugged off the hand and sulked on the balcony. Meanwhile, Robin was out in the middle, taking root. He took his time, played with the spin, and used his feet to counter the slowness of the pitch, advancing to drive or stepping back to paddle the ball gently behind the wicket. Chaughiri spread his field and for a while Robin was quiet, content to push for the single and let the bowlers exhaust themselves on the dead pitch. Towards lunch Chaughiri removed himself and Robin lashed out against the weaker bowlers with fours through mid-off and cover point. The crowd loved it.

When he returned to the dressing room for lunch he had lost Cowper (caught behind off an attempted sweep after a frustrating run of scoreless overs) but was forty-five not out. We were seventy-one for two, not a brilliant score, but with Robin in form, not a bad one.

As was his habit, Robin retired to a dark cool corner and silently drank his herbal tea. He ignored our mumbled 'Well played's. Discussion revolved, as so often, around the umpires. Ernie had a theory.

'It's not part of their culture, you see – fairness, impartiality.

They don't expect it like we do.' There was general agreement. I thought of arguing but couldn't be bothered.

Dougie roamed the dressing room like a busy nurse. He questioned first Walker then Cowper about the state of the pitch and the quality of the bowling. Robin's opinion was not sought and was not offered. Taking me aside, Dougie purred into my good ear, 'You can make runs on this one, Davie. Not as easy as it looks, mind. But if you bear down it'll be a nice score for you to take home.'

Poor Dougie. He still hoped for a miraculous recovery in my career. Why I had failed, when others with no more ability had succeeded, was a mystery to him, an affront to his professional judgement.

'How's the head then?'

My ear was still tender but the swelling on my forehead looked worse than it felt. I told Dougie I'd be all right.

'On this pitch you will,' he said. 'But I want you to wear a helmet just in case.' It was one order I had no intention of defying. The truth was that though my injuries were, as the paper said, 'superficial', the memory of yesterday's events haunted me. Why, why, why had anyone taken the trouble to follow and conk me on the head? The police had asked if anyone in Madras might have a grudge against me. It seemed impossible. I'd only been in the bloody town twenty-four hours. Yet in that twenty-four hours I'd become part of a cricket conspiracy both vast and vague. I'd spent the afternoon with the foremost Indian cricketer of his generation, and a potential politician, and the evening with a journalist. What did it all amount to?

A knock on the head.

'Siva, Siva.' I heard the slithery syllables snaking inside my wounded ear. Can it happen again? What's to stop the young man having another go at me, outside the hotel or even here at Chepauk? And would he come better prepared next time? Would he come armed?

Suddenly the thought of walking out unprotected in front of thousands of screaming Tamil cricket fans frightened me. Never mind the bowling or the pitch, damn straight I'd be wearing a helmet.

In the mess of last night and the business of this morning I seemed to have lost track of Lakshmi. It all seemed so dream-like now. Perhaps she had been a mirage? God knows, I'd been missing a woman more than enough to start having visions of one. But of course she was real. Had the broken glass and the rock and the blood and the cops put her off? Did she think I was just another westerner out of his depth in India? But then I remembered she had said yes, she would come to the match, and yes, she would go with me to Siva's party.

I took up a position on the balcony to scan the crowd. Where was she? Had she collected the ticket I'd left for her at the club office? Below, Siva sat in the sun, signing autographs and holding court. His youthful praetorian guard made a tight circle around him and kept the pushing crowd at bay.

Then something caught my eye. Cuthbert, a broad-brimmed white sun hat not quite obscuring his large red nose and thick waist, stood below me, hands on hips, surveying the spectators very much as I was surveying him. He sat down and chatted to the man on his left, whom at first I could not see. Then the man raised himself – a bulky Indian in suit and tie despite the heat. With a start I recognised Mr Narayan, of the Commercial Trust Bank of Southern India.

I thought about it. Cuthbert was rich enough to have acquaintances everywhere. On the face of it, there was nothing strange about him sitting with Narayan.

I watched Robin, alone in his corner. No doubt he was contemplating a grand innings. His strategy was clear: a dramatic break with his old club, a big innings in Madras, a tight-lipped return to Heathrow – the perfect build-up to the new breakaway league. My ear ached and I asked Dougie to change the dressing.

The Consul popped in towards the end of the luncheon interval. He was a nervous, brittle fellow who clearly felt uncomfortable among athletes in various stages of undress. Laughing and shaking hands gingerly with the robust Ernie Fairbanks, he enquired after my health with a trained display of personal concern. I assured him I would survive.

'It's Chaughiri he's worried about,' said Ernie.

'You know, this could be the start of a diplomatic incident,' said Paul Walker, giving me a wink behind the Consul's back.

'Oh no, I rather think not,' said the Consul. 'I mean, it is most unfortunate, really quite unprecedented, in my knowledge, for a British subject to be assaulted in the streets in this way. I mean, you did say nothing was stolen . . .'

'There was no attempt to steal,' I corrected him.

'Quite. It's all rather mysterious. But the police here are pretty thorough. They've never let us down in the past. Of course, I shall be chasing them up, you know, putting on the pressure. Behind the scenes, of course.'

He gave me a strained smile and glanced out of the window at the pitch, where Robin was re-marking his guard. He held out a thin hand. I shook it.

'Really, Mr Stott, if there's anything we can do . . .'

He made a quick exit, saying, 'Looks to be quite the captain's innings, don't you think?' But he was gone before he could notice the minimal enthusiasm with which the prospect was greeted by the rest of us.

I took out a note that had been delivered to me during lunch and read it again. 'David! I was so distressed to read what happened to you last night. Are you OK? Look forward to seeing you tonight so we can talk. Heads will roll, I promise you. S.'

It was a nice thought, but I couldn't really see whose head would roll, and precisely for what offence.

CHAPTER EIGHT

The haze in the air cleared in the afternoon and though the heat was intense the atmosphere was more comfortable, at least for the spectators. Out in the middle Robin resumed command. He lost another partner (bowled Chaughiri, caught at short leg), but hardly blinked an eye. For him the occasion was one to relish, and he swung his bat in an arrogant full arc. He disdained easy singles now, which didn't make life any easier for his partners. Fours rolled off his bat to all corners of the field. Even the wily Chauhgiri suffered, though as always Robin treated him with respect. It was an innings of deliberation, as much a part of his Grand Prix plans as the elaborate charade he'd been playing with the press. This was his answer to the old men who had dumped him unceremoniously in the off-season while he was toiling on a second-string tour of India. Between balls he patted invisible rough spots in the pitch, ignored everyone (including his batting partner), and managed to act as if he was alone and unobserved – in front of fifty thousand people.

I left the balcony and sought distraction in the old newspapers scattered around the dressing room. But all I found were cricket reports and articles about the disturbances in Madras, articles that made even less sense to me after talking to Lakshmi the evening before. I returned to the balcony, put my feet up on the white-painted railing, and watched, from under a large, floppy sun hat, tiny figures play out a finicky, infinitesimal drama in the centre of a baking concrete oval.

Robin moved inexorably towards his century. The crowd cheered for him, the same crowd that would bay for his blood if he gave any of their bowlers half a chance. Meanwhile, other batsmen came and went, concluding the pitch was impossible and Chaughiri unfathomable. Dour Donald Blackburn joined him and had limited success pushing the ball off his legs. But the show was Robin's. At tea he was 123 not out and returned through the members' enclosure to rapt applause. Cuthbert and Narayan stood in their places and roared 'Well played', and 'Good show'. We all clapped him into the dressing room. Kidleigh gave him a cup of his special tea and babbled about the umpires and the wicket. Robin said nothing. Sweat matted his thinning grey hair and dripped from the refined point of his nose. His gloves were soaked through and he tossed them aside with a wet thud. Dougie, suddenly softened by the spectacle of the exhausted captain, replaced them with a pair of new ones, clean and dry, from Robin's kit.

From the balcony I watched the milling, stretching, jabbering crowd. Suddenly I caught a flash of long brown hair, a swirl of white blouse and brown arms. I leaned over and shouted.

'Lakshmi!'

The long hair fell aside and above the white blouse was revealed an unfamiliar, middle-aged face. It disappeared in the crowd.

'That your bird then?'

I whirled around. Kidleigh had sneaked up behind me.

'Didn't know you fancied these coloured birds, DTS,' he chortled.

'Leave it out.' I spat it at him.

He backed away nervously, still wearing that stupid grin.

I looked at the crowd. How absurd to think I could pick a single woman in this sea of strange faces. I was annoyed with myself. I should have dropped Kidleigh over the railing and let the spectators tear him to pieces. Instead I had acted as if Lakshmi were some guilty secret. I had my hidden secrets, but Lakshmi was the least of them. She had probably gone to work today as usual. Why should I expect anything else?

After tea Robin batted on for twenty minutes. He seemed determined to punish the bowling and hammered thirty more runs before being caught in the covers for 155. It had been a classic innings on a slow pitch. The applause lingered after his return to the dressing room and he was forced to acknowledge it from the balcony with a raised cap – his (former) county cap.

Of course, they weren't clapping a simple display of batting, however skilful. The applause was about other things. It was about Robin's dismissal by his county club; it was about his status as captain-in-exile of the English Test side; it was about his age and the near certainty that never again would he grace the ground at Chepauk. They were as much a part of the innings as the late cuts and off drives.

Soon after Robin's dismissal Donald spooned a catch to midwicket and it was my turn in the middle. I walked down the cool concrete corridor and emerged through the small door into the glare of the sun, the noise, and fifty thousand pairs of eyes.

I had my helmet under my arm and, suddenly conscious of my bruise and red ear, I pushed it on my head and pulled it down over my face. A murmur spread through the crowd and gathered like a little wave into a gentle ripple of applause.

It was the story in the paper. I blushed. The applause continued as I stepped on to the brittle, manicured outfield and made my way to the wicket. I felt I ought to acknowledge the crowd's apparent good grace and ever so slightly I raised my bat. Embarrassed enough already (it had never occurred to me that my injuries would be of the least concern to anyone else), I was tongue-tied when Chaughiri himself came up to me.

'It's terrible for such a thing to happen to you in Madras. It's not like that, you know, not usually.' And he sighed and wandered slowly back to his mark, fingering the seam of the ball thoughtfully. Even the square-leg umpire shook my hand, said he hoped I was feeling all right and then opined that something really must be done about all this violence.

At the other end, leaning on his bat and barely suppressing a smile, Ernie beckoned to me.

'They'll clap you to the crease, but see what happens when the ball catches a nick on the pad.'

I shrugged and walked slowly back to my crease. As I did I allowed myself to become aware of the crowd surrounding us like a vast saucer brimful of humanity. They were separated from us by a sea of empty grass, not to speak of wire fences and slouching police patrols, but they seemed to bear down heavily. Go slow, go slow, I told myself, as I usually did, largely because there was no alternative. Hold out to the end of play. Keep wicket intact. Keep score ticking over. I took my guard and steadied my head to receive my first ball from Chaughiri.

Like a hovering, apparently motionless bird, it hung in the air for ages, then dropped outside my off stump and moved into my front pad, which I had luckily stretched well down the pitch.

The noise, as Ernie predicted, was deafening, though Chaughiri himself showed no interest whatsoever. For the rest of the over I attempted to conceal my inability to decide whether to play forward or back to the leg-spinner and somehow survived. I was relieved when the strike passed to Ernie at the other end.

I managed to avoid Chaughiri for a few overs and even took

some easy runs off the other bowler, which made me feel better. Though the sun was beginning to set behind the top of the stand, the heat was still intense and in no time my clothes, gloves, hair were soaked with sweat. I removed the helmet and passed it to the umpire, who placed it behind the wicket keeper. Injury or no injury, it was just too hot inside the damn thing. In any case, I felt peculiarly safe out there in the middle, among fellow cricketers, and the crowd seemed far away.

One of the fielders stared at my wounds.

'You look like you've been playing West Indians, not Indians,' he said.

'I think I'll save that thing,' I answered, pointing to the discarded helmet, 'and use it off the field from now on.'

They laughed.

At the non-striker's end I watched the famous Chaughiri action close up. After a run-up of four stilted paces, he brought his right arm over from behind the small of his back in a looping arc. His wrist turned over so fast I could never make out exactly what he was doing with the ball and certainly could never read the googly. Ernie coped well enough at the other end, though his scoring was only slightly faster than mine. He played back more often than not, used a lot of bottom hand, and poked his nose at every ball as if a very nasty smell was coming from it.

It's supposed to be easier for left-handers to play leg-spin, but against Chaughiri there didn't seem to be much advantage. My sole intention was survival. Nonetheless, I clipped one off my legs for two and the next ball I sneaked past square-leg to the boundary for four. I began to relax. The longer I stayed out there, the more it felt like any other cricket match. I listened to the Indian players talk amongst themselves in their curious argot, a mixture of Tamil and English in which phrases like 'extra cover', 'well bowled', and 'good length' popped up incongruously.

I felt I had re-entered a private world, and yet here I was in front of a huge and utterly alien crowd, as public as if a spotlight had picked me out on a stage. I know some cricketers for whom the whole game is an intensely private matter. Batting especially breeds this attitude. Total concentration is required. There can be a long wait between balls and the only way to deal with it is to turn inward, to conduct a kind of dialogue with yourself. This can become all-absorbing and even block out any consciousness of the paying customers. You know they're out there, but they seem not to matter, because in the end it's you who's got to decide how to play the well-pitched-up ball, whether to step down the track, or to glance the ball away to fine-leg.

My footwork, slapdash at the best of times, was well out of synch on this pitch. Somehow my score reached eighteen. I could hear Dougie mumbling under his breath. 'Keep your head down. Don't worry about runs. Runs will come. Concentrate.' But with each ball from Chaughiri the middle of my bat seemed to shrink and it was always a relief not to hear the clatter of stumps or the hysterical shout of appeal.

I escaped to the other end. Ernie coiled himself into his cramped, tortured-looking crouch. Chaughiri delivered. The ball hung in the air for the longest time, then turned outrageously wide of the off-stump. Ernie prodded at air, then swore. I avoided his eye. It's bad enough everyone else watching you without your team-mates looking on as well.

Ernie tapped the bat impatiently as Chaughiri flicked the ball from hand to hand like a card sharper. He turned and began his run-up, looking for all the world like a stiff-legged teenager learning to waltz.

In the air the ball looked to be a replica of the previous one. Ernie was already high into his backlift and followed through with a savage swish in the direction of mid-off.

A tiny click echoed round the ground. Chaughiri's indecipherable googly had sneaked between swinging bat and static pad and gently knocked against middle stump, barely dislodging a single bail. There was a silent split-second as the crowd craned necks to confirm what had happened, then uproar. Ernie stiffened and walked back to the pavilion with a glum, mortified stare. The cheering was prolonged and passionate. It was what the crowd wanted to see, and Chaughiri had delivered the goods with all the élan of a master magician calmly making a volunteer from the audience vanish into thin air.

The funny thing about this kind of spin bowling is how hostile it is. Its gentility, its sheer artful slowness, disguises aggression and violence. When you bat against it you are under a very personal form of attack, in which any weakness you might have ever displayed will be used against you. The bowler wants you and no one else; he wants you removed from the field of play and he is willing to lie, cheat and flatter to get it.

I was joined at the wicket by off-spinner Geoff Robinson.

Geoff has a casual slouch on the field, like a lean, ghostly version of Clive Lloyd. As he approached me he wore a surprised look, as if amazed to find himself the object of so many foreign gazes.

'Skipper says shut 'em out for the rest of the day,' he informed me when we met in the middle.

I nodded agreement.

'How's the face?' he asked brightly, as if injecting a personal note in a business conversation.

My glove moved automatically towards the tender ridge on my forehead. 'I've got enough to worry about out here without that,' I said, and brought the hand rapidly back where it belonged.

Geoff dealt with the remainder of Chaughiri's over with rock-like immobility. Then it was my turn against a younger bowler at the other end. His gentle off-breaks looked easy enough, but somehow I couldn't get the ball off the square. Suddenly Chaughiri seemed to have blocked all the gaps. The young bowler's reward was a maiden over and a round of applause. He looked quite pleased with himself.

As the fielders switched over and arrayed themselves in their menacing spider's web of close-catching positions, there was a disturbance at the far end of the ground. A man had climbed and mounted the wire fence and held a banner aloft between outstretched hands. He shouted fiercely.

The umpire at the bowler's end muttered under his breath. The players exchanged glances. They seemed to shy away from me and Geoff, who were left baffled by the incident. On the man's banner were flamboyant, circular, swirling Tamil characters, and from his high, uncomfortable perch, he declaimed something equally incomprehensible in a loud, hoarse voice.

Within seconds a mob of police had converged on the man. Swiftly they mounted the fence to pull him down. There was confusion in the crowd, some cheers and some very aggrieved booing. The man struggled with the first policeman to reach him, flailing and twisting away to keep his banner aloft. In the meantime, a second policeman had made enough room to grab him from the other side. With a sudden lurch both policeman and demonstrator fell off the fence into the crowd behind. The police were now separated by the fence from their comrade and the demonstrator. There were shouts and screams. Police filtered through gates into the crowd, lathis held threateningly across their chests. Five of them frog-marched the demonstrator along the aisles and out of sight under the stands.

The ground was seething. The booing and shouting came to a stop and were replaced by a furious murmur, as if the simmering cauldron of the ground was not quite ready to boil over. The police formed a neat ring around the boundary fence.

'Come,' said the umpire, looking at his watch. 'Enough time wasted. Play, please.'

Chaughiri flicked the ball in the air absent-mindedly, his eyes wandering vaguely over the agitated crowd.

'What was that all about?' I asked him.

His head tilted ambiguously and his mouth twisted into a pout.

'The banner said ''Release Imprisoned Strikers'',' he answered in the neutral tone of someone translating for an illiterate foreigner.

I watched Chaughiri torment Geoff Robinson while Geoff struggled to maintain his perfectly strokeless defence. But my mind was elsewhere. Arrests and disruptions at cricket grounds aren't so uncommon anywhere in the world, but now my hand unconsciously touched my damaged forehead. I kept thinking of the young man in the T-shirt. Strangest of all, I found myself worrying about Siva's party tonight. Who would be there? What would they expect of me? If Lakshmi didn't turn up, would I even bother to go? And now I was supposed to stand out here and block the ball for another thirty-five minutes. I felt I had been cast in a role I wasn't suited to play.

I felt vulnerable, and not just to Chaughiri and his close catchers and the (purportedly) unreliable umpires. For all I knew my erratic attacker might be lurking somewhere in the stands. And if he wasn't there, then perhaps someone else with the same intentions was. There had been no reason for my being attacked in the first place, so what was to prevent me being attacked again? Strange as that logic sounds, it was what I was thinking when my musings were interrupted by Geoff's breathless call for a single following an edge to third man.

I reminded myself of Robin's injunction. Chaughiri bowled one on the off-stump, nearly over-pitched, but it caught me by surprise. I met it with the bottom of a hastily-lowered bat. It dropped and spun at my feet. I picked it up and tossed it back to the bowler. The next delivery turned into me, not very fast, and I pushed it gently to the on side. Short leg pounced on it. There was no question of a run.

I played two more deliveries defensively back down the pitch. I looked at my name on the scoreboard and the feeble figure next to it: 23. That had been my typical innings these last few years. A slow, somewhat chancy progress to the mid-twenties, abruptly terminated.

The next ball was short. I moved easily out of the crease, legs criss-crossing comfortably, and drove it firmly along the ground between the bowler and mid-off. A four. Scattered applause. At least they hadn't completely forgotten I was out there.

I felt better. I felt I was at last taking matters in hand.

Chaughiri seemed unconcerned. He skipped in, precariously balanced, and delivered. I followed the ball out of his hand on its high trajectory and began moving forwards to drive.

Then I saw the thing dip and swerve, as if it had a life of its own. Too late I saw the idiocy of my intended stroke. Still lurching forwards I didn't have to look behind to know the keeper had the ball in his hands and was whipping off the bails. The cheers said it all.

My exit was accompanied by the same polite applause that had greeted my entrance. It was a bad time to lose a wicket. Dougie pointedly ignored me as I showered and changed. Robin, luckily, was busy elsewhere.

'Checking his shares,' said Paul Walker, who was sipping cold tea and rocking in a chair by the balcony.

Dougie at last condescended to acknowledge my existence.

'This came for you.'

It was a typewritten note on thin, tissue-like paper: *I will pick you up in front of your hotel at seven. L. Kumbaikonam.*

I was careful to hide my delight from Dougie. He would have regarded it as unbecoming in a man who had just been comprehensively stumped.

Forty minutes later we gathered in the club room in the pavilion for the daily meet-the-press ritual. Robin joined us. Tea and lemonade were served (fresh lemonade, loaded with sugar and ice). Players from both sides mingled, chatting about the heat and the pitch and the standard of hotel accommodation. Everyone remarked on my injuries and everyone apologised that 'such a thing' should happen 'in our city'. Did Indian mugging victims in London receive similar treatment? The Indian players wanted to know all about the cricket scene in England and in particular the situation in the northern leagues, where several hoped to play as professionals in the coming year. They were full of admiration for Robin's innings and keen to know my opinion of Indian cricket. I was happy to tell them I was most impressed.

In one corner Robin held court. The reporters quizzed him over the latest turn in his county dispute. He answered with a face as straight as his bat. He spoke in his most deferential manner but was, as always, full of quotable material.

'All I've ever sought is a contract that reflects my contribution as batsman and captain. I've spent my whole career with one club and I would much prefer to keep it that way. I'm no advocate of football-style transfers and big fees. That sort of thing only destabilises the game and creates an élite of highly-paid super-stars. I want to see better conditions and fairer rewards for everyone in the game.'

When Robin had finished with the press (abandoning Chaughiri to their merciless probings), he spoke to Mr Narayan, who flitted about shaking hands and smiling at everyone. For a moment I watched them in conversation. Then Robin looked up and caught my eye. Excusing himself, he walked over and pulled me to a quiet corner.

'You spoke to Siva?' he asked out of the corner of his mouth, while smiling stiffly at a gang of passing cricket officials.

'Is this a good place . . .' I stared nervously around the crowded room.

'Never mind that,' he snapped, keeping his voice low and his face expressionless.

'Well, I talked to him. I told him about . . .'

I spoke into a craggy, sunburnt ear.

'He's not interested. He's going into politics. He doesn't need it now.'

'Yes, I'd heard that,' Robin mused. 'They're mad enough here to elect him, I'm sure.'

'He said to wish you luck. He thinks the idea is workable.'

'I'm sure I don't need advice from Siva Ramachandran. Thank you. You'll be seeing him tonight?'

'How do you know?' I was startled.

'Narayan mentioned it,' he said casually. 'I'd go myself but I have some business calls to make.'

'I'll bet you have.'

He looked at me sternly. 'Sarcasm can be an unpleasant character trait, David. I suggest you avoid it in future.

I smouldered but said nothing.

'You know my commitment,' he was lecturing me, his freshly scrubbed features haggard at the end of the long day. 'If I have a plan I stick to it. There's little point in moving the field to cover the gaps.'

Ostentatiously I looked at my watch.

'Tell Siva,' he commanded, 'the last thing we want is to interfere in his political career. It's his support we're looking for, not his time.'

'He's not interested.'

'He might be yet. Remind him of the Coromandel Coast Investments scheme. That should set his mind at rest.'

'What?'

'Just remind him.'

I agreed, but swore to myself it would be my last flight as carrier pigeon. The two stars could pass their own cryptic messages in future.

'And get Fraser to have a look at that head of yours.' He moved closer and whispered, 'There's a great deal at stake here. Our little proposal could stir up quite a hornets' nest.'

He plunged back into the crowd, receiving compliments on his century with the blank politeness of someone too used to both praise and blame.

CHAPTER NINE

Siva's party was unlike any party I'd ever attended. I was pitched in at the deep end and if it hadn't been for Lakshmi I would have drowned. She was my interpreter in more ways than one.

It started outside the whitewashed walls guarding the colonial mansion like the ramparts of a fort. We arrived in Lakshmi's Ambassador. She was dressed in a green and gold sari over a black bodice. Her eyes were framed in mascara and her lips painted deep red. I had shaved, grimacing at the battered face in the mirror, and put on my best clothes. I left my tie at the hotel. It was just too hot.

Standing in front of the gates was a group of young men, quite different from the journalists I'd seen there the day before. They wore slick western clothes, some had close-cropped heads and a few wore red sweat-bands around stubby scalps. They inhaled deeply on cigarettes and joked among themselves. Two stepped forward and pushed against us as we approached the gate.

They asked questions and Lakshmi answered firmly, indicating me with a bangled forearm and pronouncing my name amidst incomprehensible Tamil.

'Well played, Mr Stott,' said one of them. Whether he spoke any English beyond this phrase was impossible to tell.

I counted some twenty of them outside the gate. They let us pass.

'Bodyguards?' I asked as we walked up the path.

The garden was illuminated with coloured lights hanging from trees and strung in circles around bushes. Incense wafted over the foliage. A cheerful babble – voices and music mingling together – emanated from the house which had seemed so sleepy and forgotten the day before. Lights burned in all the windows throwing weird shadows across the garden.

'Goondas,' Lakshmi answered as we neared the giant veranda. 'Gangsters. Political muscle-men. All the parties use them. Sometimes factions within parties have their own little army of them – individuals and businessmen as well. Sometimes they're just bodyguards. Sometimes they're much more, and much worse.'

Our host greeted us at the door. His dress was casual but elegant – pale blue trousers and a silk shirt to match. A gold medallion hung round his neck. His welcoming grin was set rigidly in his face, as if he was afraid it might slip off.

'David! David! What a pleasure! Let me look at you. Oh dear, you know it is worse close-up. What a thing to happen to you!'

He clapped me on the back and then looked Lakshmi up and down with mock astonishment.

'And you've brought a female companion! You're trying to upstage me, I know it.'

I introduced Lakshmi as a friend and journalist (I couldn't be bothered to lie about this). He insisted he was familiar with her work, but neither Lakshmi nor I believed it.

'We must talk,' he said seriously, before running off to mingle with his guests.

Inside people overflowed from one room to another. Where-ever possible they sat down, not just on chairs and sofas, but on stairs, steps, cushions. All the women wore saris. About half the men were dressed (expensively) in western garb and the other half neatly turned out in lapel-less tunics and baggy trousers. Here and there a white face beamed out of the crowd. Conversation was animated and laughter loud. Alcohol (real, foreign-made wines and spirits, not the unpalatable 'Indian Made Foreign Liquor' which had been our diet on tour) was served, the first time I'd seen this in Madras, a dry city in one of the driest of India's many dry states. Servants in red livery – immaculate white dhotis neatly tied under the crotch – passed round drinks and food on silver trays. They were adept at making themselves invisible, appearing and disappearing in the throng like automated ghosts. Manni and her children were nowhere to be seen. The guests gorged themselves on samosas, spicy peanuts, chick peas, pieces of aubergine, onion, potato, chilli pepper fried in a nutty tasting batter. Food smells mingled with the odour of incense and perfume and floated in the heavy air, while music was pumped out endlessly by Siva's state-of-the-art stereo.

He conducted himself with lavish gaiety. Incessantly making the rounds, he shared jokes with a booming, brittle laugh and commanded servants with aggressive authority. He was a far cry from the Siva I'd known struggling in the Second XI.

What impressed me most about the guests was how unbelievably rich they looked. In England – against the background of a higher standard of living – I wouldn't have noticed it. But then in England I wouldn't have been invited to such a party. Here the clothes, the jewellery, the haircuts, the plump features all stood out. And amidst the spectacle of wealth lingered the scent of something else – power.

Most of the talk was in Tamil, but English words leapt out, just as they had among the Indian cricketers, only now they were different words: sterling, dollars, Rover, Rolls, stereo, video, computer . . .

'It is a scandal that such a thing should happen in Madras,' said a man with gold cufflinks who stared aggrieved at the inky blotch on my forehead.

'This is the pass we have reached . . .'

'A fine thing for the British press to write about us.'

'These people!'

'There is no respect. None whatsoever.'

'Damn bloody hooligans. The police should take it in hand.'

I felt my wound growing redder and more prominent by the minute. In an attempt to change the subject I asked about the lone demonstrator at the match.

'This whole strike business has been greatly exaggerated.'

'Our enemies in Delhi wish to use the poverty of the people against us. They have been stirring up all this trouble.'

'You must understand our people. They are ignorant. They listen to agitators.'

'You have your Brixton and Toxteth, no? Your football hooligans?'

One gentleman insisted repeatedly to no one in particular: 'Overpopulation. Too many mouths to feed.'

Lakshmi drifted away. I remained surrounded by middle-aged men, eager to persuade me that all Madras's ills were the fault of the central government and the ruling party in Delhi, whom they accused of obstructing 'all the good work of the Party on behalf of the masses'.

The prospects for Siva's candidacy in the coming by-election excited them.

'You approve of cricketers entering politics, Mr Stott?'

'Why not?' I answered. 'There are plenty of amateurs in politics already. One more won't hurt.'

My joke was not appreciated.

'Siva will be a most professional candidate.'

'He will raise the standard of public life.'

'He is incorruptible.'

'He will bring the Party closer to the people.'

Some of the goondas from outside had joined the party and appeared to be making themselves at home. I tried to avoid staring at them.

The conversation turned, inevitably, to cricket. Was Siva the greatest all-rounder since Sobers? Would the Indians beat the Australians? Should Chaughiri go to England to play county cricket? Mostly I gave them the answers they were looking for. (A bad habit of mine, nurtured by years on the county circuit.)

'You English must understand what cricket means to our people. It expresses their hopes and dreams. They look to our great cricket heroes as natural leaders.'

This met with general and ardent agreement.

'The British may have taught us cricket but we have made it our own.'

Of that there could be no doubt.

'And Siva has been denied the captaincy that is rightfully his!'

'Is it not true that all the world recognises Siva as the true leader of Indian cricket?'

I said I didn't think I should get involved in domestic disputes.

'But he is a natural leader. The people know it.'

'Like your Robin Barnett.'

'Yes, a magnificent player.'

'And a true gentleman.'

'Why has he never been appointed captain?'

I tried to explain why Robin had never been made captain, but it came out sounding improbably byzantine and conspiratorial. They looked dubious as I struggled with the ins and outs of selectorial fashion at Lord's.

I was extricated by the arrival of an Englishman, a man in his thirties in a blue blazer and high open white collar, carrying a large whisky in one hand. There were jokes about the English taste for whisky and a strange assumption that I was already acquainted with my fellow countryman.

'Peter Shrapley,' he introduced himself in a modest, middle-class voice.

I felt relieved. Shrapley looked and sounded so familiar, so understandable in the midst of these high-flying Indians. I could picture him at the members' bar after a sunny day at Chelmsford or Taunton. Public school, pleasant manner, keen on cricket but modest about it. The sort of businessman who can deal with a cricketer as one professional to another.

He said he was disappointed to have missed the day's play at Chepauk.

'But business will be business . . .'

He seemed on familiar terms with all of them. They said he was a decent opening bat and quick between the wickets. He admitted to 'playing the odd Sunday' and 'occasionally' opening the batting.

He was pressed to give his opinion of Siva's electoral ambitions.

'All in all, yes, I think it will be a good thing,' he said. 'A fresh image for the Party. The key point now is stability, of course.'

The others waggled heads in agreement. I suddenly felt less easy with him. He spoke this opaque political language like a native.

I excused myself to join Lakshmi. She was standing in a corner with Gopal Srikkanth, the sports journalist from the *Madras Banner*. They sipped glasses of iced coffee and exchanged venomous whispers. Gopal was short and stocky with neatly trimmed hair and large spectacles. It was a surprise to see him at Siva's amidst all the politicians and businessmen.

'I see you found your compatriot,' Lakshmi said. 'How these Englishmen stick together.'

I didn't like her tone and felt I should defend myself against whatever slur she was implying. But then it was true: the Englishman's company had been as welcome to me as a glass of water to a man in the desert.

'He seems a friendly bloke,' I shrugged.

'Shrapley?' she said. 'Friendly? No one's ever called him that before. He's the managing director of the plant where all the trouble started.'

I was surprised. I must have showed it.

'A few weeks ago some of the strikers surrounded him in his office,' Gopal explained in a low voice. 'They threatened to cut him up into little pieces and post them back to England one by one.'

My mouth dropped open.

'Don't look so shocked,' Lakshmi chided me. 'Not all Englishmen come to India to play cricket.'

Shrapley, they explained, was a supporter of the Party – or rather, the parent company which sent him out here was. It was impossible for any group to take power in Madras without at least being tolerated by the foreign firms operating in the city. To Lakshmi and Gopal, Shrapley's presence here tonight was the seal of approval on Siva's candidacy.

'It's all beyond me.' I shook my head. 'Who *are* all these people?'

Lakshmi and Gopal were happy to give me a run-down on the guests.

Standing next to Shrapley was the man who had inveighed against overpopulation. He was a cigarette manufacturer who had only recently switched his allegiance from the central government. His two sons – too unreliable for jobs in the cigarette business – had then secured responsible posts in the state administration.

Next to him was a film producer. Lakshmi had interviewed him once and run a feature on one of his leading female stars. Despite rumours about casting-couch conquests he was a Hindu zealot and sponsor of the extreme anti-Muslim faction within the Party. His goondas had broken up a strike of film extras – one of the few paying jobs open to Madras's hundreds of thousands of unemployed – with scythes and switchblades.

On and on they went. Oil importers, coir magnates, 'official' trade union leaders, civil servants, judges, surgeons. All contributors to the Party. All here to show support for Siva's adventure in electoral politics. All, at least according to Lakshmi and Gopal, concealing some debt, favour or felony.

'And Siva?' I asked. 'What are you going to tell me about him?'

'Pure as the driven snow,' Gopal insisted. 'The best thing to happen to the Party in years.'

The house was packed by now. Guests lined the walls and sat shoulder to shoulder on settees and stairways. The music had been turned up and the red-liveried servants slipped in and out with food and drink. The men from outside – the goondas – insinuated themselves everywhere.

'And how are your wounds?' Gopal asked jovially. 'Even Siva had to wait longer to make the front page.'

'He wanted Siva,' Lakshmi interrupted. 'This boy, he didn't want David. He wanted Siva.'

Gopal looked startled, but before he could say anything we were joined by the great all-rounder himself.

'So here you are! Blabbing to the press?' He turned to Lakshmi. 'Has he told you of our torrid nights in Worcester and Mansfield?'

His face was flushed and his shoulders bent. His rigid grin was frayed at the edges.

'Srikkanth,' Siva pressed the journalist, 'you must write a wonderful piece about David. He is already something of a celebrity. We must show him the Indian press are more honourable than the Fleet Street hounds. And I have always said he is a first-class batsman.'

'That wasn't a first-class stroke I played today.'

'Ah, but against Chaughiri . . .' Siva sighed.

'Robin seemed to have him sussed,' I said.

'Robin!' Siva snorted.

'It was a fine innings,' Gopal observed.

'To hell with Robin Barnett!' though he hadn't touched a drink all evening, Siva was acting like a drunken man. 'He is an anachronism, a ghost. Who needs this man, eh?'

He stared defiantly at the three of us, daring us to disagree. Lakshmi, pursing her lips in a polite smile, wondered aloud, 'For an anachronism he attracts a great deal of publicity.'

'I am sick of it!' Siva raised his voice. 'It was a fine century, yes, yes, who can deny it? But what does it mean? Can you tell me that? What does it mean?'

'He's an admirer of yours,' I said quietly.

'With admirers like Robin Barnett . . .' Gopal began making a joke but seemed to lose heart.

Siva's behaviour made me nervous. 'He said to remind you of something,' I blathered merrily, 'Coromandel Coast Investments. That's right. He said it would put your mind at rest.'

There was a single pronounced beat of Siva's long dark lashes. Suddenly he was sober. Looking straight at me and very calmly he said, 'Robin is mad, don't you think?'

He turned to Lakshmi with his famous flirtatious smile and added, 'A relic. Very pukka sahib. Very proper.' He tried to imitate Robin's public school drawl.

'I wouldn't know,' Lakshmi replied in a girlish, flighty manner that was new to me, 'David is the only real cricketer I've ever talked to.'

'Well, you must shop around.' Once again he was the bantering host. 'Old David is certainly not the best we have to offer.'

He made as if someone else in the crowd had caught his eye and turned to go. 'We must discuss this mysterious attacker of yours,' he said quietly, then rejoined his other guests.

For a moment the three of us were silent.

'*The Banner* will support this candidacy, I assume,' Lakshmi said wearily.

'Of course. We must. It's better than letting those dogs from Delhi get away with murder.'

It was an argument they'd had before. I listened, not fully understanding, but admiring Lakshmi more than ever.

Mr Narayan strutted towards us beaming as if we were long-lost relatives. He greeted Gopal with familiarity and a touch of condescension, pronounced himself enchanted with Lakshmi, then turned to me.

'Mr Stott, I cannot tell you how sorry we are about this terrible incident. I was so distressed to hear about it. And the tour has been going so well. It has been such a success.'

I made polite noises.

'We're all baffled, you know. I've spoken to Robin and he has given me all the details. If there is anything we can do, please . . . As the sponsors we feel very much responsible.'

He went on in this vein. Gopal made a show of listening respectfully. Lakshmi stared into the middle distance, not completely disguising an amused smirk.

'It is these agitators, I am sure, these Naxalites. They want to discredit the Party. I shouldn't be surprised if they were goondas working for Delhi.'

However much my injuries had upset him, he expressed himself highly pleased with the day's work.

'Chaughiri was marvellous, don't you think?'

'I'd be the last to deny it!' I said.

'And Robin's century . . . What can you say? A master! Don't you agree, Srikkanth? As a paid observer?'

'Yes,' said Gopal, 'a masterful century. If you read tomorrow's *Banner* you will see that is exactly what I have called it.'

'Indeed,' Narayan resumed, 'what poise the man has!' He turned to me. 'I am not ashamed to admit being a fan, Mr Stott. It was a privilege to watch him play.'

'What about this poor umpire of yours,' Lakshmi interrupted. 'Have they found the killers?'

Narayan lowered his head sorrowfully. 'You know the man worked for me? Yes. In our foreign section, for quite some time. A tragedy. We have made some provision, of course, for the children and the widow. She is distraught. A Muslim family, very devout. I believe the police have a few leads.' Narayan looked earnestly at me. 'Siva knew him,' he said. 'Yes, I believe they were old acquaintances.'

'And the by-election candidacy?' Gopal asked.

'A loss to the cricket world, certainly. I can't help feeling Siva should wait. You know the captaincy might still be his.'

'Never,' said Gopal.

'You are a pessimist, Srikkanth.'

'I am a realist. Siva will never captain the Test side. I can tell you this as a fact.'

'You cannot imagine what he means to us,' Narayan said to me. 'He has a real place in our people's hearts.'

I said I was well aware of Siva's stature.

'I can never understand why Robin Barnett does not enjoy the same kind of following in your country.'

'Neither can Robin.'

He ignored the remark. 'A man of authority, a cricket aristocrat. Like Siva, an individualist, but also a leader, a born leader.'

Beyond Narayan's low, rounded shoulder I saw Siva's face floating towards us as if detached from his body and borne along in the current of restless party-goers.

He touched me on the shoulder.

'Come, I want you to see my newest videotape.'

We climbed the stairs and entered a room with a large bed covered with an embroidered slip. A glass chandelier hung overhead. Light spread from a small electric lamp made out of an antique vase. Billowing muslin curtains fell over the windows. In one corner, sitting proudly on a teak cabinet, was the video. Next to it, in a long rack, was a collection of boxed tapes, each one neatly labelled in Siva's minute handwriting.

He pointed to the bed and I sat down on it. He made no move towards the video but pulled up an armchair and slumped in it. From downstairs came the muffled sounds of music and talk. His face was transformed. The buoyant gaiety that had imprisoned it had vanished. It hung from his long, sinuous neck and seemed to hover in front of me, the eyes wide and dull. He looked suddenly away, and his mouth twisted in a grimace.

'Now tell me your story.'

'What story?'

'The story of how you were attacked outside my house.'

'I wasn't attacked outside your house.'

Baffled by his hostility, I recounted in a cold voice exactly what had happened: the young man's first approach; Lakshmi's intervention; our dinner; the fight outside the car; the rock in the face. I thought I felt my bad ear start to ring.

'And – you say – this young man in the T-shirt had a message for me?'

'Apparently.'

He stared grimly at me. 'I do not understand you,' he said in an angry spasm. 'You come to my house as a friend. I invite you to my private party. Can you understand what that means? Can you understand what these people in this house means?'

I started to ask what on earth was wrong, but he gave me no chance.

'You would blackmail me? You would threaten me? You would concoct allegations, you and that madman, Robin Barnett?'

He seethed with indignation, and under the indignation, showing in the sad, brown eyes, was fear; and that scared me. An umpire had been murdered. I had been recruited to some far-fetched millionaire's cricket circus. I had been beaten up. I had even been bowled by Chaughiri. But up till now I hadn't been afraid. Fear is a contagious thing. You can be blissfully ignorant of the most lethal peril, until you see it in someone else's face, and then a trap-door swings open beneath you.

'What are you talking about?' I shouted. 'I've done nothing to you. I've been knocked on the head by some bloody little thug and I've got the bruise to prove it. What the hell is the matter with you?'

He stared at me long and hard. I met his eyes as squarely as I could.

'You know nothing . . .' He said it wearily, like a man who has given up a chase and sunk exhausted by the side of the road.

'Siva, what's going on here? Tell me.' He looked so despondent I forgot my own rage and felt sorry for him.

He was silent. The noises of the party drifted up. They seemed miles away. Siva asked, 'What do you know about Coromandel Coast Investments?'

'Nothing. Robin said to remind you. You told me they would ask another favour and they did. All I've done is pass on a message.'

He slipped out of his shoes and softly paced the floor.

'And Cuthbert?' he stopped and asked. 'What do you know about him? Where does he get his money?'

'I told you. He runs newspapers.'

'But where does he get his other money from?'

I didn't know what to say.

Siva sat down again and uttered a guttural cry. Then he made a high-pitched sound like an anguished grunt and bit his knuckles.

'Damn,' he said, looking at me now with pity rather than anger. 'Damn. I have given you bad advice, David, I'm sorry.'

I smiled. I was relieved. He was no longer the grinning superstar of downstairs, nor the wild, fearful man of a moment ago. He was the old Siva, gentle, considerate.

'Whatever is going on,' I said in the mildest tone I could muster, 'whatever it is I've got myself into, it's my doing, Siva, not yours.'

He nodded vacuously. Then, with renewed urgency, 'But you must separate yourself from these people at once. Make an excuse. We'll find another job for you. Don't worry. I have friends. Friends everywhere.'

'But what's the matter? If you need help, tell me.'

'No,' he answered firmly, 'I don't think there will be a problem. I can handle it.'

'Yesterday you thought Robin's plan was great. What's gone wrong?'

'It would do you more harm than good to know.' He gave an embarrassed laugh. 'It's something from a long time ago. But I will not be pushed and I will not be threatened.'

I thought for a moment he was going to turn indignant again, but he mastered himself and went on in a low voice.

'Tell Robin I will be in touch. But tell him I will have no part in his scheme. I have people depending on me. I have a role to play.'

His sincerity was painful. He was a man struggling under a weight of fear to remind himself of his own dignity.

'Listen to me, David. I gave you bad advice. This is politics – real politics, not cricket politics.'

'Is there a difference?'

He smiled. 'Maybe not.'

CHAPTER TEN

Lakshmi and I left the party together. Outside the wrought-iron gates we walked silently past the few remaining guards – goondas – sullenly patrolling the high white walls. In the car, Lakshmi started the engine and let it idle for a moment.

'Come back to my flat for coffee.'

It wasn't a seductive invitation. Lest I entertained any confusion on that score, she added, 'We must talk.'

I didn't argue, though the hour was late and I was dimly aware that I was expected to take the field tomorrow morning before fifty thousand people.

She drove carefully through the dark streets. At large intersections and bus stops the police stopped passing pedestrians and shone torches in their eyes. The city was quiet. The traffic seemed thinner than the night before.

Her flat was the top half of an old house in the Triplicaine area between the seafront and the big shops on Mount Road. Here there were more people on the streets, though Lakshmi remarked that even so it was quieter than usual.

'Why?' I asked.

She shrugged. 'It's just the rhythm of these things. The ebb and flow. People are scared. The police have been harsh. Maybe everyone just needs a rest. Maybe it's just an intermission. I don't know. I can't give you an answer to everything.'

Her flat was small and crowded with objects. A stereo, shelves lined with books in Tamil and English, wooden boxes and carvings, a typewriter, cups with pencils and pens. The walls were covered with Indian film posters: gaudy images of well-fed, well-groomed men and wide-hipped, large-eyed women. I sat on a settee decked with brightly coloured textiles.

Accommodation of any kind is hard to find in Madras. She had been lucky. An uncle owned the building and let the rooms at a reasonable rate. It would not be uncommon for a family with four children to live in such a place.

The small windows looked out over the high road, where people made their way hurriedly up and down.

'Normally,' she said as she put a pan of water over a gas flame to boil, 'people sit outside on a night like this. You see all those front stoops? People sit there and chat. They shout to each other. They make jokes.'

'But not tonight?'

'No.'

She shook her head and spooned tea into a pot. 'You must have drunk more than enough coffee the last few days.' She laughed hesitantly, as if unsure whether a return to lightness was the right thing at the moment.

'At the party they all seemed pretty confident it would blow over,' I ventured, knowing it was hopeless to avoid the subject that had been hovering in Triplicaine's warm evening air.

'They would.'

She poured out two cups of tea and absent-mindedly stirred milk and sugar into both.

'They have to. Especially with people like you.'

She handed me a cup and sat down in a modern swivel chair (a cast-off from her office).

'People like me?' I was hurt. 'You mean English people? White people? Any old white person, Robin Barnett, Dougie Fraser? Shrapley? We'll all the same, aren't we?'

'No, you're not,' she soothed me, then grew terse again, 'but you represent the same thing, whether you like it or not. These people need your approval. They've inherited the British Raj and they've made it their own. The black Raj. The Tamil Raj.'

'You knew what the party would be like,' I reminded her, half annoyed and half afraid she would turn her anger on me once again.

'Yes, of course I knew what the party would be like. I've been watching these people for years.'

She said she had tried to make her peace with them.

'After all, I am a journalist, and it's hard enough being a woman without being branded an extremist.'

I didn't know what to say.

'They're a pack of wolves,' she spat out.

'Surely not all of them,' I argued. 'Not Siva.'

'You're so sure?' She glared at me.

And I was sure, at least of that. Everything else was chaos. Here I was sitting within reach of her sari-clad body. The hour was late. It should have been so intimate. Yet I felt further away from her than ever. I stood up and looked through the window at the street. A bicycle crept round the corner and disappeared out of sight. Teenagers chased each other with muffled laughter. A cry was heard, a scream floating across the rickety houses. An old man hobbled past singing to himself. He stopped to examine a broken toenail, then continued on his way.

It was Lakshmi's street, Lakshmi's city. The more I saw of it the less sense it made to me.

'What's a Naxalite?' I asked her.

'Naxalites,' she answered with cold, restrained impatience, 'were young revolutionaries who led poor peasants in uprisings against their landlords. In the late sixties. They were accused of all kinds of atrocities. Some people use the term for any kind of radical or agitator.'

'I see.'

'No, you don't see.' She got up from the chair and poured herself another tea. She was more restless than I'd seen her before.

'David,' she said, 'the man who attacked you was not a Naxalite – not an agitator and not a leftist and maybe not even a hooligan.'

'Then who the hell was he?' I demanded. For a moment it seemed to me she knew the answer and had been deliberately hiding it from me.

'He certainly wasn't what any of those people told you he was.'

Her eyes were fixed on me. I looked away. Then she seemed to soften.

'Does your head still hurt?'

It took me a moment to realise she was referring to my bruise and not the headache I was getting trying to figure out what was going on around me.

'Yes, it hurts. A little.'

'Do you want something for it?'

What was there for what ailed me? I didn't know.

'I think you might feel better if you told me what's going on,' she said.

'I don't know what's going on.'

Saying it aloud was a little scary, but it did make me feel better, as Lakshmi had predicted. I needed to talk, and there was no one else in this city to listen.

Lakshmi is the sort of person who gets the whole truth not so much by asking for it, as by settling for nothing less. Bit by bit it came out: Robin and Cuthbert, Grand Prix Cricket, my mission to Siva, Coromandel Coast Investments. She listened as I knew she would. Whenever I got cold feet, thinking what Robin would say, or even Siva or Dougie, she urged me on. She would ask a precise, neutral question that would force me back on the track until the whole story was out.

I thought: All these things are happening around me. There must be a link between them, but I seem the one person destined not to know what it is.

'You haven't mentioned the umpire,' she said after I had sunk into bemused silence.

I looked blank.

'The one who was murdered the night you arrived.'

'That was just a coincidence.'

'You think so?'

We were both quiet for a while. Lakshmi was deep in thought. I was too tired to think anymore. My hour facing Chaughiri, and the hapless end to my innings, weighed me down as much as anything.

'Narayan is something of a power in Tamil cricket,' Lakshmi said.

'I saw him with Cuthbert at the match today.'

Her eyebrows jumped but she changed the subject.

'You know it was Narayan who first sponsored Siva when he returned from England? Most Indian cricketers have a business sponsor; it's financially essential. Without Narayan, they say, Siva would have had to go back to England.'

'To county cricket? It would have destroyed him.'

'Perhaps. But some people say it ruined his chances of the captaincy.'

'Why?'

'Narayan channels funds to the Party through his bank. People say he's not always very fussy where they come from. Being so close to Narayan was no help to Siva with the selectors.'

It was late now and I dared not think what Dougie would say if I turned up at this hour. Lakshmi asked me to stay the night – on the settee.

'You'll be comfortable?' she asked anxiously.

'I'll be all right,' I said coldly.

'We're different, the two of us,' she said, as if explaining something.

'Doesn't mean we can't be friends,' I replied stiffly.

Lakshmi looked pleased.

'But what will they say?'

'About me staying out? If it wasn't the end of the tour I'd probably be sent home in disgrace.'

'For bringing the game into disrepute?'

I laughed wearily. 'Something like that.'

CHAPTER ELEVEN

It was another hot day. The sun pierced the clear sky and poured through the streets. Triplicaine overflowed with people going about their business amidst traffic snarl-ups and arguments. I asked Lakshmi to come to the match again today (I needed an ally), but she said no, she must work. She wasn't a cricket correspondent, after all. She would meet me later. I took one of the little auto-rickshas – a motorcycle engine mounted on a three-wheeled trolley – and went directly to Chepauk. I was pleased with myself. None of the other players would even consider arriving like this.

As it happened, Kidleigh saw me ride up and watched me haggle with the driver over the fare.

'Going native, DTS?'

I disregarded it.

'Dougie'll have you for this one. He's steaming.'

There was only one way to handle Dougie in that kind of mood. The longer I avoided him, the worse it would be. I found him knocking slip catches to three players in the middle of the pitch. The big empty bowl echoed with the crack of bat against ball. Policemen and cleaners wandered through the empty stands. Dougie acknowledged me with a glare. When he had passed the bat to Donald I went up and made my speech.

I said I knew I should have called. I was sorry. I had stayed at a friend's – no late night, no drinking, nothing out of order.

'But if I'm out, I'm out. No complaints.'

He looked me up and down like a farmer examining a piece of expensive livestock.

'Well,' he asked aggressively, 'do you want to play?'

'Yeah, I want to play.'

'Then get changed and warm up.'

'Cheers, Dougie.'

He turned on his heels and waved me away. For the first time I felt Dougie had given up on me. All his hopes for me had come to nothing. He didn't have to say it. Just by not telling me off he had let me know.

I changed and joined Robin jogging steadily round the

boundary. He asked if I'd enjoyed the party. I said I had and asked if his meeting had gone well.

'Yes, indeed,' he replied, 'very well.'

I waited for him to ask me about Siva, but he said nothing. When our jog was finished we gathered in the dressing room for the captain's instructions.

'This may be the last match of the tour but it's also the most important. We can win if we have a decent total to bowl at. Tailenders, get your heads down and for god's sake cut out the extravagant strokes unless your timing is perfect.'

I was being unsubtly reminded of my dismissal the previous afternoon. I didn't care.

Secretly I hoped our last wickets would fall quickly. I was looking forward to spending a day in the field, though I knew it would be hot, thirsty work. Somehow I preferred it to the dressing room. It occurred to me that if the Indians had a long first innings I might not bat again in the match and, with no contract in the offing, I might well have played my last first-class innings. I wasn't panicked at the prospect. It seemed a relief. Why had I jumped at Grand Prix Cricket? Did I really want to play the damn game, or was it just that I couldn't think of anything else to do?

Meanwhile, the ground had once again filled to capacity and more. The noise of the expectant crowd drifted across the dressing room, where players struck poses of indifference. The police lined the wire fence in a great circle running round the ground. Their backs, today, were turned towards the middle. Their lathis were poised. It was an unsettling sight, even from the safety of the players' balcony.

Two wickets fell quicky. Disgusted, Robin settled in a corner with the *FT*. The crowd bayed. Our last two batsmen were at the wicket and the rest of us prepared for a long stretch in the field. But Kidleigh, our number eleven, held out for over an hour. Not many runs came, but he kept Chaughiri out with a backward jig and a forward stab of the bat that was somehow right for the pitch. The Indians crowded the bat. They appealed wildly. Still Kidleigh survived; he even pinched the strike at the end of the over. The players gathered on the balcony to watch and encourage.

Dougie chatted to himself. 'No, forward to that one . . . Wait for it now . . . Ah, the arm ball, that's it . . .'

'So he's not just a pretty face,' said Ernie.

'The demon's turned all-rounder,' said Alan Cowper.

'Beginner's luck,' was Paul's verdict.

The crowd went quiet. Much as they wanted the last wicket to fall, they were riveted by the young Englishman's performance. When he was finally out they gave him an ovation, which he duly acknowledged with a gingerly raised bat.

He walked into the dressing room with a face split by a gleeful grin.

'Pitch is easy enough,' he said.

The rest of us, set to applaud his effort, turned away. Dougie was in despair. His protégé was turning into a crude, adolescent shadow of Robin Barnett.

We gathered behind our captain and walked through concrete corridors out to the open field. Robin despatched me to cover point. The Indian openers, two young players out to make an impression, took their guards. Kidleigh opened the attack, tearing in off an absurdly long run and bowling a no ball.

I was aware of the spectators looking down on us. I tried to concentrate. Kidleigh's next ball was better, surprisingly fast off the pitch, and it was greeted with a laconic clap by Robin standing at first slip.

Robin's field placings were meticulous. His long arms traced arabesques in the air as he directed players from one position to another. In accordance with his latest assessment of the pitch, he sent me from cover to shortish square leg.

Kidleigh worked up some pace. Paul passed me between overs and whispered, 'He'll be unbearable now.'

The openers were clearly determined not to give their wickets away cheaply. With key players retiring from the Indian side in the near future, they could scent a Test place up for grabs. Soon they were coping comfortably with Kidleigh's slingy pace and letting half his deliveries pass harmlessly wide of the off or leg stump. Robin took the demon off and sent him down to third man to talk to himself. Donald Blackburn came on and contained the batsmen with his reliable medium pace. I fielded the odd push off the square, but luckily nothing dramatic or demanding came my way. The ball obliged me by following the other players.

At the lunch interval we retreated from the increasingly oppressive heat to the cool of the dressing room. They were forty-three without loss in answer to our 355 all out.

On the way in Robin stopped to talk with Narayan, who was sitting with his cronies in the members' enclosure. I lingered for a moment, but was dismissed by an imperious turn of the captain's head. I walked on without protest. Maybe the forelock-tugging mentality was more deeply ingrained than I cared to admit.

I collapsed on a stool in the dressing-room and sipped the juice Dougie had provided. Kidleigh sat morosely in a corner, while Dougie talked quietly in his ear, like a trainer in a boxer's corner between rounds. I remembered the times he had poured his wisdom into my ear. Now I felt, sadly, all that was over, and not just because of my cricket failures.

In the afternoon I patrolled a large swathe of outfield and spent much of my time retrieving balls from the boundary and sending back high, lazy throws to the keeper. We took two wickets but it was hard going and our bowlers were soon exhausted. The heat was worse than on the previous day and the wicket even more lifeless. The batsmen peered suspiciously at the ball and immured themselves behind careworn defences.

Standing at long-on I heard the cries of vendors from the stands selling fruit juices, soft drinks, chat poori, aloo chat, crisps, tea, coffee and all manner of white, glutinous-looking sweets. Late in the afternoon there was a flurry in the crowd. Boys selling newspapers wriggled and pushed their way through it, tabloids held aloft, afternoon headlines chanted rhythmically. What news was it that distracted them from their cricket and set a trail of argument in its wake? I edged closer to the square.

At tea I practically ran up the steps to escape from the murderous sunshine. I grabbed a cup of juice out of Dougie's hand before I became aware of two men standing behind him, one a cricket official, the other a policeman.

'Mr Stott,' the official said nervously, 'the police would like you to visit them.'

'The police?'

'Yes. This afternoon, after the match. We will arrange a car. Terribly sorry. Forgive this inconvenience. A terrible accident.'

'Accident?'

'Yes, your head . . .' He pointed to my injuries. 'I believe the police have arrested a suspect. You will see them?'

'Certainly.'

The official apologised again. The policeman asked for my autograph, then went round the room with his little notebook collecting everyone's signature and bowing his head and smiling.

Only Kidleigh refused. He told the policeman to 'Fuck off out of it' with a snarl that shocked even Dougie.

At last Robin entered, signed the policeman's notebook, and sat down. The official apologised to the captain for summoning one of his players to the police and insisted it was merely a formality. Robin assured him that all of his players would always be happy to co-operate with the authorities.

I waited for this little comedy to finish, then drew up a stool close to Robin and spoke in a hush so that no one else could hear.

'You've got to tell me the story,' I began, trying to control the desperate whine that crept into my voice against my will. 'I'm off to the police and I haven't a clue what to say.'

Robin kept his face turned sideways to me, the thin angular nose held high, the mouth taut, betraying nothing.

'If you don't know what to say about this mugger of yours I don't know how I can help.' He kept his head in profile as if he was talking on the telephone.

'When I passed your message to Siva last night he went mad. I can't help feeling there's something I should be told.'

He turned and looked me in the face. Involuntarily, my head drew back.

'David, we have nothing to do with their squalid local politics. I don't know what Siva told you, but my advice is to stay clear of the whole mess. It's their game, not ours. We play cricket. And next year, remember, we'll play it our way.'

His expression was static, his blue eyes immobile, his mouth a thin line chiselled into his granite face.

Before returning to the field, I called Lakshmi's office and left a message.

I passed the evening session in a daze. The crowd calmed down and enjoyed the increasing ease with which the Indian batsmen scored off our tiring attack. More police had been called to the ground and they patrolled the stands and kept watch over the fences. The heat tapered off, thank god, and Robin brought himself on to bowl for the last half-hour. Though he regularly took fifteen to twenty wickets a year in the county championship, it was said his good figures were largely the result of his uncanny knack of bringing himself on when pressure was minimal and the prospects of punishment reduced.

His run-up was short and crisp, his action high and jerky. He could cut the ball off the pitch when conditions were right and this evening, miraculously, they were right. He took two wickets before stumps were drawn to leave us in a better position than we could have hoped for at tea. They were 253 for six.

I marvelled at the man. Here he was, embroiled in a grandiose plot to transform world cricket, and he could come on at the end of a gruelling day and bowl a spell like that. Yet again he had assured himself of a place in the headlines.

CHAPTER TWELVE

The official car took me to the Georgetown area of the city. In the old days the British called it 'Black Town', and the names of the streets were redolent of its heyday as a colonial port: Armenian Street, Francis Joseph Street, Popham's Broadway, Parry's Corner. It's a dense, busy neighbourhood, its shop fronts and street stalls loaded with goods of every description: fresh food, dry goods, motorcycle parts, shoes and sandals, books, newspapers, luggage, 'suiting' and 'shirting', those ubiquitous Indian words for cloth by the yard, shipping agents, warehousing, packaging.

In the midst of this commercial mecca stands the police station, a Victorian complex surrounded by high walls topped with barbed wire. Police carrying pistols and rifles stand guard outside. In the courtyard more police stroll nervously, occasionally prodding one of the women who sit with their babies in the shade of the wall.

'They're waiting for news of their husbands and sons. Many have been detained since the disturbances began.'

It was Lakshmi. She had used her press card to gain admission and had been waiting for me there. She looked reassuringly professional in her neat white skirt with a black bag slung over her shoulder.

'You came,' I said smiling.

'You think I'd leave you to cope with this alone? You cricketers are babes in the wood.'

'Thanks.'

'Have you seen . . .'

She held out the afternoon paper.

There was a small article on the bottom of the front page. MURDER SUSPECT HELD. It said the police had apprehended a man in connection with the murder of the umpire designated to officiate at the Commercial Trust match at Chepauk. The man was said to be an 'associate' of Siva Ramachandran.

'What the hell does that mean?' I asked, '*Associate?*'

'Anything. Everything. Nothing.' She shrugged.

We ignored the pleas of waiting women ('Sahib, sahib, husband . . .') and entered the reception area, a long, cold hall like a mausoleum, populated by men and women in grey-green uniforms, none of whom appeared to be doing anything in particular.

The desk was staffed by three officers (one, I was sure, would have been sufficient) who ignored us for what seemed an eternity. Finally, replying to Lakshmi's polite but increasingly insistent enquiries, one of them rose and with a sudden air of authority led us up a marble stairway and through several corridors to the accompaniment of typewriters hammering and distant voices pleading and shouting. We knocked on a door with a frosted glass front and were admitted by the policeman who had collected autographs in the dressing room. He greeted me like an old friend and guided us through a small ante-room (in which were squeezed two desks and a wall of filing cabinets) into a well furnished office. There he left us.

We sat in front of a large desk piled high with paperwork and ornamental objects: a miniature ivory elephant, a papier-maché tobacco box, three medals with ribbons displayed in a glass case, and an old cricket ball on a polished teakwood tripod. A transistor radio was perched on top of a pile of papers. On the walls were photographs of men in uniform, and framed scrolls and diplomas, some in English, some in Tamil.

After a moment, in which neither Lakshmi nor I breathed a word, we were joined by an older policeman who approached us briskly, shook us both by the hand, and introduced himself as Inspector Mohan. His uniform was neatly pressed. The gold embroidery on his epaulettes shimmered under the strip lighting. His full white moustache was clipped to set off his wide mouth and red lips. He hitched up his trousers at the knees and made himself comfortable in a big chair behind the desk.

'I understand, Mr Stott, you wish Miss Kumbaikonam to join us?'

'If that's no problem.'

'No problem at all,' he smiled. 'We simply want to review this whole nasty business with you one last time. Then perhaps you could identify a suspect we have detained?'

He grinned and I grinned back.

'I must say in my opinion the applause for you yesterday at Chepauk was a splendid gesture. And most sincere! This whole incident is so regrettable. These are irregular times, Mr Stott. I have hardly had a moment to spare these last weeks and have missed all the play at Chepauk. I am particularly disappointed to have missed your Robin Barnett. What a century it must have been.'

Why was it always 'my' Robin Barnett? Were all English people held responsible for the Robin Barnetts of this world, and would it be held against us?

'This ball,' Mohan plucked the old ball from its tripod, 'with this ball I did the hat-trick – for Madras Police against Southern Railway Staff. Many years ago, of course.' He showed us his grip for the top spinner which he claimed had trapped all three of his victims.

The cricket chatter was irritable, if expected. It's the middle level people – the clerks, the professionals, the skilled workers, the teachers, the civil servants – who are the real cricket followers in India, even if they are poorly represented on the boards and committees which run the game. I listened politely to Mohan's recollections and was thinking of how to bring him back to the subject in hand, when suddenly he slapped the desk and said, 'Now, your story again, please.'

'I've already made a statement.'

'It's not that we doubt you in the least, Mr Stott, but it would be most helpful to hear it in your own words. If it's not too much trouble.'

I sighed and recounted the events as briefly as I could. He listened with eyes focused on the ceiling and hands folded in his lap.

'And Miss Kumbaikonam, I understand, is a witness?' He turned his smile on Lakshmi, who confirmed my account with an indifferent nod.

He examined a paper on his desk. 'There is a reference in my officer's report to your assailant referring to Siva Ramachandran. That is correct?'

Why had I left it out? Was it the story in the papers this afternoon? Had it made me feel uneasy mentioning my old friend's name in a police station?

'Yes. I'm sorry. I forgot about that.'

'A natural mistake.' He leaned over the desk and looked straight at me. 'I understand you and Siva are old acquaintances?'

'That's right.'

'A great cricketer,' Mohan said, doodling with a biro on his desk blotter. 'Many times I have seen him demolish strong bowling attacks. There are few sights in cricket to equal it, you would agree?'

'Not many would disagree,' I said affably.

'And you attended the party at Siva's house last night?'

How did he know that? I nodded, feeling distinctly uneasy.

'Again accompanied by Miss Kumbaikonam?'

He bestowed on her a broad, chivalrous grin. She seemed not the least surprised that he should be so well informed.

'She is your guide in our city. I am sure you are in capable hands.'

No reaction from Lakshmi.

'You are also acquainted, I believe, with Mr Narayan of the Commercial Trust Bank of Southern India?'

'I ought to be. He organised the tour.'

'I was wondering what you could tell me of Mr Narayan's relationship with Siva, Mr Stott. As an old friend?' He placed the question before me gingerly, taking care not to prejudice it with any shade of intonation.

'Can we return to the matter of Mr Stott's assailant, please?' Lakshmi interrupted. 'He does have commitments this evening and is pressed for time.'

'Of course,' Mohan smiled at her. 'You will be pleased to know we have a man in custody whom we believe may have been one of those involved in the attack.'

'One? There only was one.'

'You only saw one, Mr Stott. But there are often many people one doesn't see.' His eyes drooped, and a dreamy look passed over his face.

'But what motive . . .' I spluttered.

'We are considering a political motive.'

I burst out laughing. 'Political?'

'It is a good thing you can laugh at such a violent abuse of your person, but the Madras Police cannot take such a view. Foreigners in our city must be protected. It's not only a matter of legality – though Miss Kumbaikonam can tell you we have great respect for the law as set out in our constitution – it is also a matter of economics.'

'I see.'

'Yes, we are considering a political motive. We believe this young man observed you entering Siva's house, and also observing your skin colour and clothing made certain deductions which, however false, were not entirely unreasonable under the circumstances ...'

'What deductions?' Lakshmi asked curtly.

'That Mr Stott was acting as an agent of South African business trying to recruit Siva to one of their pirate cricket tours.'

He looked into my eyes and gave no hint of his own thoughts on the matter. I was stumped. I didn't know how to respond to such a suggestion.

'Bloody ridiculous!' was all I could manage.

'I am sure it is,' Mohan smiled sweetly. 'But I am afraid we have a small number of people in our city – dedicated, dangerous people, fanatics – who distrust foreigners, all foreigners, and would take the law into their own hands in a matter of this kind. Siva is a national hero. They would do anything to protect him, to warn off potential enemies – people they believe to be enemies.'

'I can't see how anyone could make a mistake like that.'

'Perhaps now you will look at our suspect?' he said genially, as if inviting me for a drink in the pub.

'If you like.' I was utterly nonplussed by this ludicrous South African connection.

'Miss Kumbaikonam, you will join us?' He stood and bowed slightly in her direction. She rose silently, smoothed her skirt, and walked ahead without looking at me.

Mohan guided us along corridors, down stairs, past policemen who touched their caps in deference to him, past clerks in uniform drowning in cascades of paperwork. Soon we left all windows, all natural light behind. Not only the dimness but the dank, unhealthy scent in the air told me we had reached the basement of the building. There were strange sounds, like a low rumble of water flowing over rocks in a stream. Lakshmi kept her eyes rigidly before her. She gripped her bag with a tense hand. Her face was taut and her thoughts hidden. I was nervous. I could no longer recall my attacker's face and was worried I would soon confront some utterly unfamiliar creature who would stare back and rebut all my accusations.

We were joined by two policemen with automatic rifles slung over their shoulders. We walked past bolted steel doors. The low rumbling, I now realised, was the sound of prisoners moaning in their cells. Mohan placed a hand on my shoulder and said gently, 'I am sure your prisons in England are similar.'

'Maybe. I haven't spent much time in them.'

'Of course you haven't. This won't take long.'

We stopped in front of one of the heavy grey doors. The corridor was lit with a single flickering tube. Mohan gave instructions to the two officers. Obediently they opened the door, then went inside and shouted at someone, who remained out of sight. One of them returned to the corridor and showed me the way with an outstretched arm, as if he were a hotel porter inviting me to inspect the accommodation.

'Take your time,' said Mohan. 'Miss Kumbaikonam, you also. I know it is not very pleasant, but then . . .'

Inside the cell was utterly bare. One fly-flecked old light bulb hung from the ceiling. No mattress. No basin. A smell of shit and sweat made me wince. With his back to the far wall stood the boy in the University of Illinois T-shirt, now streaked brown with dried blood.

For a moment his eyes were dead. Perhaps he was used to being looked at. Then he seemed to remember me. His eyes opened wide and he let out a piercing, animal-like cry. I recoiled. The two policemen jumped across and pinned him against the wall. One raised a rifle butt and crunched it down swiftly on his right foot. There was a howl of pain. Tears ran down cheeks puffy and purple with bruises. The foot the policeman had struck had already been painfully hammered. The toes were nearly swallowed in folds of grotesquely inflated flesh.

The boy shouted in Tamil. Mohan, in a low but urgent voice, gave an order to his men, who grabbed the prisoner's arms and held them fast. With a silent gesture, the Inspector ushered us out of the cell. As we walked down the corridor we heard another howl, then a whimpering, like a child crying alone in its bed.

Lakshmi looked straight through me. She marched, close-lipped, one step behind Mohan, back through corridors, up stairs, and once again into the office with the large desk, the diplomas, the photographs, the hat-trick ball.

We sat down as before, but it didn't feel like before. The boy had hit me, for no reason I could see, and my first instinct was to want to hit him back, or at least be glad they had locked the little bastard up. But now it looked like whatever Mohan and his men were doing to him was a lot worse than anything he'd done to me. I felt sorry for the bloke.

'I regret, Miss Kumbaikonam, you should have to see such things. It is not a proper place for a lady.'

'I've seen it before,' she said, with stone-cold-sober calm.

'Mr Stott, you can make a positive identification?'

'No question of it . . .'

'Ah, but I'm afraid there is some question.' He raised his hands apologetically. 'You see, this young man, for whose further rudeness to you just now I must offer apologies . . .'

'I didn't understand what he said.'

'That is just as well. You see, this young man – his name is Sartar Paravassina – is being held also in connection with the killing of Bharat Pannedimbi, the umpire who was so atrociously murdered two days ago.'

I gaped. Mohan seemed to find nothing extraordinary in this development and pursued his own line of thought.

'I cannot help thinking of this umpire's tragedy. One day a man is standing in a white coat in a green field giving people out with his finger, and the next . . .'

'Siva's *associate*?' Lakshmi asked.

'Yes. Something of a part-time, irregular employee, I gather. I believe he acted on occasion as Siva's bodyguard.'

'A hired goonda,' I said.

Mohan laughed. 'Mr Stott, you are beginning to pick up our language. That is very good.'

'How did you find him?'

'We received information regarding the whereabouts of this young fellow and his connection with the murder and the little incident in which you were involved. It was not difficult to find him and make the arrest.'

'He's confessed?' asked Lakshmi.

'Not yet. Certainly not as fully as we would wish.' Mohan turned with relief from Lakshmi and addressed himself pointedly to me. 'It is strange that this young man should commit murder and then loiter about Siva's doorstep, as it were, and approach a complete stranger to get a message to the great cricketer, don't you think?'

I felt cornered, though I had done nothing criminal or in the least worthy of police suspicion. There was Grand Prix Cricket in the background, and Siva and his politics, and that seemed to leave me in limbo and make the questions increasingly difficult to answer.

'You knew the dead man was a Muslim?' Mohan said lightly.

'Yes. I'd heard. Does it mean anything?'

'It might. I regret to say we have our fanatics here as elsewhere. A communal atrocity cannot be ruled out.'

He stared as if expecting me to confirm or deny this hypothesis. I resisted the temptation to turn to Lakshmi and appeal for help because I was certain it would do no good. Before I could begin to splutter a response there was a knock at the door.

'Enter!' Mohan shouted, without taking his eyes off me.

The autograph-collecting constable darted in with a file of papers bound with an elastic band. He placed them cautiously before his superior as if they were a volatile plutonium specimen.

'Ah, here we are.' Mohan dismissed his subordinate with the merest inclination of the head. He removed the elastic band and turned the pages over one at a time. Silently he handed me a sheet. I took it with a question in my eyes which Mohan refused to answer.

It was headed paper from the Commercial Trust Bank, emblazoned with their crest and a motto in English: 'South India's Largest Lender'. There was a number handwritten on the top, a lengthy series of digits and letters that looked like an account code. On the lefthand side of the page, in the meticulous copperplate handwriting still practised by Indian clerks, was a list of names. On the right, opposite each name, a figure in rupees. I'm lousy with numbers, but it wasn't hard to see by the number of noughts involved that the sums were substantial – many *lakhs*. The shock came as I scanned the names. Half a dozen leading Indian cricketers were among them, including Siva Ramachandran.

My face must have been a study in confusion. Mohan smiled broadly, revealing red, betel-stained gums under his elegant moustache.

'Odd, isn't it?'

'Where's it from?' I passed the document to Lakshmi, who scrutinised it in silence.

'Sartar. We found it with other papers when he was arrested.'

Lakshmi handed the paper back to Mohan. 'So the alleged murderer worked for Siva. And the dead man worked for Narayan,' she said.

'That is correct,' Mohan replied. 'What do you make of it?'

'Bugger all,' I said, and wondered how Paul or Ernie would handle this situation. Then I realised they would never have got themselves into it in the first place.

Mohan disregarded my remark. 'You see, this young Sartar, how can I explain it? Son of a large family, semi-employed, ambitious, tough . . . Yes, we have our juvenile delinquents here, too, I'm not afraid to admit it. This young man was identified by the dead man's widow, poor creature. She says he entered their house and threatened her husband and made all kinds of demands, then beat his brains out with a cricket stump – apparently a souvenir of a match he umpired some time ago in the Ranji trophy.'

He talked in a detached, mournful manner like a man delivering the eulogy at a funeral. All the while he carefully studied my reactions, which I did my best to disguise.

'You may see the stump if you wish. We are analysing blood and fingerprints. There is little doubt they will confirm the woman's story.'

I said I would take his word for it. I could live without seeing the lethal stump.

'Quite right, Mr Stott, a gruesome business. The stump entered the eye and shattered the skull. Blood everywhere. The wife ran out of the house and hid with neighbours. Not the kind of thing we associate with cricket.'

I nodded agreement. Laskshmi shifted in her seat.

'So perhaps you are really rather lucky, Mr Stott. Sartar was capable of giving you far worse than a bump on the head.'

Mohan swivelled in his chair and tossed his ancient hat-trick ball from palm to palm.

'Perhaps now you can think more clearly about the young villain's reason for attacking you. The motive, eh?'

'Well, it's obviously not a communal atrocity, is it?' I said.

He grimaced at my cheekiness. 'No, that is unlikely,' he frowned. 'However, in the case of the murder victim it is still a possibility, much as I regret to say it. Miss Kumbaikonam will agree with me that Madras is a city known throughout India for its tolerance. But we have our problems, our bigots, just as you do in England. We hear disturbing reports of attacks on our kith and kin in the East End of London.'

Mohan's heavily lined, bird-like eyes assessed me, weighed me, and I couldn't help trying to avoid them, as if by meeting his gaze I would incriminate myself in this mysterious plot.

'So you see we cannot rule out the possibility that Sartar murdered the umpire because of his religion. And a communal murder can turn into a very complicated affair. Revenge killings, perhaps more disturbances – our state ministry would face a grave threat. Central government might be forced to intervene. On the other hand, if the people were to learn that such a crime had been committed by agents of the ruling party in Delhi, for just such a political purpose, there might be a terrible backlash.'

I was baffled. 'Ask the boy, Sartar. He's better placed to give you an answer than I am.'

'In one sense, yes, you are right. And we will certainly continue to question him very closely. But in another sense our prisoner is a blank, a cipher. How we fill him in depends on other factors.'

'Such as what?' Lakshmi asked and cleared her throat, the first sign of nerves I had seen in her.

Mohan ignored the question. Knitting his fingers together and resting the clasped hands on his desk, he asked, 'Mr Stott, have you ever heard of Coromandel Coast Investments?'

I felt the blood drain from my face. Aware as I was of being closely observed, I could not check the panic spreading through me.

Deliberately and carefully I lied. I said I'd never heard of it. I could have come clean with the Inspector, as I had with Lakshmi the evening before. But I didn't. Perhaps it was a dawning conviction that you didn't hand a man like Mohan the truth on a plate.

'And these names on the list? What do you make of them?'

'Haven't a clue. Why don't you ask Mr Narayan. It's his bank.'

'Quite so.' He perused papers from the file. 'Mr Narayan has assured us it is a list of contributions to a cricketers' pension fund. The Bank, as you know, is a great supporter of cricket in this part of the world.'

I said nothing. I knew Mohan didn't believe Narayan's story any more than I did.

'A cricketer like Siva is virtually a national asset to us,' Mohan was saying. 'His life is not his own. He is a public figure. He is of great value to anyone who would wish to influence the people.'

'I can believe it.'

'His involvement in this incident, you understand, however remote, however coincidental, is unfortunate. There might well be repercussions.'

'Surely you don't suspect Siva?'

'Suspect Siva? No. It could not be countenanced, not in the Madras Police Force.'

Was he being ironic? I looked at Lakshmi. The full red lips were reduced to a thin, colourless line.

'No, what we are looking for – it is our first principle – is who gains from such a murder? For example, if the umpire was blackmailing someone . . .'

He looked hard at me, as if he expected me to confirm by a twitch of the eyelid that it was indeed a matter of blackmail. But my mind was leaping ahead, and I didn't at all like the path it was taking.

'And if the young hoodlum, the goonda, Sartar, thought his master – his hero, the people's hero – was being threatened in some way, perhaps by South African agents, or by someone acting on their behalf . . .'

Again he studied me. My face was blank. It wasn't a pretence. It was simple, befuddled despair.

'Information is power,' Mohan went on. 'To know something about someone can give you more power over them than money, or even goonda. A simple bank statement, a list of names – who knows what they are really worth?'

He opened his eyes wide as if appealing to my better judgement.

'I'm sure you're right,' I said. 'But who would want this information?'

'Not, I think, our prisoner,' he replied.

'Which means?'

He grew impatient with me. What he apparently considered my false naivety was wearing thin. How would I persuade him I was completely out of my depth, that I only understood him in fits and starts? In a world where everything is disguised it is impossible to prove one's innocence.

'Sartar clearly acted at someone else's behest. We will ensure that he pays for his criminal acts – of which not the least is his unwonted attack on your good self – but we will not assume he acted alone. We in Madras have an excellent record in this regard. Miss Kumbaikonam will confirm this. We employ the most up-to-date detection methods. I myself have completed a degree in forensics in my spare time.'

He indicated one of the diplomas on the wall.

Now it was my turn to lose patience. I wanted out of this police station, in which I now felt as imprisoned as the brutally treated Sartar. And I wanted to be alone with Lakshmi. I wanted her to tell me what it all meant, and that I had nothing to worry about. It was all just politics, local politics, like Robin said . . .

'Inspector Mohan, I'm anxious to help. I'm grateful you caught the man who hit me, but really all I know about it is that he did hit me. I don't know why and I'm not really bothered. Maybe it's a communal thing, maybe it's blackmail, maybe Sartar just hated this umpire's guts, and for some reason mine as well. You have your own disputes here and they've got nothing to do with me.'

'Refreshingly honest, Mr Stott,' he said in manner that implied he thought I was anything but. 'Nevertheless, there are ways you can help. Before we proceed further with this case there are certain determinations we need to make. We would like to know, in the first place, the meaning of this list and to whom it is of value. We would also like to know,' and here he pronounced his words with care and watched steadily to make sure I grasped them, 'the precise value of this information to those to whom it is of concern. You see, murder is a delicate business in such circumstances. The police must act with due care for public order, for the interests of the nation and the state. Of course we are politically neutral. But we have our responsibilities. You are aware of the political situation in Tamil Nadu. You will also be aware that this crime might be seen in any number of different lights, which might cast different shadows on different people. A communal murder, for example, might turn out to be a much better thing – if it was handled properly – for the people of Madras than the political murder of a blackmailer.'

I felt myself sinking again into that murky pool of Indian meanings. He was asking for something and he expected me to know the answer, but I was lost. I must have looked quite stupid. He pushed his chair back from the desk and stood up.

'Tell Siva,' he said crisply, 'tell him I don't know everything, but I know enough. I will keep the little goonda on ice. And tell Mr Robin Barnett also. I understand he takes an interest in these matters.'

He extended his hand. I shook it in a daze. I wanted to ask 'Why Robin?' but knew he would only treat it as more false naivety on my part. He bowed politely to Lakshmi and called his minion, who held open the door.

'And good luck tomorrow. I shall be listening on my transistor.'

CHAPTER THIRTEEN

Madras beach runs nearly the entire length of the city, from Fort St George – the original English colony from behind whose walls Clive set out to subdue Southern India – south for over a mile towards San Thomé. It falls in a broad, gentle slope of fine pink sand between the Marina Esplanade and the waves of the Bay of Bengal. No one swims in the ocean, inviting as it looks, because of sharks. But at all times, and especially on warm winter evenings, people come here from their offices and shops and factories to breathe the cool air and stroll among the coiled ropes and heaped nets of the fishermen, whose long grey, wooden boats, at this hour, are beached and deserted on the sand's upper reaches.

Lakshmi and I joined the evening promenade. She had guided me there in silence from the police station. The air was clear and smelled of brine and fish, augmented, when the breeze died, by a hint of rotting vegetable. As far as I could see I was the only white person on the beach, but I was growing less self-conscious of this and felt protected, in any case, by Lakshmi's company. The little kids playing in the samd stared at us. One followed, asking for rupees, but ran away when Lakshmi replied with a few blunt words that were not hard to understand, though spoken in Tamil. Her hair tossed in the breeze and her skirt swayed. The evening gleam shed a deep brown lustre on her skin. Strange, the interview with Mohan had left so many questions, so many dilemmas, and yet all I could think of there and then was how nice it was to be with this woman, and how much I wanted to stay with her tonight, and not on the settee. I had known her two days and of course she was right (her most infuriating habit), we were different. Yet on that beach in Madras she seemed my only friendship, my only warmth, in a world that was growing alarmingly cold and hostile.

Pausing by a boat, wood warped and cracked, gaps plugged with a red, mud-like cement, Lakshmi asked, 'Why did Mohan want you to tell Robin?'

I thought of reaching out and touching her on the shoulder, that delicate shoulder, but turned away instead.

'I don't know. Why did he want me to tell Siva? What did he

mean by keeping Sartar on ice? And why should the little bugger attack me after murdering an umpire? You tell me.'

We wandered off again, down toward the waves slapping the sand and leaving cusps of black detritus. She picked up a small stone and threw it into the water.

'It means they're biding their time,' she said. 'He wants you to tell Siva he's open to negotiation.'

'A bribe?'

She laughed. 'That's the going price of justice in India. But it's more than that. It's a warning. The police follow politics closely. They have to. They need to make sure they're on the winning side. Right now the situation is volatile. With the elections coming up, and the strike, and Siva entering politics, they're marking time. That list of names could turn out to be worth a lot more than a bribe.'

'But what is it? I know Mohan didn't swallow that rubbish Narayan told him about pensions.'

She stopped and held my arm. It wasn't the way I wanted to hold hers, with a soft caress, but violently, the way you grab someone, without regard to their feelings, if you want to stop them blindly stepping into the path of an oncoming car.

'You don't understand what is happening.'

Once again I felt a stupid, startled look on my face.

'Mohan is right. Sartar did not murder anyone on his own. He is a flunkey. He did what someone else told him to do.'

'But who?'

'Someone who was at risk, someone threatened by the umpire and that piece of paper. Siva's name was on the list.'

'So were others.'

'Siva is the only one I know with a political career, or at least the prospect of one. That's a risk, a big risk.'

I refused to follow her line of argument. It made me furious.

'It is absolutely impossible,' I insisted. 'You don't know what you're talking about.'

'Do you?'

I turned away, stymied, frustrated, fed up. I waved my arms helplessly, like a crippled bird trying to fly.

'Look, I know this bloke who hit me is a murderer. I think I know that. I think I know that he hates my guts. And it scares the hell out of me.'

'And now you want it all to go away?' She said it with

something very like contempt, and it hurt. 'David, you haven't a clue!'

'Then tell me.'

She held me in her sights. 'What about this South African business?'

'You don't think for a moment I'm a bloody South African agent, do you? Mohan's crazy.'

'No,' she said calmly, 'he's not crazy, though he's certainly wrong about that. But do you really have any idea who you're working for?'

'What do you mean.'

'Just that. How do you know who you're working for?'

'I work for Robin.' I stopped. 'For Cuthbert.'

'You know Robin Barnett played cricket in South Africa?'

It was common knowledge. 'So has Dougie Fraser,' I shouted angrily. 'So have lots of cricketers. But not me! God damn it, not me. I've had the offers, but I turned them down.'

She touched my arm again, more gently, and said, 'I knew that.'

I looked at her quizzically.

'I've been doing some research,' she said airily. 'I've been to see an old friend, a friend of the family. He knows everything there is to know about South Africa, especially the sporting connection. It's his life's work.'

'You checked up on me?' I was shocked. I suspected she thought of me as a simple cricketer, but I hoped she knew me well enough not to have to vet me.

'Not just you, others as well. I asked some questions. The answers are pretty disturbing.'

'You told this old friend about Cuthbert and the rest?'

'No, not everything. That's up to you.'

I felt betrayed. I cursed myself for ever trusting a journalist. And a woman at that. Why did she have to blow everything out of proportion? I asked questions and she gave me vague, enormous answers, too vague, too enormous for me. It wasn't right. It didn't fit.

'And the umpire? What about that?' I argued fiercely, but to no particular end. 'And the list? What's all that got to do with South Africa? Make sense of that!' I puffed myself up to challenge her authority.

She thought for a moment, drawing a wiggly line in the sand

with her small, pointed foot, then wiping it out with a quick kick.

'I'm not sure. That's why you must talk to Srini. If you want an explanation, you're more likely to get it from him than from anyone else. All I know is that there have been rumours – rumours about money in Narayan's Bank, about Siva.'

'Hold on.' I had to stop such reckless speculation. 'That's just too much. You're not saying Siva's mixed up in this South African thing? That he had the umpire murdered to keep him quiet about it?'

Even as I said it I could hear how strangely, shockingly plausible it sounded, how much it explained. Yet it was impossible. It gave me a queasy, nauseous feeling.

'You don't know Siva,' I insisted. 'You don't know how he feels.'

'He's your friend, David,' she tried to soothe me. 'To you he is Siva the innocent and always will be. Maybe you're right. It would be nice to think so. All I'm saying is let's find out. Come with me now. We'll talk to Srini.'

For days I had been pushed and prodded – by Robin, by Dougie, by Mohan – and now Lakshmi had joined the ranks. She was pursuing her own obsessions and I felt I had to make a stand.

'What does it have to do with me anyway? Why does everyone treat me like a glorified messenger boy? I'm a foreigner here. I don't want to interfere.'

I sulked and walked ahead of her. She trotted and caught up with me.

'David, don't you see? It's too late for that. You carried one message for Robin and now you can't stop. Mohan talked to you precisely because you are a foreigner, a reliable intermediary – because you know Siva, because you know Robin. Why did Sartar attack you? Don't you understand? You're in the middle of it all. And if you don't sort it out you'll just get in deeper and deeper.'

'Deeper and deeper? But how? Where?'

She made me sit with her on the side of one of the boats.

'What did you think of Mohan, with his cricket ball and his diplomas? Maybe to you he seemed a bit of a joke. But listen to me. Some years ago, during the emergency, they locked up ten thousand political prisoners in Madras. The station was full of people coming and going all night. Women filled the courtyard waiting in the queue with their pitiful bribes: a bunch of bananas, a ring, a necklace, a ticket to the Test match. They locked up everyone – trade unionists, shopkeepers, Muslims, untouchables, yes, even film stars and journalists. They were beaten and insulted and tortured. They put small stones in their rice and fine sand in their millet. They made them live in their own filth. Then the emergency ended. The election was called. No one knew for sure what would happen. The police waited, and decided in the end to co-operate with the new powers. Mohan was named in one of the judicial enquiries as an instigator of round-ups and a torturer. But like all the other criminals he was given a slap on the wrist and allowed to get on with the job. That's the man you're dealing with. That's the man who's got Sartar, and the list, and knows something about Coromandel Coast Investments, which is more than you do. And he knows you and he intends to use you.'

She had begun mildly, as if reproving a slow child, but ended fiercely, as if she was angry at me for making her spell it out.

But I was angry as well. I wanted to walk along the beach with her and talk about personal things and forget about politics and cricket. I wanted my Indian interval to be sweet and fragrant and painless.

'Robin was right,' I said bitterly. 'He told me not to get mixed up in your crazy politics.'

I regretted it instantly.

'It's not "our" politics, David. It's Robin's politics, and his friends', and God knows who else's. And now it's yours, too, whether you like it or not.'

'I don't like it. I don't bloody like it at all.'

'But you're the link, don't you see? You're the one who can put the pieces together.'

I wanted not to argue with her. I wanted to please her. But I resented being 'the link'. Tears filled the corners of my eyes and I couldn't bring myself to look at her.

'Lakshmi,' I said in a hoarse voice, 'all I want to do is take a walk on the beach. Just look at the fishing boats and not think about it all. Just for a little while. Is that too much to ask?'

'Yes,' she said, standing up from the boat. 'Yes, it is too much. You think these little boats are charming? Picturesque? You know who owns these boats? Not the fishermen who rise before dawn and sweat to bring home a few rupees a day and die in countless accidents before they're forty; whose children go blind from disease and lose their hair; whose wives commit suicide when they're evicted from their homes after their husbands die.

You think they own the boats? No, not the boats, not the nets, not even the live bait – all owned by traders ashore, who lend them the money to hire the boats so they can go out and catch enough fish to pay off their debts and hire the boats again. So each day's work is chopped into little pieces. One for the traders, one for the banks, one for the police, one for the goondas. And a last little bit for the fisherman and his family. But at least they know who they're really working for, which is more than you can say.'

'Yeah, I'm just an ignorant bugger and I want to stay that way.'

She continued as if I hadn't spoken. 'And the Party makes a big concession. It lets the fishermen keep their boats on the beach for free. Why? Because the traders, the banks, the businessmen who make money off the backs of the fishermen all support the Party. People like your friend Narayan . . .'

'He's not my friend. You know that.'

'. . . Narayan and Siva and their Party. That's why they have to win the election – to keep up the flow into their pockets of bits of other people's lives. Fishermen, the workers at Shrapley's factory, the million people living in the slums, not to mention the ones sleeping in the streets and gutters and out here on the beach, the ones they don't even bother to count, the ones who can never even hope to get into Chepauk to see their idols play cricket for them.'

'You want to write a big story? You want to expose corruption and scandal? Make a big name for yourself? Fine. But use someone else. Find another sucker.'

I was hurt and I wanted to hurt back. I felt humiliated by her – and by all the other events over which I had no control – and I stormed off down the beach, digging my feet into the sand and leaving a trail of dark patches. I hadn't got very far before I began to feel rather foolish. But when I turned around to apologise, she was gone.

CHAPTER FOURTEEN

I was alone. The darkness closed in and strollers abandoned the beach. I crossed the flower-lined avenue that separates city from sand and wandered through small streets until I reached a broad high road. Here the crowd was thick. Talkative clusters constantly formed, dispersed, and re-formed further on. The street lamps burned a yellowish colour, made hazy by swarms of flies. Police, huddled in groups of five or six, swung lathis and watched the crowd with anxious eyes. I thought of Mohan and what Lakshmi had said of his role in the emergency. I walked in what I hoped was the general direction of Mount Road and our hotel. In the back of my mind I imagined myself stumbling across Lakshmi's flat, running up the stairs, pounding on the door and . . . what? Ask to be forgiven? Visit her old friend, the expert on apartheid? I still didn't know.

I had been alone in Hyderabad and that had been strange, but now I saw a different India. That protection I had felt – the protection of white skin and a foreign passport – was seeping away. I passed a tall temple streaked with orange and purple paint in slapdash fashion, the entrance thronged with worshippers and beggars. The houses surrounding it were run down, plaster and paint peeling off, and children leaned over first-floor balconies and spat into the street below. On the shabby walls between the shopfronts lurid film posters alternated with political graffiti, in both Tamil and English. In open doorways groups of men and women lingered with string bags full of groceries. Everywhere I walked I was noticed. You can't miss it: the turn of the head, the naked stare. But no one spoke to me.

I entered a small shop selling newspapers and magazines and a variety of used paper, envelopes, notebooks, and colour prints, all stacked to the ceiling on narrow shelves. A bare electric bulb illuminated the long, thin faces of men in lungis with gnarled black legs. They went silent. One picked his teeth with a knife. I scanned the fading coloured magazine covers and wondered which one was Lakshmi's.

Hesitantly I asked for the latest edition of *The Banner*. A man who appeared to be the owner, sitting in a rusty metal chair, promptly pulled out a tabloid from a wooden board on which the main titles were displayed. As he handed it to me, smiling and wobbling his head from side to side, I told him I wanted to check the cricket scores.

'You are English?'

'Yes.'

'You go to match at Chepauk?'

'Yes.'

They conferred in Tamil. For a moment I thought a fight was going to blow up between them. Something about the Tamil language sounds contentious to a foreign ear. But a barrage of questions followed, all polite, eager, earnest.

'You like Chaughiri?' 'Indian spinners are very good?' 'The pitch is too slow?' 'Siva should be Test captain?'

I took a chance and asked about the umpire's death. This provoked an argument, and though it was in Tamil this time I knew it was for real. I stood in the middle clutching my newspaper, grinning foolishly.

'But is it a political murder?' I asked.

Yes, it was political, they all agreed, but could not agree precisely how it was political.

'It is the Prime Minister's swine who have done it,' offered one, spitting his betel juice in the street, as if the very words turned his stomach.

Another disagreed. 'No, my friend, do not listen, they are always blaming Prime Minister. It is the Communists, I am sure.'

Uproar followed, and the man who had accused the Communists was practically driven from the shop. The others apologised. They were ashamed I should have to listen to such nonsense. They offered me a cup of coffee, but as politely as possible I declined.

'But why an umpire?' I asked.

Again they conferred.

'It is to discredit Siva. To say we Tamils are barbarians. To say we cannot govern ourselves.'

The rest wagged their heads in agreement.

'Our Siva is too great. They are afraid to make him captain.'

Back in the dark streets I examined the paper by the light of a street lamp. Robin's wicket-taking was, predictably, headline material. There was no mention of Sartar's arrest, or of anything else to do with the murder. There was renewed speculation about President's Rule. The strike at the factory continued. I looked around and was utterly lost. I tried to guess my way back to the hotel. I wanted to talk to Dougie. I didn't know exactly what I could tell him, but I kept thinking that despite everything he was the one person out here whose loyalty was to me and not to his pocket or to some cause, except maybe cricket.

It was through Dougie that I had first been approached to coach in South Africa. He thought he was doing me a favour and I took it that way. South Africa is a common topic among cricketers. Every year more and more take winter work coaching or playing there and return with tales of fabulous wealth, long, sunny days, and high-standard cricket. To a cricketer who feels lucky if he can keep up the payments on a small house and one car, the stories of swimming pools, patios, double garages and cheap domestic servants sound pretty enticing. We play with black cricketers on a daily basis in England and it's rare to hear a kind word said about apartheid as such. Nonetheless, there are more than a few players who clearly believe there is something innately more rational about the social order in South Africa than in England these days. In this they are encouraged by a posse of journalists, commentators, and administrators who still feel the exclusion of South Africa from Test cricket was unjustly foisted upon them by a bunch of upstart third world politicians. Of course there are cricketers who are well aware of conditions in South Africa and feel strongly about it. But discussion tends to focus on why poorly paid cricketers are expected to pay the price of South Africa's isolation when companies and governments continue with business as usual. More than one of English cricket's major sponsors is a heavy investor in South Africa.

The offer that had come to me via Dougie, to coach in Western Provinces, was a good one – plenty of cash, and a house, car, pool and servants thrown in. My off-season job with the estate agency was already up the spout. A winter work-out would have done me no harm at all. But I knew from the start that I wouldn't take it. I had played cricket with black and brown-skinned people all my life. Siva was my friend. He had talked to me at length about apartheid and the feelings of West Indian and Indian cricketers. I gave the appearance of thinking over the offer, if only to show Dougie I was taking it seriously. But when I turned it down I made my feelings clear. If I hadn't, if I'd made up some excuse, more offers would have followed. I wanted to avoid temptation. And I had succeeded . . . until now.

The crowd thinned out. The streets grew quiet. None of the figures hurrying past looked like they would or could tell me the way to Mount Road. The houses grew poorer, interspersed with corrugated iron shacks. Small families washed at public stand-pipes; children scavenged from piles of rubbish. It looked like the wrong direction.

I heard sounds of shouting or cheering – I couldn't tell which – and tried to follow them. An old woman rushed by, dragging two squealing children through piles of cow and donkey shit. Others passed, going the opposite way, looking up at me in surprise as they went. I turned a corner and about a hundred yards ahead I saw a large crowd, lit up by flaming paraffin torches. They shook their fists in the air and screamed themselves hoarse.

Police lined the road. They were armed with riot shields made of bamboo and wicker, lathis, and heavy, old-fashioned looking rifles.

'You sir, what are you doing here?' said one of them, stepping in my way.

'I'm lost. I want to get back to Mount Road.'

'You are journalist?' he asked suspiciously.

'No, a tourist. I want to get back to Mount Road,' I repeated.

'Tourist? No tourist comes here. This is not for you.' He waved a hand, indicating that not only the demonstration but the whole area was off-limits to the likes of me.

'You are businessman, you do business in Madras?' he asked, now joined by three others, looking nervously over their shoulders at the increasingly restive crowd.

'No,' I decided my best bet was the truth. 'I'm a cricketer. I'm playing at the match at Chepauk.' I told them my name.

They were quiet for a moment, perhaps confused by this unexpected information. Then one of them pointed to the bruise on my forehead, which had by now turned almost black, and they all exclaimed and smiled.

'Sir, you must not stay in this part. It can be dangerous.'

'Yes, yes,' I assured them. 'But how can I get back?'

They looked at each other. There was a brief, low-voiced exchange, then one went off to consult with an officer further down the street.

'A demonstration?' I asked.

The officer who had first stopped me waggled his head. 'Communist agitation,' he muttered mournfully. 'Is a big problem.'

I asked no more. Shortly a police car emerged from one of the sidestreets, as if it had been hiding itself there until needed. I was ushered ceremoniously but firmly into the back seat. My hand was shaken in turn by the officers who had spoken to me and by their commander, who assured me 'complete safety of transport'. As soon as the door had closed the car took off and turned into a narrow street.

Our way was blocked by a small cart carrying an enormous load of hay, spilling over its sides and trailing in the street. My driver leaned on his horn, then leapt out and disappeared round the front of the cart. There followed an almighty row in which, as far as I could tell, the invisible cart driver gave as good as he got. Then came the sound of a stick swishing through air and meeting flesh, a brutal noise accompanied by curses in both voices. The mule brayed. The cart staggered a few feet forward. Another swish and another thud. More cursing. A bare-chested boy leaned out of a window and shouted at the men below. Then there was another, quite different sound from the opposite direction – a noise of running, screaming, scuffling, falling, getting nearer moment by moment. Looking round I saw men and women rushing past the entrance to the narrow alley. A lamp dropped and a stream of fire spread across the road. Demonstrators turned into the alley and charged towards the car.

I slid down the back seat and hid my white face. Huddling on the floor of the car, I squinted up but could see little in the darkness. A mob surrounded the cart, which lurched from side to side. Suddenly it overturned. Straw fell over the car windows and I could see nothing.

I heard a crash, more screams and hostile shouts. I curled myself into the smallest round object I could manage.

Then the shouts died down. There was an interval of quiet, which scared me more than all the noise. A hand moved to clear away the straw. I looked up and saw a policeman's cap. The face beneath it blinked at me and an arm signalled to others. Before I knew it I was being pulled from the car. Officers stood breathless in a circle round me. I looked down and saw the tip of one of the lathis, red with blood. Hay from the overturned cart was everywhere. One of the policemen held a lantern up and by its light I could see clearly their sweating, frightened faces. Behind them two others dragged something along the ground. I recognised the body of my driver; a wound in his head left a red smear across the yellow hay.

Before I could utter a sound I was hustled back into the car. An officer leapt into the front seat, removed his cap, and with a crunching of gears reversed the car at speed back down the alleyway and into the broad street, which no more than fifteen minutes before had been filled by the shouting, fist-waving crowd. It was now deserted. A fire burned uncontrolled on one side of the road. Policemen attended injured colleagues lying on the other. Riot shields, stones, broken sticks were scattered in the dust. A young woman crouched in a doorway, holding her head and wailing. The car roared off down the street and away from the carnage.

'You want Mount Road?' the new driver shouted at me, swivelling his head and giving me a glimpse of red eyes and quivering moustache. 'I take you Mount Road. Is no problem. No worry.'

Phantom figures dashed across the silvery beams of the car's headlights. There were sirens in the distance. The streets were empty.

We were in front of the hotel. Had the ride taken five minutes? Ten? I had no idea. I thanked the driver as I got out. He said nothing and sped away.

I wandered into the lobby. The solicitous clerk smiled behind his desk. The young boy carried tea into the lounge. Snooker balls clicked. Cricketers laughed. It was a world away from the unholy ruck taking place on the other side of town.

Paul, Kidleigh and two other players sat in chairs in the lounge. They looked up as I entered. I made no effort to answer their enquiring glances and ordered myself a cup of tea. I sank exhausted into a fluffy armchair.

'He's been with that native girl,' said Kidleigh. 'He looks shattered.' As usual, he was the only one to laugh at his joke.

'What happened to you when they were handing out brains, Kiddo?' said Paul, at the same time eyeing me as if I were a creature from another world.

'You lot take everything so seriously,' sulked Kidleigh.

'Coppers the same here as everywhere else, then?' Paul asked.

'They've caught him. The bloke who hit me.' I reported plainly.

'You sound excited,' said Paul. 'What'll they do to him?'

'I don't know. I don't care.'

'Bloody send the little cunt down, I hope,' said Kidleigh.

I ate scrambled eggs and listened to the players talk. No one wanted to discuss the match or the tour. The conversation flagged.

'I'm thinking of jacking it in,' said Paul, in one of his sour, late-night reveries. 'One more summer' had been Paul Walker's motto for years now. He was past love of the game, or even of the money; it was an addiction.

Kidleigh said he had big plans for next year.

'Test selectors already been in touch, have they?' said Paul.

Kidleigh turned up his nose and left for the snooker room. At that moment I knew he was another of Robin's 'pioneers'. I wondered who else might be involved. I no longer wanted to talk to any of them.

Upstairs, sitting on the edge of his bed, Dougie confronted me. He wagged his bald, furrowed head from side to side, like an Indian, but with a very different meaning.

'What have you got yourself mixed up in, son?'

I wanted to talk to him. I'd planned to. Now, I didn't know where to begin.

'Trouble, lad?' It was his softest voice, reserved only for his special pupils.

'It's all right.' I wanted to reassure him. He looked old and worried.

'I've got a lot on my mind,' I added, feebly.

'It's bloody Robin, isn't it?' he sighed. 'Man only knows how to ruin talent. Shouldn't mess where he isn't wanted.'

'No, Dougie, it isn't Robin. Not really.'

I lay awake for a long time. I was exhausted, and I wanted to sleep, but I was afraid of what the dawn might bring.

CHAPTER FIFTEEN

'Message for you, sir, message for you.' A boy's voice called. Dougie leapt out of bed, slung a towel round his waist like a lungi, and opened the door.

'For you, lad.'

He tossed a white envelope on my pillow. I sat up, opened it, and read. *I'm outside in a car. Have breakfast? Roy Cuthbert.*

I promised Dougie I would meet him at the ground, threw on some clothes and bounded down the stairs (the lift had packed up overnight). I dashed through the lobby and staggered into the morning light. Cuthbert sat in the back seat of a gleaming grey Rover. He acknowledged me with a smile and opened the door.

'Morning, David,' he bellowed as I slid in next to him. 'Looks like another hot day in the field.'

He ordered the driver to move on and gave me a hearty slap on the thigh.

'Hungry?'

I mumbled a reply. It wouldn't have mattered what I said. He was going to take me to breakfast where and how he liked and my job was to follow. This morning I would play the role of loyal retainer, but only up to a point. I wanted to know what Cuthbert knew and what he thought I knew. I would not allow myself to carry any more messages.

'Seen the headlines?'

He passed me a copy of *The Banner*. Giant letters screamed: WHERE IS SIVA? It took me a moment to focus. AUTHORITIES INVESTIGATE.

I was aware of Cuthbert watching my reaction. Skimming the columns I picked out details. Siva was thought to have vanished from his house in San Thome sometime the previous afternoon. 'Business associates' had found him missing when they arrived for a meeting. The police expressed 'concern'. They urged the public to remain calm. A Party secretary was quoted: 'We must pray for the return of our beloved Siva.'

I turned the page. Inside was a short article on the umpire's murder. Police were questioning a suspect whose identity had not yet been confirmed. There was an unattributed suggestion that it might have been a communal killing. In a small box at the bottom of the page a report read: 15 HELD IN MADRAS AGITATION. POLICE INJURIES.

The Rover dropped us in front of Cuthbert's hotel, the most expensive in town. It was a modern construction with magnificent palm trees adorning a vast semi-circular drive. Amidst the swathes of reinforced concrete were strange oriental touches: Mogul arches over doorways, striped parasols on the lawn, carved wooden screens around the patios. A gaggle of over-uniformed footmen and porters attended the entrance. Inside the atmosphere had the refrigerated tang of permanent air-conditioning. Telephones, telexes, tobacco stalls, barbers, valets, travel agents all lined the main hall. Around the news-stand a small crowd gathered. As we made our way to the dining suite we heard the name 'Siva' passing from mouth to mouth in excited whispers.

'If anything's happened to him this town'll blow apart,' I hissed just loud enough for Cuthbert to hear.

'Let's eat in the small dining-room,' he said brightly. 'They do a proper English breakfast. All the trimmings.'

We took seats in a darkened oval room with long red curtains, patterned black and white marble floor, small tables with starched white cloths and a single red rose in a narrow vase. There was a formidable array of cutlery assembled on either side of an elaborately folded serviette.

'A sight better than the place the Bank stuck you in, I should say.' He winked conspiratorially. 'When you play Grand Prix Cricket you'll only stay in the best.'

Cuthbert ordered a massive breakfast: cornflakes, eggs, tomatoes, fried potatoes, bread, orange juice. I settled for toast and marmalade. As a rule I don't eat much before playing and the headlines made me even less hungry than usual. We shared a pot of coffee.

'So where's your mate taken himself off to, then? That seems to be the question of the hour.' He munched a mouthful of cornflakes.

'It's who he's been taken off by that worries me.'

'Abducted?' He shook his head. 'Not likely. Who would do a thing like that?'

'Ask your friend Narayan.'

He held his next spoonful suspended in mid-air.

'I saw you sitting with him at Chepauk.'

'Ah, I see.' The spoonful completed its trajectory and was deposited in a broad mouth. His face and hands were heavily sunburnt and his green eyes were clear and healthy. 'Narayan is an old business acquaintance. A useful chap actually. Easy to deal with. No monkey business. What makes you think he knows anything about Siva's scarpering?'

'This dead man, this umpire,' I answered wearily, 'worked for Mr Narayan. The bloke they picked up for the murder – he's just a kid – worked for Siva. Or so they say.'

Cuthbert pushed a forkful of egg, toast and tomato into his cavernous mouth, chewed thoughtfully and wiped his lips with the serviette. All very calm. All very deliberate. The man was a faker of terrifying proportions.

'Why should anyone harm Siva?' he asked innocently. 'These people want him for their political thing. Narayan told me so himself. He's worshipped in this city. Anyone would be mad to interfere with him.'

He drained his coffee. The cup was promptly refilled by an assiduous waiter, who then scurried round the table to do the same for me. I picked it up and gulped it down.

'No, Dave, I'll tell you what I think. In my opinion it's a stunt, that's right, a stunt. Something Siva's cooked up to get himself a little publicity. A little drama. Remember, I'm a newspaper man. I've seen it done before.'

So this was how you made a million quid by the age of forty. You learned to state the outlandish with as much calm and complacency as the truth.

'I want to know about Coromandel Coast Investments,' I said.

He sighed wearily, almost affectionately. 'David, David, listen to me. You know how much our little project means to people in cricket, people you know, your friends, as well as yourself. Grand Prix Cricket is just too important for us to let petty difficulties get in the way. We're pioneers together. We have to trust one another . . .'

'Bollocks.'

Undeterred by my rudeness he ate and talked at the same time and signalled to the waiter for still more coffee. I could see why the unions hated him. He was steadfastly affable and apparently reasonable while giving absolutely fuck-all away.

'You know politics and sport ought not to be mixed. I've

always felt strongly about that. And believe me, politics and business don't mix either. But we have to face facts as they are. I speak from experience, Dave. When you make an investment you have to know your local conditions. You have to know who's who and what's what. Wherever you go you'll find a small group pulling the levers. Narayan and his lot pull them here.'

'For the moment.'

'For quite a while, yet, I think.'

'I got a taste of their opposition last night – by accident. They're not going to go away.'

He shook his head dismissively. 'They know how to handle that sort of thing here. Don't worry.'

'Yes. I got a taste of that as well.'

He smiled an enigmatic smile, half ingratiating charm and half utter contempt. 'You see? That's my point. You find yourself getting mixed up in things you don't understand because you don't know your local conditions. You wouldn't play cricket on a wicket you hadn't properly examined, would you?'

'Don't patronise me.' I was fed up with pompous businessmen treating cricketers like mental midgets.

'Look, Dave, I know this thing with Siva has got you upset,' he proceeded smoothly. 'It's got us all upset. But that's just the point I'm trying to make. We have to watch ourselves carefully here. There are many factors that need to be taken into account. Above all, we must stay well clear of local politics. It's a quagmire.'

'It's Grand Prix Cricket that got me involved in this quagmire in the first place.'

'How can you say that?' A look of wounded innocence. 'All we're trying to do here – and it's all we ever asked you to do – is recruit a few local players to our new venture – a business venture; a sporting venture. Nothing to do with all this other nonsense. We put our proposals to people and they make their own choices. We encourage them to pursue their options.'

'By blackmailing them?'

He frowned gently, like a patient psychiatrist. 'It looks to me like it was that dead umpire who was trying blackmail. Perhaps that's why he was killed.' He paused. 'Perhaps that's why his murderer – his alleged murderer – attacked you in the streets the other night. Perhaps you're just blinding yourself to the facts. I can understand that, David. You and Siva go back a long way. I respect loyalty.'

I stared silently at the crumbs in my plate. I felt utterly mastered by his silky ruthlessness. Everything he said was logical. Everything he said was backed up by something else. And yet it was a lie. It had to be a lie.

'I should imagine that's the way the police are looking at it,' Cuthbert added casually. 'Of course they might choose to play down the blackmail aspect.'

I said nothing.

'We were curious about your talk with Inspector Mohan.' He buttered yet more toast. His appetite seemed inexhaustible.

I stared passively around the room. Some Americans in a corner wanted to know why you couldn't get any 'real bread' in India. I heard a German voice ask for fresh orange juice. An elderly Japanese couple sat silently at the table next to ours.

'Inspector Mohan is a powerful figure in these parts,' Cuthbert went on. 'Since you've already established a working relationship with him, we thought it would be helpful if you could meet with him again, informally, just to explore . . .'

'No way,' I interrupted.

'But I don't think . . .'

'No way, Mr Cuthbert. I'm finished being a carrier pigeon for you or Siva or Mohan or anyone else. It's over, understand? I'm going back to England next week and I never want to touch a cricket bat again. I'll be telling Robin the same.'

With that I dropped my serviette in my plate, stood abruptly, and walked as steadily as I could out of the room.

CHAPTER SIXTEEN

I ignored the doorman's obsequious offer to hail a taxi and instead procured myself an auto-ricksha. The driver was reluctant to take me to Chepauk.

'Is dangerous. Siva gone. Many, many police.'

The offer of a double fare revived his courage and we set off through dense traffic. With a combination of lightning reflexes and blind bravery he manoeuvred the vehicle through columns of backed-up traffic, down narrow sidestreets, round donkeys and overburdened old women, grumbling at anyone and anything that got in his way. The day was hot. A haze, part sea-vapour and part pollution, enveloped the city. Tempers in the street looked stretched to breaking point.

About a quarter of a mile from the ground the driver stopped and refused to go on.

'Police. Many police. Siva gone.'

I paid him off and walked the rest of the way. Sure enough, the entire ground was surrounded by police, perhaps three times as many as on the day before, all armed with bamboo and wicker riot shields as well as long, menacing lathis. There were no demonstrators, no placards, no banners, no chanting. But the atmosphere was unmistakable. The atmosphere of India embroiled in its own politics. The atmosphere of a nation whose rulers, despite all their disclaimers, live in constant fear of those they rule over. The police circling the ground looked almost like toy soldiers, uniforms immaculate, moustaches twitching under dark sunglasses. The crowd in lungis, casual western dress, a few suits and ties, swirled around them – ignoring and, for the moment, ignored.

I made my way to the private club entrance which leads to the dressing rooms. Here a special cordon of police had been established. I looked neither right nor left as I walked between them, wondering if any of them would recognise me from the evening before.

As the crowd filled the stands we loosened up in the outfield, taking catches, bending and stretching in a circle, jogging in place. The players were quiet and tense. Dougie tried to relax us, urging one player to 'Stretch your limbs, boy,' and another to 'Slow down, you'll do yourself an injury.' In groups of two and three we talked about the disappearance. As soon as a group grew larger the topic was dropped, as if talking about it in a crowd would only make it worse.

'He's your mate, isn't he, DTS,' Kidleigh said. 'You ought to know what's happened to him.' He said it resentfully, as if he suspected me of withholding information.

'I don't know where the hell he's gone or who he's gone with,' I said bitterly.

Everyone agreed there must be more to the story than met the eye. We had all seen enough of India by now. The general opinion was that it was a shame a good bloke like Siva should get mixed up in these absurd political shenanigans.

Robin stood alone on the players' balcony, surveying his team from afar. I knew what Dougie was thinking: a balcony was no place for a captain when his team were about to go into a match with deaths and disappearances on their minds. He should have been on the field, among his men, setting those minds at rest.

By the end of the warm-up the stands were full, only today the horns and bells were ominously silent. Robin remained at his perch and I wondered what new strategy he was hatching for us.

In the dressing room he called us together.

'We want to bowl this side out by lunch and then bat for the rest of the day. Anyone who is thinking about anything else is not doing their job. Forget about the crowd. The police are here for that. We're here to play cricket. Kidleigh, you'll open the bowling. I want no no-balls, no short stuff. We can't afford to waste a delivery on this pitch. All right then?'

Paul Walker stood and stared at the captain, hands on hips. For a moment I thought he would take a swing at him, but it passed. Alan Cowper's head hung so low it nearly vanished in his high starched collar.

'Cheer up,' Ernie said as he passed the young opener, 'You've only got one life to give for your country . . .'

We jogged through the members' enclosure and on to the pitch to distinctly muted applause. We tried not to look around. We tried to act as if it was a mid-week match at a provincial ground in England, the only spectators a few friendly journalists, some old age pensioners, and a couple of kids bunking off from school. One or two of the younger players looked up at the stands in trepidation. Do they blame it all on us? they seemed to be thinking. Do they think it's our fault?

The Indian batsmen followed us, and they too were greeted with scant applause. They took their guards, made their marks in the crease, and examined the field with the look of men determined to stay there all day. Kidleigh ran in fiercely but had no more luck than on the previous day. The ball kept low, the batsmen miscued, but no catches came to hand. I stood at mid-off, strutting back and forth, nervously eyeing the crowd. Squads of police wandered through the stands, prodding the odd spectator with a lathi, making their presence felt. They stood in a ring between the boundary and the wire fence, except in front of the members' enclosure, where they were absent. In the sponsors' box at the top of the enclosure, I could make out Narayan and his cronies, sharing food and chatting merrily.

When Kidleigh had exhausted himself for no wicket, Robin brought on our spinners, such as they were, and pulled me into a close fielding position. At the end of the over I sidled up to him and we walked the length of the pitch side by side.

'What do you make of it all?' I asked.

'Siva?' He shifted his eyes sideways, peeping at me from behind his wrinkles. 'Baffling, I should say.'

'And Coromandel Coast Investments?'

He was not amused. 'I should have thought Roy Cuthbert explained all that to you this morning.'

'He explained nothing,' I said. 'But anyway, it's you I want the explanation from, Robin. It's you who got me into this.'

Another over passed, a good one, a typically mean maiden from Geoff Robinson, before I could get close enough to continue the conversation.

'Quiet today, isn't it?' The crowd in the stands milled about and talked among themselves but there was a mute pall over the ground that affected everyone.

'Yes,' Robin agreed, 'they've lost their leader, their Siva, and they're not quite sure who to blame it on.'

'Nor am I.'

'Ah, but it's different with you. You think you'll find out simply by asking, even if you have to ask again and again. The trouble is, old boy, I can't really help you. You see, I just don't know where the living legend has got to, and what's more, I don't really care.'

'And if the crowd lose their patience and invade the pitch?'

'That's what the police are here for.'

The overs ground away and no wickets fell. Then Robin and I teamed up for a run-out. I made a quick pick up at point and threw on the turn. Robin, poised over the stumps, eyes glinting with mad, competitive hardness, caught the ball and tore off the bails.

Seven wickets down. Kidleigh came trotting in from third man, sweat streaming down his pale face. 'They're getting a bit excited down there,' he said in a shrill voice. 'They got coppers all round. I might get hit.'

Robin, suppressing a sneer of contempt, turned to me.

'Take his place, will you, David? You're not so easily intimidated as some.'

I took up a position near the boundary. Behind the wire fence was a wall of faces, engrossed in conversation, apparently indifferent to what was happening on the field. A good ball or decent stroke brought only a smattering of applause, an unusually subdued response on an Indian ground. When the next wicket fell – to a ball that turned on a full length – there was virtual silence. I could smell the crowd's food: little pooris wrapped in paper, bowls of sauce and pickle, packed up in cylindrical metal tiffin containers. Coconuts were being eaten, the shells tossed into a pile at the foot of the wire fence.

Was it my imagination or did I hear a dim refrain, 'Si-va, Si-va, Si-va,' a meaningless mantra emanating from the heart of the crowd and floating out over the pitch?

It was a slow morning. The pitch grew more and more uneven. The thought of what Chaughiri would do on such a wicket began to preoccupy our front-line batsmen. At gully Paul looked deep in thought. Young Cowper stood in the covers like a statue. At lunch Robin led us back to the dressing room. This time even the members failed to applaud. It was as if Madras was preoccupied. Siva was missing and suspicion was rife.

I met Gopal at the top of the stairs.

'A simple game of cricket?' he looked up in despair.

'Yeah,' I said, 'dead simple.'

'You've heard nothing?'

I shook my head, the western way, a long, sad, negative reply.

'There are demonstrators outside his house. They blame the

government in Delhi. Another attempt to interfere in Tamil politics.'

'And you?' I asked. 'What's your bet?'

'I wouldn't like to say.' And with that he excused himself and rejoined his fellow journalists.

In the dressing room the players sprawled everywhere. The haze had intensified the heat. They were drained.

'Thank god tomorrow's a rest day,' Ernie moaned.

'We've got to do more today than wait for tomorrow,' Robin scolded him, then resumed reading the correspondence he had removed from his briefcase.

If it hadn't been the end of the tour Robin would have been faced with a full-scale mutiny. As it was, Dougie made the rounds, soothed ruffled feathers, massaged tired shoulders, taped bruised feet and blistered toes. I used to think cricket would be much better if it was run by the Dougie Frasers of the world. But watching him potter around the dressing room that day made this seem perhaps the most pathetic of my illusions. The Dougie Frasers would never be a match for the Narayans and Cuthberts.

Outside there was a tremendous roar. I moved, along with some others, to the balcony. Spectators had torn down a part of the fence and a stream of young men poured through the gap, shouting and waving fists. They carried a banner. It was a home-made affair with large Tamil characters in red and gold. 'Something, something Siva!' they shouted in Tamil, 'Something, something Tamilnad!'

Police advanced from all sides and trapped the protesters near square leg (when the bowling was from the members' end). Lathis were raised high overhead and descended as one, whistling through the heavy atmosphere and landing with a smack on exposed brown flesh. There were about thirty protesters, young men in trousers and open-necked shirts, and they kept shouting as the lathis cracked down on them again and again. A detachment of police ran to block the gap in the fence. They stood in a row, six deep, lathis at the ready. There was screaming, cheering, booing from the crowd, though no one made a move to help the stranded demonstrators, now enmeshed in a huddle of green uniforms. Only a few heads were visible and soon they were obscured in a thicket of yellow cane.

'They know how to use those fucking things,' said Kidleigh, looking feverish and ghostlier than ever.

We watched in stunned silence. It was the sound of the beating that held us there. Not the sweet music of leather against willow, but the sickening drumming of cane against flesh. Below us Narayan waved his hands frantically, bellowing at the police and bullying those around him.

Dougie cleared us off the balcony. 'That's enough of that now,' he said. 'Won't do any good gawping like that.'

I was the last to move. The police had almost finished their work. The protesters were frog-marched across the ground, arms twisted behind their backs. The unconscious ones were dragged by their feet. I thought of what awaited them in Mohan's cells. Dougie tried to pull me away.

'I should think you've had enough of this sort of thing.'

'Maybe I'm just beginning to really see it.'

Dougie could make nothing of such an odd remark.

'For god's sake, let's just try to get back to England in one piece. It's not our country. Not any more, at least.'

An hour later we returned to the field. In the dressing room Narayan had assured us of complete physical security.

'On behalf of the sponsors may I say how very much we regret this morning's incident. It is only a small group of troublemakers who wish to exploit Siva's popularity for their own ends. We are all terribly concerned by his disappearance. Believe me that our officers are sparing no effort to locate him. But such outbursts as this morning are a shame to the Tamil people. Of course we have these elements in our society as you have in yours. Our police are the finest in the country. I can assure you of their complete support and readiness. You need have no fear for your own safety. The troublemakers have been escorted from the ground.'

'What a load of rubbish,' whispered Paul Walker behind me.

Dougie was not pleased. 'It's not right,' he told Robin in front of us all. 'Some of these lads could get hurt. You don't know what these people will do. It's not like an English crowd. I've seen it in the Caribbean. They all go bloody mad sometimes.'

It was his first overt act of defiance since Delhi.

Robin stared down at the old manager from what seemed a great height, though in fact it was only a few inches.

'We have a duty to complete this match. We have a duty to the sponsors. The police have handled the whole thing efficiently. There is no call whatsoever to go on like an old woman. We shall return to the field and we shall win this match. Is that clear?'

I'd never seen Dougie look so worn out. Nothing had gone right for him on this tour. Robin, Kidleigh, me, the crazy Indians, none of it. He retreated to a corner and for no apparent reason sorted through a bag of practice balls.

Back on the field we played with one eye on the crowd. They were restive, but quiet, as they had been before lunch. More police made rounds through the stands and a large contingent blocked the gap in the fence. For the first time empty seats appeared here and there among the crowd. What had been a capacity audience this morning was now clearly something less. I returned to my lonely patrol at third man. I couldn't resist the temptation and had a look at the crowd behind me. They stared back. Perhaps they were as puzzled by me as I was by them. A little boy standing near the fence shook the wire mesh and called to me. His father dragged him away and scolded him. Nonetheless, everyone seemed to be smiling at me, reaching out hesitantly, and I suddenly felt a surreptitious bond with them. On an impulse I waved and grinned. Row after row of spectators broke into polite applause. Was it such a big deal to acknowledge them, the paying customers? Siva's people? Rapidly the police ploughed into the section and the applause stopped.

It took us another hour to capture the last two wickets. The pitch was increasingly unpredictable but our bowlers strayed wildly in line and length. As we made our way at last to the dressing room and out of the heat haze I passed the patch at square leg where the police had surrounded the demonstrators. Dry brown blood stained the grey grass.

The next period of play promised to be one of the most interesting of the match. Before long our openers would be facing Chaughiri on a turning wicket. And the leg-spinner, in front of his home crowd, would be at his craftiest. The batsmen looked a picture of misery as they changed out of their sweat-soaked shirts into the fresh ones Dougie laid out for them. I didn't envy them. The best they could hope for was survival. We needed runs, sure, but more important we needed to bat out the day and save our wickets for the resumption of play after the rest day tomorrow. On this pitch, in front of this crowd, it would be an uphill struggle. What's more the heat was still intense. The freshening breeze from the sea had failed to arrive.

As the openers settled down for the first few overs of medium pace there was a knock at the door. Dougie answered it and I heard a low voice ask for me.

It was Gopal. I ignored Dougie's advice to talk later and met him outside the dressing room on the small landing that separates it from the members' clubhouse. From behind his newspaper Robin watched me leave.

The journalist was agitated, almost breathless.

'My friend,' he began, 'I am sorry to disturb you but really I am most concerned. People have been arrested outside Siva's house. The Party has accused the central government of trying to destabilise the State. The police are rounding up more strikers, those they haven't already got in prison. Rumours are flying. Some say Siva has been taken by Delhi goondas. Some say he has been kidnapped by dacoits. I heard one man say Muslims are holding him to ransom in return for favours from the Party. There are even rumours of a faction-fight within the Party, that Siva has enemies within the Party.' For a moment he ran out of breath. Then he paused, inhaled, and said, 'And now the police have issued a statement saying they wish to interview Siva in connection with the umpire's murder.'

He looked up at me. His broad, sweaty forehead was creased with anxiety. I said nothing.

'For god's sake, man,' he pleaded, 'if you know anything about this tell me.'

'Christ, it's your country not mine. People keep asking me questions but I don't know the answers.'

'You are Siva's friend?'

'Yes.'

'You spoke to the police last night?'

'Yes.'

'Lakshmi told me the boy who attacked you is the same one who murdered the umpire?'

'Yes.'

'And you know nothing . . .' He let out a disgusted sigh. It reminded me of my parting with Lakshmi on the beach.

'You know I am not like Lakshmi,' he explained, trying to calm himself, 'I am no cynic. I support the Party because they are the only alternative to the monsters in Delhi. They may also be monsters but at least they are our monsters. What is happening now has me worried. One man, a little man, is murdered. Another man, a greater man, disappears. The people are confused. They feel they are being tricked and they are right to feel this way. When the dust settles someone will pay for this.'

'Gopal,' it was my turn to plead, 'I just don't know what I can do. You know Siva is my friend. I want to help him, but how?'

'Yes, yes,' he had resigned himself to my predictable reply. 'I must go watch the match. Chaughiri will bring himself on soon. Your openers will never survive.'

I returned to the dressing room. Outside, Chaughiri had already begun his spell. He tiptoed in, back arched, arm whipping over, and sent the ball on its looping way towards the tense batsman. I thought of Lakshmi. Of the riot the night before. Of the blood on the pitch. Of the fishermen on the beach. Where was Siva? I was convinced that someone had done something to him, but who, what, how? I was only just beginning to realise how high the stakes had risen.

Cowper and Walker survived until tea. Cowper's attempted cuts and sweeps had been played, for the most part, at pure air. Walker had been strokeless, mired in suspicion and doubt. For the modern English batsman there is something deeply unsettling about leg spin. We hardly see it in county cricket these days and when we do all our habits are against us. The ball is there and yet not there – tempting, tantalising, always floating just out of reach.

Robin gave his usual advice. Keep your head down. Don't try to drive. Take your time. Dougie told them not to be afraid to play back.

'Easy to say,' Cowper groaned.

They returned to the wicket and settled in for the last session of play. It had been a long day. The crowd had gradually shrunk. Had they heard of the disturbances outside Siva's house? Even the Indian cricketers seemed affected by the rumours. They moved about the field hesitantly, sluggishly, hardly speaking to one another. Robin, padded up to go in when the first wicket went down and watched play from a position just inside the balcony. Here he could see without being seen.

'David,' he called me over.

I approached from behind. He seemed to know without looking when I had reached the back of his chair.

'We must get together later,' he spoke softly, in his best elder-counsellor's voice. 'We must have a chat.'

'About what?'

'About your prospects, boy,' he spat out. 'Your future.' He was barely audible, but it had all his force and venom.

'You must be joking.'

'Not at all. There are many things you simply don't understand.'

He sat in his chair, like a Mogul emperor too exalted to appear in the eyes of his subjects. His gaze, directed to the players in the field, never wavered.

I walked away. It wasn't Robin I needed to talk to, it was Lakshmi. But would she talk to me again? Had I disgraced myself in her eyes forever? I had felt she was pushing me further than I wanted to go. But really it was the others – Robin, Cuthbert, Mohan – who were pushing. So far I had let them get away with it.

Robin called to Kidleigh: 'Pad up, son, you're going in next.'

A nightwatchman to protect Robin – he was our best batsman, the only one who could really play Chaughiri; and if he needed protection at the hands of the pale boy wonder, what about the rest of us?

Kidleigh, delighted with his recent elevation to all-rounder, strapped on his pads and rehearsed a few forward defensive strokes in the centre of the room. Dougie was fuming. This was definitely not what he'd had in mind when we touched down in Delhi.

The first wicket fell a few minutes later. A googly from Chaughiri transpired not to be a googly at all. Cowper found his body in a terrible tangle, feet pointing in opposite directions, bat half-forward and blade half-cocked. The ball sailed clean through to nick the off stump. He stormed back to the dressing room, head down, speechless. Kidleigh nearly sprinted to the crease. Paul did a good job of disguising his surprise and dismay at the sight of the nightwatchman. Kidleigh played and missed dramatically in the first over, then settled down to a repeated forward prod. At stumps he was five not out. Walker had meanwhile compiled twenty-five runs in his pragmatic, invisible manner.

The exhausted players packed their kits and looked forward to the next day's rest. It was unmistakably the fag-end of a long, dispiriting tour. Dougie tended various niggles, pulls, abrasions and strains. Kidleigh, though flush from his batting triumph, looked distinctly ill.

'All right then, Kiddo?' I asked as he tottered towards the bog.

The sound of retching filled the air. Dougie bravely rushed to comfort the youth. Certainly no one else would have made the effort. More than one of us was thinking it served him right.

Outside the ground the police presence remained heavy. Most of the crowd had dispersed. A few young people dashed from car to car thrusting leaflets through open windows. The police, looking as tired as the players after their long day in the field, trooped after them, but the youngsters, shouting slogans and waving fists, were too fast. One ran up to our coach and dumped a pile of leaflets through the open door before scarpering at high speed, vaulting two barriers, and leading three policemen a merry, and futile, chase across the congested avenue.

Kushwant, who had waited patiently in the parked coach for over an hour, angrily kicked the papers away.

'Tamil people all bloody mad. Talk, talk, talk, all the time.'

I picked up a leaflet and read. It was in English, cheaply printed on what looked like recycled newsprint. 'Cast aside false leaders of Tamil people! No more Government lies! No more Party lies!' It mentioned the events I had witnessed the previous night. 'Madras proletariat charged down by police.' Further on it asked: 'Where is Siva?' and warned the people against publicity stunts staged by 'greedy power-brokers who run our state'. It was issued by something calling itself 'Student Left Democratic Front of Tamil Nadu'. I passed it around. The players studied it carefully, curiously. It was the closest thing we'd had to an explanation of the turmoil surrounding us.

Robin stood at the front of the coach.

'Just had a word with Mr Narayan. He's arranged for us all to be guests tomorrow at his country house. I gather he's got a rather nice swimming pool. Food and drink laid on, of course.'

No one cheered but Robin carried on as if they had.

'We'll have a good rest tomorrow and then a final crack at Chaughiri the next day. There's no reason why we can't win this match.'

No one listened to his cheerleading. We were all just too tired, too defeated.

The captain picked up one of the leaflets and read it.

'Well,' he snorted, 'I'm sorry to see they have to put up with the same left-wing hooligan rubbish we have at home.'

The drive to the hotel took twice as long as usual. The police had barricaded several major intersections and were searching cars, donkey and bullock carts, and lorries. Kushwant reviled them. Newspaper headlines screamed: SIVA STILL MISSING. *Cricketer's whereabouts to be raised in Lok Sabha*. Everywhere people seemed to be running for cover, though as yet there was no sign of outright violence.

Outside the hotel we were met by the inevitable battery of press. After respectful enquiries about Chaughiri's bowling, Robin was inundated with questions about Siva. He handled them in his usual manner.

'We hope this matter will be cleared up as soon as possible. In the meantime we are grateful to our sponsors, the Commercial Trust Bank of Southern India, who have done everything possible to make our stay a comfortable one.'

He passed into the lobby, head held high, followed by his exhausted flock. I straggled behind, wondering how I would get hold of Lakshmi and promising myself if there was one thing I would refuse to do it was go and swim in Narayan's pool like a pet seal.

There was a tug at my sleeve. I turned, but before I could see who it was the doorman leapt out and with a back-handed swipe knocked a small human object from my side. I saw an old person of undefinable sex sprawled on the dusty ground, face tense with shock and pain. The doorman continued to threaten the old creature with a raised hand and a volley of Tamil obscenities. When I looked closer I recognised Manni, Siva's housekeeper, now sitting on her haunches and weeping. There was already a red bruise coming up on her cheek where the doorman had slapped her. As I reached down, her ochre, skin-enfolded eyes looked up at me in terror. She pressed a piece of paper into my hand and fled, slithering along the ground for a yard or two before getting to her feet and stumbling off between cars. Instantly, my hand went into my pocket and deposited the paper.

Some of the players remonstrated with the doorman. They told him there was no need to be so harsh. He was unmoved.

'These people are not allowed,' he explained. 'Hotel guests must not be bothered by beggars and other kinds of dirty peoples. This is my job.'

CHAPTER SEVENTEEN

Alone in my room (Dougie was tending to Kidleigh, near paralysed with diarrhoea) I pulled out the crumpled paper Manni had given me. *I need your help*, it read. *Tell no one.* Then a long Tamil name and an address.

Though the handwriting was unmistakable (and little changed after ten years of wealth and fame), my first reaction was to suspect a fraud. Someone was trying to set me up. No, I wouldn't let it happen again. But then, I looked at the note, and yes, it was his handwriting. It was addressed to no one in particular, like a message in a bottle. Somehow this bottle had been washed up on my little island and now I alone knew what all Madras wanted to know. I remembered what Inspector Mohan had said: Information is power. I had information, but I felt no power. I felt scared and weak and utterly inadequate. This scrap of paper weighed more than a jumbo cricket bat and no matter how I tried I couldn't lift it off the ground.

Had I been seen? Was Mohan watching me? Would he have me followed? Narayan? Was he watching me? Or did he leave that to Robin? Or was there yet another actor in this drama, someone I didn't even know, someone who had trailed Manni to the hotel, watched her wait patiently in the dust, invisible in this city of battered old women, invisible except to someone who knew her relationship with Siva, or Siva's relationship with me.

I looked again at the note. It stared back at me with a life of its own. I might have been the only person in Madras to know the whereabouts of the great Siva, but far from making everything suddenly clear it plunged me into even greater darkness.

I wanted to burn the note. Standing alone in my hotel room with the filthy thing was like being cooped up with a dangerous criminal maniac. Anything might happen. The door might burst open and . . . I tried to calm myself. I refrained from burning the note. I folded it neatly in quarters, then unfolded it and pressed it flat on the table. At last I pulled a money belt from my travelling bag, an ordinary looking leather belt with a long zippered pocket inside.

I folded the note again and placed it inside the pocket, then threaded the belt through the loops in my trousers and buckled it. Now if they wanted the note they would have to cut it off me. This thought brought little relief. They would probably be prepared to cut off a good deal more than my belt.

One thing made me glad. Siva needed my help. It gave the lie to all those people who dismissed his vanishing act as a stunt. It showed I was as important to him as he to me. But what help could I give him? And what help did he expect of me?

It was barely twenty-four hours since I'd left Lakshmi – or rather, since she had left me – on the beach. In that time everything seemed to have changed. Except one thing: I still had no idea what was going on. All my thoughts now went back to Lakshmi, not as an object of desire (though I won't pretend I'd given up on that), but as the only person who could or would explain it to me.

I opened the door slowly and peeked into the corridor. It was empty. I walked rapidly down the stairs, stopping at the landing to listen for voices, then drifted as casually as I could manage through the lobby and into the street. Was I being followed? I checked over my shoulder, walked to the corner, turned, and walked back again. It wasn't sophisticated, but it was the best I could do. I hailed an auto-ricksha and told the driver to take me to Popham's Broadway, where I simply sat in the back for ten minutes, after guaranteeing the driver an extra ten rupees. Then I gave him Lakshmi's address and asked him to hurry. This was a mistake. He careered around corners and nipped between giant lorries at high speed, at times lifting the rear wheels of the contraption right off the ground. I imagined myself splattered across the pavement and a coroner reporting a mysterious note in the dead cricketer's money belt.

Triplicaine was tense. The ricksha slowed down as we entered the district. Police patrols with automatic weapons stood on every street corner. Outside Lakshmi's house it was obvious the driver was keen to get rid of me. I paid him off and looked up and down the busy street. No one appeared to be following me. Just the usual street kids skipping around hassling the foreigner. Was it possible for Mohan or someone else to use them as spies? I shrugged off the thought. If it was true there was nothing I could do about it. I rang her bell. She was surprised to see me but not (to my relief) displeased.

'For god's sake, David, get out of the street.'

We sat on the settee. She looked as nervous as I felt. I didn't know where to begin so I started taking off my belt. She jumped up and looked at me wildly.

'No,' I stammered, 'there's a note . . . in the belt.'

As I removed the belt and unzipped the pocket her apprehension disappeared. When I took out the note and spread it before her like a prize she sat down again, fascinated.

'Siva?'

'No question.' I told her how it had been delivered.

She examined the address. 'I don't know it. Somewhere in the countryside. We'll have to look it up.' She stared at me and slowly smiled. 'Poor David, you can't keep out of this, no matter how hard you try.'

The smile was all I needed. I swallowed hard and said what I had to say. I told her what I'd seen the night before. I told her of my talk with Cuthbert, the protest at Chepauk. I said I had been wrong yesterday. If I was to be a puppet I had to know who was pulling the strings.

'And I'm sorry I said that about you last night, on the beach,' I concluded.

'No, no.' She was brisk, dismissive, strangely distant, I felt, after such a confession as mine. 'You were quite right. I do want to make a big story of it. I want to expose a scandal. It needs exposing.'

It was a strange reconciliation. It seemed we had been led into it by a series of accidents. Yet I wanted it more than anything else. It was more important to me (at least for the moment) than Siva's safe return, which I guiltily felt should be my main priority. For Lakshmi, too, it was strange. She wanted her story and without me it would be hard to get. But I began to sense that, almost in spite of herself, she had grown fond of me.

'If you are serious about wanting to know who's pulling the strings,' she said, 'we must visit my friend.'

She had known him from childhood, she explained as we drove through deserted streets in her Ambassador. (She drove slowly, but not so slowly as to attract undue attention.) He was one of her father's old colleagues, though more radical, and had been detained for several weeks at the start of the emergency. He was a political independent (Lakshmi's words) who had been born to Tamil parents in Natal, South Africa, and returned to India in the wake of Independence, shortly after the new National

Government in South Africa had passed laws restricting the right of Indians to move and settle freely. According to Lakshmi he was a veteran of many political battles. An enemy of corruption in Madras as well as Delhi ('and not many people will oppose both') he had defended 'communists' ('mostly illiterate villagers') arrested during the repression of peasant rebellions in Telengana in the early fifties. During the emergency, he had despatched letters to newspapers and civil rights organisations detailing atrocities committed throughout Tamil Nadu. He was a thorn in everyone's side.

'He's obsessed with apartheid. He's been watching for years – keeping an eye on the traitors, the frauds. He knows all the links.'

We entered a grey, industrial district unlike others I'd seen in Madras. The streets were narrow, the buildings three and four storeys high, facades streaked with rust from vanished drainpipes and smeared with graffiti. Here and there could be seen the remains of political posters, torn away or daubed over with paint. Children scampered across the roofs or climbed up and down the wooden balconies which ran across the tenements on every floor. There were few shops, but a great many people on the street, old and young, men and women, congregating in groups of a dozen or more and talking in loud voices. There wasn't a policeman in sight. Behind the tenement roofs a giant brick chimney loomed. No smoke issued from it.

'Shrapley's plant,' Lakshmi said. 'The workers live here.'

We passed the remains of a barricade in the street. Burnt rubber, twisted car fenders, bamboo poles had been thrust together in a tall heap. An old man scavenged the pile, looking for pieces of tyre rubber to make sandals to sell in the market. A passageway had been cleared through the middle of the barricade and Lakshmi carefully squeezed her Ambassador through it. There was no other car in sight.

'Is this all right?' I asked anxiously.

'Normally, no, it wouldn't be all right,' she replied. 'But as long as we can say we're visiting Srinivassan, we'll be safe.'

'Srinivassan?'

'My friend. The old man. He's been helping the strike committee – drafting press releases, writing letters, that sort of thing. He's lived in this district a long time. The people know him.'

On top of everything else I was being driven through what

appeared to be a no-go area for the police in the middle of a heavy industrial dispute. I didn't like the look of it, but knew it would be pointless to protest. Besides, I'd said I wanted to know, and it was becoming clearer all the time that I'd learn nothing in Madras without taking a risk.

We parked outside an old building in a crooked row of tenements. People in the street stared as we walked through the low, narrow doorless entrance. The hallway smelt of burning butter, urine, and rich spices. A fat woman sat on a step on the first floor and peppered us with questions in Tamil, which Lakshmi answered briefly, almost (for her) shyly.

The old man lived on the top floor in a single room filled with dented filing cabinets, stacks of books, and typewritten sheets spread everywhere. A single-ring gas cooker hooked up to a blue bottle of paraffin stood on a bench in the corner. A battered aluminium kettle rested on the ring. Chipped cups stood in a row next to it. A simple bed, made of a wooden frame with twine wound round it supporting a thin, beaten mattress, was pushed against the wall. A white sheet was folded neatly on top of the mattress. A little table with an electric lamp stood at the end of the bed and a thick book was folded open beside it. I glanced at the cover and saw an unfamiliar language, neither Tamil nor English, perhaps Russian.

Lakshmi introduced us. 'This is Srinivassan, but we call him Srini.'

He extended a thin, bony hand at the end of a long, shirt-sleeved arm. His grip was surprisingly firm. He wore rimless glasses and his white shirt was crumpled and yellow round the collar. His small, childlike face was lit up by a genial smile.

'So this is the young cricketer who was given a taste of Madras goonda?' He stepped back and looked me up and down. 'I used to watch cricket. In South Africa. But really I have no interest at all in it now. Do you know, I've never even seen this famous Siva whom everyone talks so much about, like some Chola king returned to save us from foreign oppression!'

We sat on wooden chairs in the middle of the room. Srini was formally, deliberately polite. His stilted manners made a strange contrast with the chaos surrounding him.

'David wants to know who's pulling the strings,' Lakshmi said. 'I told him for that kind of information you were the best person in Madras.'

'The only person! Information I have, as you see, in quantity.' He waved an arm majestically over the scattered contents of the room. 'But there is little point in knowing who is pulling the strings unless you are prepared to cut through them!'

He smiled as he said it though there was no misinterpreting the challenge in his voice. Strangely, it put me at ease. Here at last was someone who would tell me exactly what he thought and not what he thought would be best for me to think he thought.

'First, you must give information to me. I must know the whole story. This includes names of people, companies, everything. If you are not prepared to trust me with this then we should not waste each other's time.'

It was said in a firm voice that brooked no argument. Despite some forebodings, I nodded my agreement. I had come too far to back out now. I didn't look at Lakshmi, but I sensed she was pleased with me, and that made it easier.

The story seemed to have grown more complex and certainly longer since I'd told it to Lakshmi the other night, and it took some time for me to divulge it all. Srini interrupted with questions and made me repeat details over and over again, often for reasons I couldn't understand. When it was finished I felt relieved. Srini removed his glasses, polished them on his shirt, and replaced them on the bridge of his small, hard nose.

He asked Lakshmi to make some coffee, which she proceeded to do like a dutiful daughter. It occurred to me that few men could get away with such a request, and I doubted if I was one of them.

'To understand all this you must forget about cricket for a moment,' Srini began. 'Cricket is important, I don't deny it. It's the thread on which all the different coloured beads are strung. But you must know that for the regime in South Africa cricket is not a sport or a game. It is a political vehicle. It is an iron crow-bar with which they hope to prise open certain doors, certain minds, certain forces. It is a battlefield. You see, in the third world, those of us opposed to apartheid, at least, are not great financiers or capitalists. We wield no great armies or nuclear arsenals. What we do have, we who are struggling for some dignity and some independence from our old masters in the West, is our athletes, our great cricketers, our sportsmen, and they represent us, you see, simply because there is no one else. On the world stage, in so many matters, we are bit players. But in this, in cricket, we take the leading roles. That is why we fight so hard to keep our sportsmen away from South Africa. That is why our boycott is so important.'

I said I understood all that. I'd always supported the isolation of South Africa from world cricket. It was Siva himself who had taught me that lesson, and I hadn't forgotten it. What I couldn't understand was what it all had to do with Grand Prix Cricket, with the Party, with me.

'No, that is not easy to see.'

He reminded me that the South Africans had managed to obtain a favourable report from the International Cricket Conference investigators who visited there in 1979. But this report had been rejected by the ICC itself, solely because of the veto exercised by India, Pakistan and the West Indies. The South African attempt to insinuate itself back into the game by making cosmetic changes (like including a few coloured or black players in cricket sides and allowing the players to drink together at hotels granted special dispensation from apartheid laws) had failed. The next step was the pirate tour of English cricketers in 1982. They had gone to great lengths to attract star players and in some instances had succeeded.

'It is said they offered your Ian Botham a blank cheque. To his everlasting credit, he turned them down.'

The tour itself was a flop. Attendance was poor and ('I'm told by those who take an interest in such things') the cricket was second-rate. But this wasn't important to the South Africans. Their real purpose had been achieved. And this real purpose, as with the rebel tours by Sri Lankans, West Indians and Australians which followed, was to disrupt world cricket.

'Their strategy, you see, is to provoke boycotts and splits amongst the Test-playing nations. They want the solidity of world cricket to crumble so they can negotiate their way back piece by piece. It's part of their grand political project. They want to divide their third world opponents from the West, whom they still regard – and they are not wrong to do so – as their natural allies. Allies masquerading temporarily as opponents for the sake of political expedience.'

'But the rebel players were banned,' I pointed out. 'People complained, but in the end they had to swallow it.'

'True. And that is where your friend Cuthbert and his Grand

Prix Cricket come in. It is the next item on the South African agenda.'

'But what would they stand to gain from it?'

'A great deal, yes, a great deal indeed.' He spoke like an old-fashioned history master and treated me like a slow but willing pupil. 'Have you asked yourself what will be the repercussions of this new set-up, this new league?'

I thought for a moment. 'If they get away with it, the TCCB, the ICC, the whole international cricket establishment will be weakened.'

'Exactly. And not just weakened; positively split. It is only the solidity of this establishment that has kept South Africa out for the last decade. The English, the Australians, the New Zealanders – they all want to play cricket with their kith and kin in South Africa. They resent being kept from it by these upstart coloured bastards, these kaffirs. Look at rugby. No third world 'blackmail', as your politicians like to call it, in rugby. Nothing to stop the tours flying out to Johannesburg and proclaiming another victory for freedom.'

'But all that's speculation,' I said, a little timidly in the face of such conviction and eloquence.

'Perhaps. But is a dead umpire speculation? Is a missing Siva speculation?'

I couldn't follow him. My face must have shown it.

'Is Coromandel Coast Investments speculation?'

'But what the hell *is* Coromandel Coast Investments?'

He rose from the chair and searched through a pile of papers on top of the cabinet. At length he produced a thick file and sat down again. Lakshmi poured coffee and joked about Srini needing a housekeeper.

'If only you would apply for the job!'

'And spend my prime years cleaning up after an impossible old man? No thank you!'

'She is wasting herself on that stupid paper,' Srini confided to me. 'Such a lovely girl!' He sighed in mock despair.

Lakshmi gave me a stern look, as if to say: Don't you dare encourage him!

Srini continued.

'You want to know about Coromandel Coast Investments? I can tell you about Coromandel Coast Investments. I am especially qualified. But you must first understand that between the Tamil people and the Republic of South Africa there has been a long and unhappy relationship. Generations of Tamil labourers have been forced to seek work abroad because of the inefficiency of our agriculture. They travelled as indentured servants – little different to slaves – to Burma, Fiji, Sri Lanka, and of course South Africa. Indeed it was only in 1911 that the new South African Republic put a stop to the practice. Not because they deplored it morally, but because as far as they were concerned they had too many of these Tamil rascals already. My father was one of those, and so terrible were the conditions of his life that all he ever thought of was returning to his native Thanjavur district – not a very rich or happy place, but at least his own. Over the years heavier and heavier restrictions were placed on us by the Boers. When I was a young man we were removed from our house in Durban and forced to live in a concrete hut miles from the centre of town. Many in the Indian community were outraged and some of the militants among us gained control of the Natal Indian Congress. This was in the forties. Before long they had us all behind bars. But meanwhile a small group of Indians in Durban had become fabulously wealthy. With the connivance of the British and South African authorities, they had secured complete control over the supplying of ships in the harbour throughout the war. They became war profiteers.'

He drank his coffee slowly, savouring it drop by drop, and for a moment lapsed into silence. Lakshmi wandered to the window and peeped out as if keeping watch.

'In 1950,' Srini resumed, 'there were riots – terrible fighting between Indian and African people in Durban. I knew then I could not live in such a place. I came here, to my family's homeland, to my own country, as I thought at the time.'

A pained look spread across his face and he once more removed and polished his spectacles.

'Some of these war profiteers also felt strongly their ties to their native Tamil Nadu. We had only recently won our independence from the British imperialists. There were new opportunities for Indian capital. There was room for investment, profit to be made. Coromandel Coast Investments was formed.'

He lifted the papers and held them under my nose.

'This is the record,' he said excitedly, 'I have watched them. I have watched this Coromandel Coast Investments from the beginning. I knew them from Durban and I have followed their progress very closely indeed. At first it was shipping and supplying up and down the eastern coast, the Coromandel Coast. Now they trade across the whole of the Indian Ocean. They have invested heavily in the so-called 'homelands' and the sham independent nations set up by the South Africans as dumping grounds for their surplus labour. South African Breweries, who put up the money for the rebel English tour, are also involved there. Their subsidiary, Sun Country Hotels, runs the big casinos in Bophutatswana, where they stage spurious multi-racial concerts with collaborators from Britain and America. Did you know that?'

Like so much he said, it was news to me.

'Now, the Indian merchants who run CCI enjoy great privileges compared to their fellow Indians in South Africa, not to mention the African masses. The whites allow them these privileges because a handful of millionaire Indians can be useful to them. Not least in entering markets where the whites themselves dare not tread.'

He showed me documents: page after page of fine handwriting; transactions, dates, places, amounts neatly noted; names of partners, subsidiaries, investors; financial profiles clipped from South African magazines. CCI was an independent Indian corporation, at least on paper. Indian laws are quite strict about foreign investment and officially there is no trade at all with South Africa. But the bulk of CCI's orders and capital flowed from the 'homelands' of South Africa. And their main channel of entry into India was the Commercial Trust Bank.

I was more than a little taken aback. How was it possible in India – not the white man's India, but modern, independent India?

'I thought the government was against apartheid,' I said. 'The Prime Minister was denouncing it last month at the Commonwealth Conference. I read it in your newspapers.'

'Ah, the great charade,' said Lakshmi. 'Secular, democratic, socialist India. The champion of the oppressed. The enemy of world imperialism. They would make a deal with the devil if it suited them.'

'It is useful for them to have people thinking we support our brothers and sisters in the third world,' Srini explained wearily. 'But for all their talk of non-aligned India and new domestic wealth, there is more foreign investment here now than under the

British. And it is important for them that conditions are favourable for these investors.'

'No strikes?'

Srini smiled, pleased with his pupil. Lakshmi went again to the window.

'You are worrying?' he asked her.

'A little.'

'She is worrying,' he said to me with a laugh, as if it was a joke between men. 'They will not come tonight. They are not interested in an old man. Now there are young people in the streets. Workers. Harijans. An old man with filing cabinets is the least of their worries.'

He laughed again.

'You know Inspector Mohan?' I asked.

He positively chuckled with glee.

'I know him. Yes, we are old acquaintances. But now his rowdies are too busy, you see? Besides, they would find it difficult to get past the big lady downstairs. Mrs Naidu is formidable when aroused.'

'I can believe it,' I said, but I still had another question. 'What does it have to do with Siva? Why is he so scared of CCI?'

'Is he scared of CCI? Perhaps rather he is scared of someone who knows about CCI.'

'It's time you accepted, David,' Lakshmi said, leaving the window and approaching me with a stern face, 'that your Siva is no innocent. Didn't you see that list Mohan showed us? What do you think it means? If something like that became public it might ruin Siva. And if Siva sinks it might be difficult for the Party to swim.'

So much of what they told me was new, so much unexpected, yet I had accepted it all. But now they were pushing too far.

'You don't know the man,' I insisted. 'He may be naive. He may keep the wrong company. But dealing with South Africa? Murdering the umpire? It's just not possible.'

Lakshmi shrugged. She had made her point. She would waste no more talk on a fool. The old man sipped his coffee and kept his counsel.

'One thing is clear,' he said. 'Robin Barnett and this Cuthbert fellow not only know about CCI but are directly involved with it. Otherwise they would not have whatever inside knowledge it is that so frightens Siva. In fact, I believe it is through CCI and our friend Narayan's bank that the South Africans intend to finance Grand Prix Cricket.'

At Lakshmi's request I showed Srini the note from Siva. He examined it carefully, then rose and after searching through a pile of yellow folders produced an old tattered atlas with broken spine and frayed covers. He leafed through it rapidly.

'Ah, there it is. I thought I knew it. A small village in South Arcot. Maybe ninety miles from Madras. We could drive there, say, in three hours.'

He looked up at me earnestly, a question in his foggy brown eyes.

'You'll go with Srini?' Lakshmi implored gently.

I agreed. What else could I do? How else could I get there? And who else would explain whatever I found there? Besides, the old man had a healthy distrust of the police. He would get us to the village in South Arcot safely and quietly. I only hoped Siva would vindicate me when I found him.

'You'll come too?' I asked Lakshmi, trying not to sound like a little boy in need of an escort.

'Of course. I intend to file an eyewitness report. You see, my story is getting bigger all the time.'

As Srinivassan rose to bid us goodnight his joints cracked. He removed his glasses and rubbed his red eyes.

'I will meet you in front of the big post office on Mount Road tomorrow at eight o'clock. Don't be late. Our roads are not like your motorways. It will be a long drive.'

CHAPTER EIGHTEEN

I wanted to go home with Lakshmi that night even if it was just to sleep on her settee. Anything seemed better than the cold hotel and trying to act normal with the other players. As usual, Lakshmi corrected my folly. I should be seen at the hotel, she said, to allay suspicion and make my excuses for skipping the outing to Narayan's pool.

It was ten o'clock. Robin and some of the others were in the lounge, drinking Indian-brewed beer and for once not complaining about it. A sour mood prevailed.

'Any sign of the great man then?' asked Ernie Fairbanks as I came in.

Surely he was only asking because he knew Siva was a friend of mine?

'No sign,' I answered and picked up an old copy of *The Indian Express*.

Siva's disappearance weighed heavily on the players' minds. It disturbed them far more than the other things they had seen in the last few days. Siva, after all, was one of our own, a professional cricketer, and if something as decidedly odd as disappearing could happen to him, then perhaps none of us was safe. Paul was convinced it was a stunt.

'Pure electioneering,' he declaimed.

Donald Blackburn's theory involved kidnapping by rival gangs of politicians. (Their picture of Indian politics had come to resemble gangland Chicago.)

Ernie was certain Siva had taken himself off with some woman and simply wanted a clear run without the press for a few days.

'You know Siva and his birds,' Ernie leered.

Robin, who had no taste for such jokes, tried to stop their speculation. 'Don't let your adolescent minds run amok,' he murmured from behind his newspaper. 'The Indian people are very respectful towards their women. They wouldn't tolerate your sort of prurience.'

No one argued, but clearly no one was very impressed. It only confirmed their view that Robin was a kill-joy as well as a tyrant.

They took turns placing phone-calls to wives, girlfriends,

parents, children back in England. It was a long and tedious process, requiring repeated instructions to the operator, long waits at the end of blank connections, much ill-tempered shouting down the receiver, and a great deal of abuse hurled at the Indian telephone system.

When the other players had made their calls and gone to their rooms, I sat myself down near Robin. I tried to do this, like everything else since my visit to Srini, in a casual manner that I hoped would mask the nervous energy buzzing through me. In this I was assisted by the mounting indifference of the rest of the squad to what was going on around them.

'I'm sorry, I won't be making the trip tomorrow,' I said.

Robin brought down his paper. His eyebrows, pale against his tanned forehead, rose for a fraction of a second.

'Really?'

'I've arranged to spend the day with this young woman I've been seeing.'

It felt odd to use her like this when there was nothing, at least nothing like what the other players thought, between us. But one excuse is rarely challenged among men and therefore provides a ready cover for almost anything: the pursuit of sex. It is an agreed priority. Even Robin, who regarded himself as above such childish nonsense, would hardly question it.

'And where will you be taking the young lady?'

'Out in the country somewhere. She's got a car.'

'Splendid. You should go to Mahaballipuram and see the stone rathas. Spectacular stuff. I'd be off myself except I have to shepherd this lot to Narayan's.'

We were silent for a moment. Was he toying with me? Did he treat me like a fool because he thought I was a fool, or did he suspect something?

'You know,' he broke into my thoughts, 'we must have a little faith in each other, David.'

I listened.

'I've had a chat with our mutual friend and he agrees with me. We owe you something for the commitment you've already shown, not to speak of your regular service in the future.'

He spoke like an automaton. We were alone in the room, but Robin always acted as if he were being watched, as if there was a video camera in the corner of every room, and for him an audience of one was little different from an audience of thousands.

'We're aware of the pressures you've been under,' he continued. 'What with this thug attacking you in the street and this business with Siva you've had rather a lot on your plate. The last few days have been difficult for us all. This is what comes of trying to organise a complex international enterprise in a country like India.'

'I thought Roy Cuthbert would have sorted all that out.'

'I assure you there are circumstances outside even Roy Cuthbert's control,' he said, with the merest hint of a smile.

'But how do you know it's all not a pipe dream?'

He assumed a shocked expression.

'Pipe dream? Hardly. Cricket is fifty, sixty years behind the times. And a man of independence like Roy Cuthbert is in a position to do something about it. Together we can boot the game into the modern world. What W G did in his era we can do in ours . . .'

He spoke at me as if I was a tape recorder, unaware of, or at least indifferent to, my rising disgust. Grand Prix Cricket would usher in a new world of independent professional cricketers, a new order in which 'people like us', by which Robin meant people like him – people of ability and the determination to make the most if it – would run the sport (and what else besides?) unhindered by petty bureaucracy and old-fashioned sentiment. He was transfixed by this future cleansed of all the impurities which had frustrated him in reality. As I listened, my disgust turned to pity. For all his fantasies of a brave new world he remained an anachronism. He was a man of the past convinced of his destiny as standard-bearer of the future. Rejected by his peers, he would be the leader of a new generation. He was in search of a place in history, a place which he felt had been denied him, despite all his successes.

'In our day skill and leadership and natural ability count for so little. Mediocrity rules everywhere. Cricket has a role to play in tearing it down. And you too, David, have a role . . .'

Much as I disliked being cast in such a role, I went along with him. I remembered Lakshmi's instructions: Don't let Robin think you're a renegade. Not yet. The puzzle was still incomplete. Robin's rambling monologue now came to rest on his favourite topic – money.

'We need only your signature – on a standard contract we issue to all our players. When you sign we can offer you an honorarium. I expect you'll be needing it on your return to England.'

For a moment I nearly pulled back. If I accepted money and signed their form, it would give them something to use against me. On the other hand, if I refused I might jeopardise whatever mission it was I was being sent on the next morning. I had learned. These people – and to me they were still a murky collection – could move fast.

I followed Robin up to his room. Outside the door he put his finger to his lips.

'The boy wonder isn't feeling well tonight,' he warned. 'Best not to wake him.'

The room smelled foul. The young bowler turned uneasily in his sleep as we entered. Robin turned on the toilet light. I saw Kidleigh open his red, rabbit-like eyes, blink once, then pull the sheet over his head with a shiver.

'Poor boy has no stomach at all,' Robin said as he closed the toilet door. 'Pity, he'd be more use to us if he'd really come off on this tour.'

The toilets were cubicles with basin, lavatory bowl, shower, and little room for anything else. A bare light bulb flickered distractingly. The two of us squeezed in and Robin sat himself comfortably down on the lavatory seat. His shaving brush, cologne, water-pick, and sun-tan oil were neatly arranged in a row on the shelf above the basin. What I took to be Kidleigh's things were stuffed in a plastic bag on the floor. Robin opened his briefcase and handed me a typed document. It was a single page and simply worded. It committed the undersigned to the sole employ of Grand Prix Cricket Ltd for a period of one year, with an option to renew, and in that year to act in whatever capacity required by the management of Grand Prix Cricket Ltd. It included the usual clauses about injury and discipline. The payment indicated was exactly what Robin and Cuthbert had promised me that first night in the restaurant. It still seemed outsize, a fantasy wage trailing off into all those noughts at the end.

I read slowly and carefully while Robin looked on with approving eyes. The document was a photocopy and I wondered how many others had seen it and how many had signed.

Robin's signature appeared at the bottom in his capacity as

'Cricket Organiser' on behalf of the management. I added my own under his, a little shakily. Then I turned to the copy underneath and signed that. I looked up when I'd finished, handed Robin back his fountain pen, and quivered slightly.

'No need for the jitters, old boy,' Robin laughed. 'It's not your soul you're signing away.'

'I'm relying on you, Robin,' I said as earnestly as I could. If I gave him half a chance to play the sponsor and caretaker he would wallow in it.

'And so you should.' He put his lean arm around my shoulders. It felt horrible, like the mechanical limb of some futuristic robot. 'And here is a little token . . .drawn on an Indian bank . . .cash it here . . . there'll be no problem with customs at the other end . . .'

He handed me a colourful, oversized cheque. The sum was considerable. It was drawn against the account of Coromandel Coast Investments at the Commercial Trust Bank of Southern India and signed V. P. Narayan.

'Narayan?' I nearly choked on the name.

'A most helpful chap,' said Robin, pleased with himself and his most recent transaction. 'Most capable.'

He placed his copy of the contract in his briefcase and snapped it shut.

'No noise now,' he said, rising and opening the door. We tiptoed through the bedroom and into the hall.

'Drink?' he asked blithely.

I yawned and stretched. 'No thanks. We're leaving early tomorrow.'

'Jolly good then.' He turned to descend the stairs by himself (and, I was sure, to place a last phone call before retiring). 'And don't forget Mahaballipuram. Excellent place to take your lady friend.'

CHAPTER NINETEEN

I left Dougie grumbling in his sleep and stole out of the hotel soon after sunrise. The haze had cleared and the skies were cobalt blue. The air was warm and for the moment the atmosphere in the city was light and pleasant. The police were already at their posts and shoppers moved quickly among them, keen to finish their business before the sun was too high in the sky. On the way to Lakshmi's I read the morning edition of *The Banner*. The headlines were all Siva. Curiously absent from the coverage was any real conjecture about where he had gone or why. The main interest was the introduction of President's Rule, said to be imminent, and the frantic manoeuvring of politicians in Madras and Delhi to either forestall or precipitate this event. In its lead article the paper, normally a staunch ally of the Party, was surprisingly ambivalent on the subject. It was as if everyone, like Inspector Mohan, was hedging a bet.

I turned to the sports page. In Gopal's account of the match he had inserted a brief note of the protest in the middle and an indication of how the police had handled it. I saw my own name, but was hardly delighted to find myself referred to as 'the quick-armed Stott, one half of an exceptional run-out team with captain Robin Barnett.' The article also mentioned Kidleigh's surprising appearance as nightwatchman. 'No one cares to guess how long he will last on the fourth day, with the pitch increasingly receptive to spin and Chaughiri in form.'

I knocked loud and long at Lakshmi's door, but to no avail. I stopped a little boy dressed in dirty shorts and nothing else and indicated that I wanted to see the lady upstairs. I gave him five rupees. He was so shocked by this that he stood stock still for two minutes examining the notes like a bank teller, certain the peculiar westerner was out to cheat him in some way. At last he agreed to my proposal. Clinging to a rusty drainpipe that looked as if it might fly loose at any moment, he shimmied up the outside wall. On reaching Lakshmi's window he leaned forwards and banged as hard as he could with a small fist, while uttering a noise like a plaintive calf. There was an irritable reply (I recognised her voice, even in Tamil, even in an early morning rage), then apologetic whimpering from the boy. He slid back down the drainpipe, fell in a heap on the ground, and miraculously popped up, still in one piece.

'Lady coming,' he announced.

Lakshmi admitted me in a swirling silk dressing-gown and complained that since I'd been in town it had become impossible to get a decent night's sleep.

'I thought we were meeting at eight at the post office,' she said, winding a wristwatch and yawning.

'I had to show you this,' and slowly, with (I must admit) a hint of showmanship I drew the cheque and contract from my pocket and presented them.

I had hoped for a triumph of sorts. At least excitement. The documents proved Srini's theory about Grand Prix Cricket. But she sat down with a bump, and fingered the cheque absent-mindedly.

'That should give you a story,' I said.

'How did you get hold of them?'

I told her about the signing ceremony in the toilet.

'You were right to sign,' she said. 'And now it is up to us to see that there is no Grand Prix Cricket to hold you to this agreement.'

She held up the cheque.

'You will certainly never be able to cash it.'

I was offended. Cashing the cheque had never entered my head, though I could have used the money. Hadn't I won any credit with this woman yet? She was impossible.

'Leave this with me,' she said.

'What about the village?'

'You go with Srini. A woman would only attract attention out there. I'll do a little more research. The more details the better. Gopal will help.'

'I thought you said he was "politically naive",' I said morosely.

'Naive but honest, and very useful at times.' She smiled for the first time. 'Besides, politically naive men are obviously to my taste.'

I brightened instantly. It may have been a back-handed compliment, but it was a compliment nonetheless.

'David, you've been really abused, you know. And I'm as guilty as anyone.'

'Not at all,' I sprang to her defence. 'I blame Robin and

Cuthbert. If it hadn't been for you, I might never have known what they were dragging me into.'

'It's nice of you to say that,' she said. 'From the first time we met I've been prying things out of you.'

'Never anything I didn't want to tell. Or need to tell.'

'You've taken it well.'

'I didn't have any choice,' I laughed.

I wanted to leap up and grab her round the waist, but in her business-like way she forestalled this by announcing she would be dressed in a minute and would take me to the post office to meet Srini.

He turned up ten minutes late in a battered old Ford. The two doors were of different colours and one wing had a deep, rusting gash. The engine continued turning over a full thirty seconds after he switched off the ignition.

'Normally I avoid motor cars,' he said. 'I hardly leave my local parish these days. But for this occasion I prevailed upon a friend to lend us this beautiful specimen.'

'Will it make the trip?' I asked anxiously.

'We must hope and pray,' the old man said, wrenching the car into first gear and pulling off with a jolt into the column of traffic moving slowly down Mount Road.

'And where is the woman?'

I told him about the cheque and Lakshmi's determination to investigate further.

'Excellent. You showed presence of mind in signing it. We could never have secured evidence of that sort without bribery. And the going rate is far beyond our means.'

'You think it costs so much to bribe a cricketer?'

'Well, I shouldn't want to have to compete with South African Breweries,' he answered, then added, 'It is good to know there is at least one cricketer we can afford.'

He seemed less forbidding than he had the day before. His frail arms, still covered to the wrists in white shirt-sleeves, held the wheel at full stretch. He peered through his glasses over the dashboard and concentrated on the slow drive south through the city. The car stalled more than once, heaving and jolting every time Srini changed gear. Thinking that perhaps I had proved myself at last to Lakshmi, and to her extraordinary family friend, I relaxed in the passenger seat and contemplated the journey ahead. Despite doubts and fears about what we would find at the end of the road, my mood was lightened by the prospect of escape. For a few hours at least I could leave behind this impossible city, with its lorryloads of police, its whispering citizens, its nervous crowds.

But first we had to traverse the suburbs of Madras. Having seen only the slums of the inner city and the regal houses of San Thome it was a shock to find the city straggling out in acres of squalid, temporary settlements. Tents and huts made of canvas, plastic sheeting, corrugated iron, wooden planks scavenged from wrecked buildings, spread in a chaotic labyrinth on either side of the main highway. People squatted around small smouldering fires, in the shadow of an enormous bunker of rubbish. The stench lingered for miles down the road and nearly made me gag.

'A colony of scheduled castes from the countryside. No land of their own, and no more labour from the owners, so they come to the city,' Srini explained. 'The Party won their votes years ago by promising not to evict them from this site. It kept its promise, for once, and actually installed a water supply of sorts – if one public standpipe for a thousand people is a water supply. At every election the Party comes back with more promises. It reminds the wretches what it has done for them, then forgets them for a few more years. Except to auction off licences for the right to sell them paraffin at exorbitant prices.'

'Why don't they vote for someone else?'

He shrugged and took his hands off the wheel for a moment, as if referring to some eternal and unfathomable mystery.

'It was overcrowded when I first came to Madras, but since then the population has grown by yet another million, mostly landless poor from country districts. It has gone beyond a question of overcrowding. We need a new word for it, not just in Madras but every Indian city. It is a new form of human life, and not a happy creation . . .'

'But they keep coming, these country people, despite that?'

'What else can they do? My friend, to understand India you must understand the countryside. Our cities are vast, as you know, and yet some eighty per cent of our people are rural villagers. Village India is the real India.'

After the teeming suburbs, Srini's 'real India' seemed a charming, inviting wonderland as it flowed past the windows of the old Ford. Rice fields spread out in endless flat vistas, broken only by thick groves of banana trees or coconut palms. Canals cut across the scene, bringing a cooling touch of moisture to sun-baked aridity. Dotted across the landscape, and almost blending into it, were human figures bent double in work or leaning on staffs in leisured poses. Close up, their black skins burned like paper silhouettes against the blue of the sky and the blonde of the fields. Bullocks trudged the earth. Whenever we stopped the swish of the cane and the patient weary cries of peasants urging their animals through the day floated around us. Srini was less than confident about his friend's radiator and we stopped frequently to top it up. Afterwards, he would close the bonnet and fastidiously wipe his hands on a rag before resuming his ordeal behind the wheel. He adopted an even more peremptory manner than usual with the peasants who passed us as we waited by the side of the road for the engine to cool. They deferred to him with a kind of exhausted indifference, and though they would not challenge this man from the city it was clear they placed no trust in him.

We passed through village after village. Srini pointed out the small hamlets, like outriders to the main settlements, inhabited by untouchables and Muslims.

'Caste is still a great force in the countryside,' he said. 'The landowners are high caste, almost without exception. And the labourers are largely so-called 'scheduled' castes and minorities. Untouchability is of course against the law in India, but like so many of our excellent laws it is honoured more on paper than in reality. Every party since Independence has pledged to reform the relationship between landlord and peasant. And every one of them has found a reason to abandon this pledge once in power. What reforms they do make are impossible to enforce because out here the high caste landlords control the police, and with a few well-placed bribes they avoid any trouble from the bureaucrats in Madras as well.'

When Lakshmi spoke of these things you could feel the anger seething in her, perhaps all the more intense because of her own relatively privileged upbringing. Srini was different. He enjoyed his little lectures. Somewhere in him there was bitterness and even hatred, but it was as if he had brought it under control years ago and now took a perverse pleasure in his self-mastery, like a reformed alcoholic in a pub.

There was no cricket out here, he informed me with a malicious grin. The poor people were too busy keeping body and soul together. The mass circulation newspapers, those bloodlines of the big cities spreading the names and faces of India's celebrities across the continent, were impotent in three-quarters of the nation. Illiteracy was still the norm.

'Radio is the power here,' he said. 'Our All-India Radio is like an octopus. It has tentacles everywhere.'

We stopped at a sleepy little hamlet, hardly a village, just a few huts and stalls selling dried peppers, bananas, bidis, and soda-water in thick glass bottles with rubber stoppers.

Srini stretched his limbs and cleaned his glasses. 'It is a long time since I drove such a distance. I must rest.'

He lay down in the shade of a large spreading tree with heavy green leaves and a thick twisting trunk. He might have been a city person by his own admission, but he was more at home in the country than I would ever be. A young man in lungi and white turban tended a stall with green coconuts. Srini shouted a laconic order and the young man silently responded. He selected one of the coconuts, held it to his ear and shook it, then with a sudden whirl of his long knife neatly guillotined one end of it. He handed the decapitated coconut to Srini, who in turn offered it to me.

'You have tasted tender coconut?'

Though I'd seen them sold elsewhere in India, until then I had never thought of trying one. I raised the heavy fruit with its hard smooth surface and poured the juice into my mouth. More like water than milk, it was cool with just a hint of sweetness. Much to Srini's amusement it trickled down my chin and dripped on to my shirt. I jumped back and wiped my face.

Meanwhile the young man had elegantly butchered another coconut. Srini tilted his head at a precise angle and delicately quaffed the liquor. The young man stared expectantly at me.

'Give him your coconut, man. He will give you the jelly.'

The turbaned youth took back the green sphere and buried his knife in it lengthwise, then cracked it apart. Using the thin end he'd sliced off earlier as a scraper, he scooped out the nearly translucent jelly and handed it to me with a broad grin.

'He thinks you are stupid for not knowing how to eat tender coconut,' Srini informed me brutally.

I tasted the jelly, a thick silky cream, and not at all like the dried coconut we eat at home.

'A healthy food,' Srini said. 'Good for the hair. Good for the skin. If you eat enough of them you might live as long as me.'

He tossed the remains of his coconut in the rotting pile behind the big tree. I followed suit. The road here was smoothly paved. I said I thought the country roads would be rougher.

'Yes, it's not too bad,' Srini agreed. 'Lucky for us with this heap. Of course it's not for the villagers. They have no cars and no business to take them anywhere. The roads are for government officials, tax collectors, for the landlords to bring the harvest they steal from the peasants to market in the city.'

Much to my relief, and despite repeated sputterings, sudden jolts, and lurching halts, the car served us well. According to Srini, we were making good time. He told me about the uprisings in Telengana, a region to the north of Madras, in the fifties.

'After Independence, you see, there were expectations. Expectations of a new world. In some areas people took matters into their own hands. They seized the land from the owners, created their own village councils and courts, organised their own harvests. For the rulers in Delhi, the fathers of the nation who had fought the British, it was too much. They put a stop to it in the usual way.'

'Which is?'

'Army massacres! What do you think?'

At last we reached our destination. It was a village very much like the others we had passed. On the outskirts was a tiny hamlet for untouchables. It was little more than a circle of mud huts with thatched roofs. People fetched water from a brown trickle that meandered between the huts. Stooped old women with milky cataracts in their eyes splashed through it.

Beyond the untouchable settlement was the main village, flanking both sides of the road, which had by now run out of metalled surface. There were small brick and plaster houses. A few small stalls sold dry grains and pulses, fruits and basic provisions: matches, paraffin, oil, tobacco, coir mats, shiny metal cooking pots. A tea shop in the centre of the village was the only place to display any sign of life. The sun was high and the hot air lay heavily on the chest. A few men sitting around wooden tables with bare crossed legs went silent as the car pulled up.

With a slight movement of his hand Srini ordered me to remain in my seat. He walked slowly toward the shop, brushing drops of sweat from his eyebrows. They stared at the man from the city with his long trousers, his shoes, his shirt with the sleeves buttoned at the wrists. Srini disappeared inside the shop.

I waited in the car. Two small children edged their way across the road towards my window. They wore faded purple shifts and had rings through their noses. They stood near the window, their round eyes, circled with some kind of charcoal ring, opened wide with curiosity and fear. To them I was a monster – a white-skinned, gibberish-speaking monster from a faraway land.

I smiled at them. Children in the cities usually ask for rupees when they get this close. Not these. They were just too overawed. I held out my hand with a few small coins in the palm. They froze for a moment, eyes quivering, then grabbed the money and ran.

'What are you doing?' Srini demanded as he strode back to the car, followed by a tall, thin man in lungi and turban. 'You have enough money to give to all these children? You think that is what is needed?'

The man had an amazing capacity to make me feel small.

The stranger in the lungi clambered into the back seat. Srini told me he would show us the way to the house named in Manni's note.

'The man who lives there is one of the village big shots,' he said. 'A landowner. They all knew him but only this one was willing to show us the way.'

From the back seat the thin man barked out directions in a nervous staccato. We came to a wooden cattle gate. Our guide climbed over the seat and backed out of the door, attenuated limbs unfolding awkwardly. He acknowledged me for the first and only time with a bowed head and a whispered farewell. I responded in kind.

Fifty yards from the gate, in a grassy field, with no trees in sight, stood a house built of whitewashed brick, fronted by a dry, cracked wooden veranda. There was silence all around.

'Looks deserted,' I said.

'It's the time of day.'

Srini switched off the engine, which rattled for a moment, then leaned back in his seat and stretched himself.

'Go ahead, now. I am waiting for you.'

I left the car and walked towards the house.

CHAPTER TWENTY

The house was the biggest for miles around. Little else distinguished it. The paint was fading and the brickwork crumbling. A heat-stricken, deathly midday silence prevailed. I crept up the veranda and knocked.

After a moment there was a stirring inside and the door opened to reveal a middle-aged man with a moustache and sleepy eyes. He wore a low-slung lungi below a neatly rounded paunch and above two finely sculpted calves. He looked at me with surprise but, unlike the villagers, without fear. Silently, I handed him Manni's note. He retreated into the interior darkness leaving me alone at the door.

There was a scuffle behind me. I turned. Two large men wearing the briefest of lungis and nothing else were dragging Srini from the car. They gripped his arms, which looked brittle in their heavy fists, and hustled him roughly towards the house. I stepped forwards to help him, but was yanked back by a strong hand on my shoulder. Before I could identify its owner I was hauled inside the dark doorway and hurled on to a hard, dusty floor.

I raised myself to hands and knees, tense and stiff and ready for the next blow – and prepared to respond in kind. To my surprise another hand, a gentler hand (though it might have been the same) helped me to my feet in the dark. The air smelled dank inside the house, like a barn filled with wet hay; it was chill after the baking heat outside. Just as I steadied myself I was pushed hard in the back, slightly winded, and I stumbled down a dark corridor and into another room. Again and again I was pushed through dark, dank, sparsely furnished rooms by a pair of large hands which seemed to exert complete control over me. By the spare light coming from narrow high windows I tried to identify my bullying escort. I glimpsed heavy limbs, a big gut, and the glint of a gold medallion. I tried to steer myself, to regain mastery over my own body, but every time I did I was shoved, tripped, knocked out of my stride, hustled at high speed from one room to another, each time almost falling on my face and each time just kept upright by those powerful hands. For a professional athlete it was galling. For Dave Stott, human being, it was terrifying. In those moments I admit I forgot all about Srini. All I could think was: Who is doing this to me? And why?

Idiot! I thought. You've been set up again.

There was a sudden burst of light, like walking unexpectedly into a cold shower, and I found myself sprawling in an open courtyard. In its centre was a heap of greenish-yellow paddy, raw unprocessed rice stinking to high heaven under the midday sun. Chickens clucked and ran in circles. Rusty scythes and an ancient looking plough stood next to the rice. On four sides the space was enclosed by the tall, blank walls of the house.

In one corner, shaded from the sun by a canvas awning suspended from the first floor windows, on a flat, low string bed, curled up in childlike sleep, lay Siva.

I stood up, ready to make a fight if I was pushed again, but we were alone. I approached the string bed, softly, as if afraid to wake the sleeping child. When I came within a yard of it Siva turned lazily, blinked twice, and opened his eyes. A broad contented smile spread across his slack, still half-slumbering features.

'David,' he purred, and stretched himself. He was wearing a lungi, the first time I'd seen him in one, and it showed off his fine, athletic legs to advantage. Over his chest he wore a Lacoste tennis shirt, an elegant cut with griffin crest on one side. On any one else the combination would have looked incongruous.

Just then I heard bare feet slapping stone floors. There was grunting and pushing and then Srini emerged into the light, still suspended between the two big men who'd grabbed him outside. They threw him to the ground. I bent down to see if he was injured. He waved me away and brought himself up slowly, bones creaking, brushing dust off his trousers and fumbling for the handkerchief he kept in his back pocket.

Siva was now on his feet, shoulders hunched like a threatened animal, looking wildly from one of us to the other.

'What's the meaning of this?' he shouted. 'Who is this?'

'Siva!' I shouted back. 'Who are these animals?'

The two men stood blocking the doorway, perusing the scene, ready to act at a moment's command.

'They work for me,' he pouted.

'Country goondas?'

'If you like.' He relaxed slightly, but kept staring at Srini, weighing him up, wondering, I could see, if his old friend had betrayed him.

'You sent for me . . .' I began.

'I didn't know you would bring a stranger,' he shot back. 'I cannot afford to be seen by strangers.'

'For god's sake, he's a friend.'

'Your friend, maybe.'

'If you don't trust me why did you send for me?'

'I do trust you. I trust no one else. There is no one left in Madras I can trust.'

He said it without affection, without flattery. It was a statement of despair more than anything else.

'Because Madras is a viper's nest,' Siva continued. 'Because I am safe only here. And because you are not one of Narayan's men. Or so I thought.'

The anger in his tone and his defiant stance alarmed one of his men, who made a move to grab Srini again. I quickly reached out and held the old man by one arm. The goonda held the other. A tug-of-war might begin at any moment and Srini's frail, flyweight body would be torn in two. He held himself erect and stared calmly back at the great cricketer.

After a moment's hesitation Siva barked an order at the goonda, who released Srini's arm. I pulled the old man close to me.

'He stays with me,' I declared. 'I need him. I trust him.'

If Siva wanted help from me he would have to accept Srini as well. Without the old man I was lost. I no longer had any faith in my own judgements and reactions.

'What do you know, David?' Siva sounded mournful, tired. 'He is no one. He could be anyone. You could easily be deceived, David. You know so little.'

'Then why tell Manni to give me the note? Why drag me out to this godforsaken place?'

'Precisely because you know so little. That is why I trust you. You are not tainted. You can act for me.'

'I know more now than I did before . . .'

I said I had talked with Inspector Mohan. I said I knew about CCI. I said I knew about the Commercial Trust Bank. Siva straightened, pursed his lips, turned his gaze away from me.

'And him?' He indicated Srini with a jerk of his handsome head. 'He also knows?'

Srini interrupted. 'I know that the strikers in Madras look forward to the safe return of the great cricketer.' The irony in his voice was deliberately ill-concealed. 'I know despite everything they are loyal to Siva.'

Siva examined him. Again the goonda, to whom this whole conversation was nonsense, edged forwards. Siva sent him back to his place with a commanding frown.

'How do you know this?' he asked Srini.

'Because he knows the strikers,' I interjected firmly. 'He knows the leaders. He's one of them.'

Srini smiled modestly and kept his eyes on Siva, who looked suspiciously back and forth between us. Then his whole body changed. The stiff, hostile readiness that had hunched his shoulders and bent his knees was gone. A languid ease replaced it. He wagged his head from side to side in the typical South Indian gesture of agreement, only to me it seemed a sad, uncertain signal. He spoke quickly to the goondas, though in a softer voice than before, and they retreated inside the house. With an elegant wave of one hand – he was now once again Siva the celebrity, the perfect host, even in this fly-populated farmyard – he invited us to sit in two wooden chairs next to the string bed.

We sat down.

'I'm sorry you were treated so roughly, David,' he said, still avoiding my eyes. 'Only a true friend would come this far. I cannot say what I owe you.'

'You owe me the truth, for a start.'

Siva stared at his perfectly manicured toes. After a moment he leaned back and let out a long, strangled sigh. There was frustration, exhaustion, defeat in it. It reminded me of something I'd heard at Nagpur when at the end of a long day in the field an experienced cricketer had inexplicably dropped a sitter.

'I cannot go back,' Siva moaned. 'They have turned on me.'

The fear in his voice, so uncharacteristic of the self-assured national hero, should have made me pity him. Instead I was impatient. I had travelled far and risked god knows what and I was in no mood for evasions. I had been buffeted by half-truths for days. Now I wanted it whole. And with Srini in attendance I knew I could settle for nothing less.

'The city is going mad, you know,' I said. 'Half the people think you're dead. The other half think you've been abducted. And everyone blames everyone else.'

Siva lowered his head. 'Narayan . . .' he cursed, a rare thing from his lips. 'I would never have advised you to get involved with this thing if I knew it had anything to do with these people.'

He said it from deep inside hunched shoulders.

'But you knew about CCI already. You knew at the party. And Robin knew you'd know. How? Why?'

He twisted in his seat and groped for words. I was still shaken by the rough welcome, still angry with my old friend – first for his mistrust and now for his childish muteness.

'They say you had the umpire killed!' I shouted at him.

'That is a lie!' his voice quaked with rage. 'You cannot believe I would do such a thing. If you think that, why have you come?'

'I've come because you asked me.'

I had many questions for Siva and one by one they tripped off my tongue. At first his answers were piecemeal, halting, incomplete. He glanced at Srini with anger and fear. The old man smiled at him complacently. Gradually his story emerged, and we began to see just what he had done, and what he was afraid of.

He had returned from England ten years ago to an uncertain future. Despite obvious talent he had made little impression in county cricket. After his long absence he was out of touch with the Indian scene, his name known only to a few insiders. In the meantime his father had died. In footing the bill for Siva's English education and providing dowries for his two sisters, the old merchant had borrowed heavily. The recession hit India and the textile business suffered. Siva found himself head of a proud, near penniless Brahmin family. His mother had grown accustomed to a certain style of life. His younger sister was engaged and in need of a dowry.

His great ambition, his father's dream, seemed doomed. Without contacts in the cricket hierarchy, without an entry to the prestigious clubs which monopolise high standard cricket in South India, and without a proven record in England, making it to the state side, not to mention the Test squad, was impossible.

'Who was I then? No one. Who were my friends? No one.'

Then a man came to him – a man who had played against him in a local match. This man offered to introduce him to people in power, people who could provide finance and sponsorship and prominence, people who could save him from a lifetime paying off his father's debts in the textile business. This man made a great show of his friends in high places and after some agonising weeks of delay brought Siva to Narayan. And Narayan, in his fluent, friendly, confident manner, took command of the young cricketer's career. Suddenly Siva met the right people and played in the right matches. And, as Narayan promised, soon there was money: money to pay off his father's debts, money for a dowry, money to keep his mother from the swelling ranks of the impoverished middle classes. And the money came in the form of cheques drawn on the account of Coromandel Coast Investments at the Commercial Trust Bank of Southern India.

'You knew what it meant?' I asked. 'You knew what kind of money it was?'

Not at first, he said. But soon Narayan had drawn the rising star into his political circle and little by little Siva was allowed to see for himself. It was the early seventies. South Africa had just been expelled from the International Cricket Conference. They were looking for a foothold in the cricket world. A small investment in promising young players might later yield a considerable return. Siva claimed that the only South Africans he ever met were Indian South Africans working for CCI.

'But I would never go to South Africa,' Siva insisted. 'I would never play there. You must know that.'

'What's the difference?' I said. 'You took their money. You worked for them.'

Srini had been right. Lakshmi had been right. I had been wrong. And I wasn't alone. I thought of his countrymen. Siva was their champion, the noble Tamil bestriding the world in their name. What would they make of the truth he had just admitted?

We were silent. Srini stared grimly at the cricketer, who looked at me balefully, pleadingly. I couldn't bring myself to return his gaze. Though if anyone had something to be ashamed of it certainly wasn't me. The paddy stank and the sun fell like a dead weight on the awning above us. The middle-aged man who had met me at the door brought us cool water in steel beakers.

'My cousin,' Siva said, then raised the beaker to his lips and drank it in one go. 'Don't worry. It's clean.'

I didn't remind him of our discussions in England years ago. They were fresher in my memory today than ever before, and I didn't believe he had forgotten them. At least he had the dignity – or the arrogance – not to make excuses. He spoke of the money from CCI as an incident in the distant past. In any case, he said, soon he was making enough money on his own and he no longer required the cheques from CCI. He became a star of the Ranji Trophy. His batting and bowling blossomed. Before long he was called to the Test side. He became Siva, the great all-rounder, the dashing leading man of Indian cricket.

And in so doing he pleased his mentor, Narayan, who treated Siva as a prize possession, reflecting glory – and power and wealth – back on his owner. But master and man could not agree on this. Siva saw his fame spread and his position strengthen. He sensed his own power and he wanted to exercise it. Siva believed he owed little to Narayan and a great deal to his own talent and intelligence. He had every cricketer's ambition: to be his own man, something apparently easy if one is rich and successful, yet surprisingly difficult.

'I knew myself the equal of Narayan and his friends. I felt I could use the Party to give something back to the people.'

'That is always the excuse for a faction fight within the Party,' Srini said. 'I presume Narayan threatened you with exposure to keep you in line? It wouldn't have looked very good – the people's champion on the apartheid payroll.'

Siva glared at the old man. It was obvious he disliked him intensely. It was obvious he resented his presence at this enforced confession. But with his customary self-discipline, his deeply ingrained politeness, he answered the query.

'Not at the time. But we both knew it was there. He made it clear on many occasions he was not pleased with the advances I was making within the Party.'

Having answered Srini, Siva turned back to me, impatiently flicking a lone dribble of sweat from his cheek.

'Narayan was threatened by my popularity. I no longer needed him or his machine. I could speak directly to the people. I can still speak directly to them. I must speak to them. They will listen. I know it. But you must help me.'

'I'm listening,' I said.

Siva resumed his tale. He told it slowly, with many silences, and many hesitations. But he now accepted that it must be told and he would tell it to the end.

One day not long ago the man who had first introduced him to Narayan paid him a call. This man knew of Siva's political ambitions. He said he now expected Siva to repay the great favour he had done him in the past. This man who had once seemed to well-connected, so influential, so terribly useful, now seemed rather lowly and pathetic.

'It was the umpire. Narayan had put him on the panel. I threw him out of my house.'

Why should the home he had worked so hard for be stained by a parasitical blackmailer? Why should such a small man stand in the way of a political career which could only bring good things for the people of Madras? Maybe not just the people of Madras, maybe all the Indian people?

'Yet I am no killer,' he glared at me fiercely. 'I would not touch a hair on his head.' He leaned forward and indicated the minuteness of such a hair with thumb and forefinger.

Then what had he done about the umpire? Nothing at first. He told no one. He simply avoided the man.

'You thought you could get away with that?' I asked.

He didn't answer. But in the sheer blankness of his response I could see at least part of the reason. The umpire was a man simply too insignificant to worry about. The distance between people of different social status in India can be so vast that they feel themselves living on different planets and subject to different laws. It was another example of Siva's innocence in which I had once so fervently believed. Now it seemed a less endearing trait.

It was around this time that the Legislative Assembly by-election had first beckoned, and with it an avenue to greater freedom for Siva, greater room for manoeuvre, and an opportunity to reduce Narayan's power over him and over the Party. Rumours were circulated. Hints were dropped.

'Then I read that the umpire had been appointed for your match at Chepauk. I had hoped to announce that I would stand in the election after the final day's play. I thought it would be fitting.'

He confronted Narayan. He accused him of having sent the umpire to intimidate him. Narayan made a great display of surprise. He denied all knowledge of the umpire, but warned Siva to restrict his political horizons and stick to cricket.

When Siva read of the umpire's murder he was worried, but spoke to no one. An enemy, an obstacle had been removed from his path, by accident or by some unknown agent. He would wait and see.

'When you came to me with Robin's Grand Prix Cricket I could see no connection. I did not know Narayan and his Bank were involved.'

My getting beaten up had shocked and baffled him. It had made him think, ask questions, but still there were no answers. Then, when I came to him with Robin's message about CCI, things started to fall into place.

'They were going to force me to play for that blasted circus. To make a spectacle of myself on the cricket pitch when I could be working for my people.'

'They expected a return on their investment,' Srini said.

Siva ignored him. 'It would be the end of my political career.' He spoke of his career as an invaluable asset, even though it had hardly begun. 'If I refused to play they would make my connection with CCI public and that would be that.'

'No doubt Narayan was under pressure from his own masters,' Srini said, 'from CCI and those who stand behind it. They were waiting for him to deliver the goods, the cricketer Siva whom they had bought and paid for.'

'He was jealous,' Siva said flatly, refusing to rise to Srini's bait. 'He could not tolerate anyone who could appeal to the people over his head. He wanted to control me.'

For Narayan Sartar was the perfect tool. He was a young man who had served Siva well. He may have been slow-witted and hot-tempered, but he watched over his master, shouted his name at rallies, even bowled to him in the nets. His loyalty was absolute. He protected his master as he protected himself, for he could see little difference between the two. When Siva learned that the young hoodlum had been arrested on the murder charge he could finally see the destiny being shaped for him. Narayan had persuaded Sartar that to protect Siva he must kill the blackmailer and retrieve the incriminating evidence. He had no doubt he was acting on behalf of his master. Narayan could have persuaded him to act with any number of excuses. It didn't matter because as far as Sartar was concerned Narayan and Siva were on the same side, members of the same Party. Narayan must have been pleased with his work. Sartar himself would say nothing to the police, but they would know he was one of Siva's men and their suspicions would be aroused accordingly.

'Sartar could not understand why I had not been in touch with him, nor why Narayan had avoided him. He had done this deed for us, this murder, and then was left alone. Yet he would not come into my house. He would not incriminate me.'

'But why did he attack me? What did he want?'

Siva shrugged. It was obviously a matter of less importance than his own survival.

'Obviously Narayan kept an eye on Sartar and told the police where to pick him up. Poor boy, he didn't know what hit him.'

'I saw him in his cell,' I said. 'He knew what hit him. He didn't know who.'

Siva winced. Was it the thought of the brutalised Satar, paying a price someone else, perhaps Siva himself, should have paid? Or was it the thought of Narayan, his erstwhile sponsor and ally, the Party boss turned mortal enemy, the back-stage manipulator who had outmanoeuvred the cricketing idol and left him isolated, as alone in this country retreat as Sartar was in Mohan's cells?

I had heard of inner-Party faction fights in India – the papers were full of them – but could it really go this far? Narayan, desperate to keep Siva out of politics and get him into Grand Prix Cricket, had set up the hapless young goonda. He had sent him on his murderous mission to the blackmailing umpire, sent him ostensibly on Siva's behalf, knowing that when he was caught the police and everyone else would draw the same logical conclusion, which only I had resisted, and then not out of logic but loyalty (misplaced?). Of course! Only Siva had enough to lose from exposure of his CCI connections to warrant such violence. Narayan had sent Sartar onto the streets and then bided his time until the moment came to spring the trap. One call to the police and Sartar was locked away and Siva incriminated. What did Narayan have to fear? He had always been a back-stage man, an invisible manipulator; in itself his bank's link with CCI might be embarrassing but of little political import. But while Narayan sat in the obscurity of the members' pavilion, Siva was in the middle, courting the public, and such a connection could well prove his undoing.

'I had to leave Madras,' he said. 'I was a liability to the Party. Even if I could prove the charges false the mud would stick. And if the South African connection was exposed the Party would suffer. Narayan had already disposed of one man. I do not put it past him to dispose of two.'

'You are right,' Srini chuckled. 'They would do to you what they liked and blame it on central government, or even the strikers. They could persuade enough of the people to believe this nonsense. And as a martyr the great Siva would be of more value to the Tamil Party, perhaps, than when he was alive. In the ensuing chaos the strike could be broken and the strikers locked away. Very convenient.'

Srini smiled into vacant space as if he found the whole idea strangely amusing. Siva brought his face close to mine, his eyes sad and pleading.

'I do not want to be a martyr,' he said. 'I can do something for the people. I can offer my service.'

Silent and utterly downcast Siva sat in the sun-filled courtyard, miles from the glamour of newspapers and cricket grounds. Disgrace, assassination even, hung over him. His normally erect razor-blade shoulders curled in towards his breast.

Narayan had played the proud independent star like a puppet on a string. The Party, riven by faction, had turned on one of its own. Of all the many friends Siva had boasted, not one reliable one remained. Only me. A foreigner. A cricketer. A man with nothing to offer.

Only Siva did not see it that way. He had plans for me. In his despair he had seized on his old friend from the Second XI.

'I know the people will hear me,' he said. 'I know if I appeal to them they will support me.'

'How do you propose to do that, sir?' Srini pounced on him. His dry lips drooped at the corners in a sceptical frown.

'My proposal,' Siva said slowly, 'is for David to go to the press. He must use his connections there to bring my story to the people, to rouse them on my behalf. They will listen. He is neutral. He has himself been a victim. People will remember. When they find who is responsible they will be enraged. Then I will return to Madras and lead a struggle against the corrupt elements in the Party. We will purge it. We will go to the people renewed.'

Srini suppressed a sneer. 'A fine scenario. But what evidence do you have? Can you prove your claim to innocence?'

I considered warning Srini to watch his tone – the old man enjoyed teasing and taunting the superstar, the titan of Indian cricket – but something in me was curiously pleased to see Siva wriggling and squirming and trying all the while to retain his dignity and self-control.

'The only person who can confirm to you what I have said,' Siva answered Srini with haughty exasperation, 'is Sartar. He will say nothing to the police or anyone else. But I know him. He will talk to me.' He shrugged fatalistically. 'That will not be possible. Not while he sits in Mohan's cells.'

'Ah, Inspector Mohan,' said Srini gleefully. 'An old acquaintance of mine.'

Siva looked at the old man. It was not hard for him to guess under what circumstances the police inspector and the old political radical would have known each other.

'I am no follower of the grand and glorious Tamil Party, as David knows,' Srini said, ignoring me and addressing himself exclusively to Siva, 'but I want to see the end of this South African carnival and the end of Mr Narayan and his gang of liars and butchers.'

Siva watched the old man. Eyes fixed, head still as if awaiting a fast delivery at the batting crease.

'Mohan is treading water at the moment. He has Sartar. He has the umpire's list of names. Yet he holds back. He plays games with the press. Why?'

With an enigmatic smile he looked from Siva to me and back again. He then confidently answered his own question.

'Because he is a wise man. Because he remembers. The police and their allies lost ground after the emergency. They are now more cautious about imposing President's Rule, the rule of the Delhi goonda, a rule of terror that is not always in their own interests. It might well make their job more difficult, their job being the collection of graft, the persecution of strikers, and so on. At the moment, they would prefer to see the Party in control. Your friend Mr Shrapley no doubt feels the same way.'

Siva said nothing, but I could see in his eyes the glimmer of hope which Srini's explanation had ignited. The afternoon heat was searing even in the shade of the awning, and we all moved as little as possible. Srini went on, sweat stains spreading from both armpits, jabbing a bony finger in the air to make his points.

'I know from experience that Mohan is no fool. I believe you can make a deal with him. Clearly he has much to offer you – protection from prosecution as accessory to murder for a start; the return of the incriminating document; perhaps more. You know better than I. But you too have something to offer him.'

Siva kicked a pebble from under his sandalled foot. 'Mohan,' he snorted. 'I know him. He is a snake in the grass. He is beyond trusting. It cannot be safe.' He turned again to me. 'You must act for me, David. It will be better that way. You must represent me. I trust you. You must expose Naryan and this Grand Prix Cricket. You are innocent. People will believe you. No one will blame you for exposing Robin Barnett. You will be thanked.'

'And where does this exposure stop?' Srini intervened. 'It is not only Narayan or Robin Barnett who will be threatened by David's revelations. It would be easy for me to supply David with all necessary information on Coromandel Coast Investments, including the names of its cricketing retainers.' The smile had vanished from the old man's face. He spoke clearly and harshly and tried to drive his meaning into Siva with the unwavering force of his gaze.

'So you are threatening me after all?' Siva said with a morose stare. 'I never expected that from you, David. I trusted you. I called you to my cousin's house. I am at risk. You know that.'

An image of Siva struggling on a wet wicket somewhere in the Midlands came back to me across ten years. Then came another image: Siva at a Cricketers' Association meeting, patiently arguing the case for a ban on South Africa.

I shook my head. 'I have to trust the people who tell me the truth,' I said. 'You told me you wanted to be independent, to be your own man. You said even a big star like Robin could be a prisoner. I didn't know then how true that was. I don't intend to be a prisoner, even though I'm no big star. I trust Srini. I want to hear what he has to say.'

Srini had quaffed a beaker of water while Siva and I had our exchange. Now he leaned forward and resumed talking, as if an unpleasant but necessary matter had been at last settled between his two colleagues.

'Go to Sartar. Talk to him. Make him tell the truth. If what you say is true Narayan can be charged with the umpire's murder. It will be your gift to Mohan. He needs a big shot in the courts. He would prefer Narayan, I suspect. There would be fewer risks than putting the great cricketer in the dock. Then the Inspector can sit on the fence and bide his time a while longer.'

Siva was silent for a moment. He retreated within himself and weighed up the situation with which Srini had presented him. He took on a vacant, distant, melancholy look. Then he returned from his solitary conference and spoke in a bitter tone.

'There is a problem. I must meet Mohan and Sartar in a safe place. I will not make a martyr of myself. If I return to my house Narayan's men will do as they like. And I will not set foot in that police station.'

'I do not blame you,' Srini answered, the grin he withheld from his mouth wrinkling the corners of his eyes. 'I found the accommodation most unpleasant during my stay. But there is another way, a safe place I know. It will involve making a deal. I know you are not averse to that.'

For a moment the anger flashed in Siva's face. His spine stiffened indignantly. Then his whole body subsided into flaccid resignation.

'You know the old field behind the assembly plant in Tandiarpet? The workers play cricket there.'

Siva knew it.

'You know the little pavilion, the little box of a place where the players change?''

That too he knew.

'Of course you know it. It is your constituency, is it not? Your electors?'

Again I thought of telling Srini to restrain himself. But there was no stopping the man. He had all the angles covered. He had thought it through and knew where he was going. And he intended to make Siva pay.

'The strikers from the plant have been meeting there. It is virtually off-limits to the police. The surrounding tenements provide excellent protection, and the workers will safeguard you, I am sure, though God knows why they should. You will be able to meet Inspector Mohan there in complete safety.'

Siva frowned. 'Who will arrange it?'

'Who will arrange it?' Even as he spelled out the means to Siva's return to Madras, Srini would not let up on the cricketer. 'Why, you will arrange it! Yes, yes. You and your friends in the Party. When you are back in their midst, safe and sound and untainted by corruption, you will approach your friend Shrapley and explain the political situation and prevail upon him to end the lock-out and call the goonda off the workers. You will even try to convince him that rescinding the wage cut will help restore order and calm to the city. I am sure if the workers knew of this commitment on your behalf they would be only too glad to arrange for your protection.'

'You can do this?' Siva brushed aside the old man's sarcasm.

'With David's help, yes.'

'Me?' I didn't like the sound of it. My role, I had hoped, was nearing its end.

'You must call Mohan,' Srini said. 'Speak carefully on the telephone. Make sure he understands. He will be expecting to hear from you.'

There was no point in arguing. It seemed I would have to make one last flight as carrier pigeon.

'Don't worry,' Srini laughed. 'You will know how to do it.'

Siva appealed to me with nervous, unhappy eyes.

'And later you will go to the papers, talk to your friends?'

I nodded. The deal was concluded.

We went indoors to eat a meal Siva's cousin had prepared for us. Several years ago Siva had lent him money. By offering sanctuary now, that debt was cancelled. The big men who had greeted us so rudely worked for him. Their usual job was intimidating uppity harijans. Now they joined us for the meal. The sight of them made me nervous at first. But they were all smiles, and as far as they were concerned we were now friends. They seemed in awe of Siva and spoke to each other in whispers. The cricketer, tense, unsmiling, ignored them and made only the odd casual comment to his cousin, who served the meal.

We were each given a shiny flat banana leaf, which we rinsed with water from a metal jug. Then a huge helping of rice was deposited on the leaf, followed by spoonfuls of vegetable curry and sambar, a thin, sweet-and-sour tasting sauce. A metal dish of hot pickle was passed around. When we'd finished we were given another helping of rice and sour, runny buttermilk to pour on top of it. My companions worked the rice and buttermilk into little balls and popped them into their mouths. I struggled until, at Siva's command, his cousin brought me a fork. I still couldn't finish all the rice. The goondas ate with gusto, leaving not a grain on their leaves. Srini, silent but obviously pleased with himself, and Siva were were not far behind.

We agreed to meet Siva that night at a rendezvous not far from the workers' pavilion. The grim-faced cricketer bade us a strained, formal goodbye. Was he thinking, perhaps, of the new people to whom he was becoming indebted, and how they might one day hold it over him?

On the drive back Srini chatted merrily.

'Very good. Yes, very good indeed. Your Siva will not dare go back on his word now. The umpire may be dead. Narayan may soon be descredited. But there will always be one or two of us around who know about Coromandel Coast Investments and their favourite cricketer.'

He laughed heartily and changed gears with a ferocious crunch. Amazingly, the car made it back to Madras in one piece.

CHAPTER TWENTY-ONE

It was seven o'clock when Srini dropped me off in front of the hotel. During the day the police presence in the city had increased. All India Radio described the situation in Madras as 'spiralling out of control' and warned that the Government might be forced to intervene to preserve law and order. The streets were abandoned with the coming of dusk. Exhausted, I trudged upstairs (the ancient lift was still out of order). I was too tired to think. I was just glad the whole thing was coming to an end.

In the shower I rinsed country dust from my skin. Brown water ran into the drain. The others were still at Narayan's country estate. I pictured them lounging round a pool and drinking tall drinks, and for a moment I envied them. In clean clothes I made my way downstairs and asked for the phone. The desk clerk, in his usual extravagant manner, summoned various minions and arranged for me to make a private call in a small room off the main lobby.

'You will be calling your family in England, sir?' he asked.

'No,' I said, 'I have no family.'

This distressed him. 'No family? All men must have family. Sir, there is no happiness without family.'

It proved easy enough to get through to Madras Central Police Station, but getting hold of Mohan himself was more difficult. Over and over again I explained that only the Inspector would do and that no, thank you, I would not leave a message for him. After two disconnections and an endless wait on a silent line which forced me to hang up and dial again, suddenly I was through. Mohan's jovial voice greeted me as an old friend.

'Mr Stott, a pleasure to hear from you. I trust no one else has gone and knocked you on the head?'

For a moment I was speechless. Srini had said I would know what to do. He had trusted me with this crucial liaison. But I had forgotten to work out what to say.

'You will be facing Chaughiri tomorrow. The wicket will turn, no? A difficult proposition . . .'

This gave me a lead.

'There is another cricketer. A mutual friend. He's not playing at the moment, but he asked me to say he would very much like to meet you and talk.'

There was silence at the other end.

'He has a proposal to make. He thinks you'll be interested. But he wants to talk first to a former employee of his. Someone you're holding in custody.'

'Well, this is most interesting,' chirped Mohan.

'My friend feels this meeting would be best held at a neutral ground. Somewhere he feels comfortable. I'm sure you understand.'

Mohan understood. I was amazed how easy it was to communicate this way, without mentioning names, when both parties shared a common interest. Perhaps I was getting the hang of India after all.

'Needless to say, Mr Stott, I can make no guarantees. But with a person so eminent as your friend I will certainly come with an open mind.'

He baulked when I named the meeting place.

'You will appreciate that for myself and my men to enter such an area after dark in the current situation will be extremely difficult, extremely dangerous. Surely we can meet at your friend's house or some other place . . .'

'Impossible.'

'I see.'

He weighed up the risks and the possible rewards. I could almost hear his brain turning over at the end of the line.

'Very well,' he said. 'I am a reasonable man. I am prepared to negotiate in a civilised manner. But of course I will take every precaution.'

I pictured Mohan with a battalion of lathi-armed police ready to charge at the first sign of trouble.

The time and place were agreed.

'I look forward to seeing you again,' Mohan finished.

I hung up and dialled Lakshmi's number at home. There was no answer. I tried her office. No answer there either. I hung up again and called *The Banner*. Gopal was out. I left a message. Would Mr Srikkanth call Mr Stott as soon as possible?

'Mr Stott, the English cricketer?' asked the voice at the other end. I confirmed the fact and got off as quickly as I could.

I thanked the desk clerk for the use of the phone and went upstairs to rest. Srini would soon return for me in his borrowed

Ford. I felt surprisingly calm. I had performed my part of the bargain – rather well, I thought. Lakshmi would be pleased. Srini would be pleased. Soon I could return to being an ordinary run-of-the-mill cricketer on an expenses-paid tour of India. Soon the big stars would occupy the crease again, and minor characters like me could retire gracefully to the dressing room.

In the hall the gaunt, chalky face of Mark Kidleigh loomed in my way. His illness made his cheeky grin sour and malevolent.

'Back from the country already, DTS?'

I mumbled about the heat and asked how he was feeling.

'Rotten. Couldn't make it to Narayan's.'

I was about to pass him when he held me with one hand and leered at me with rheumy eyes.

'Your girlfriend was round here today.'

His breath smelled of stale vomit.

'Sniffing round the rooms she was, poxy bitch.'

'Fuck off, Kidleigh,' I whispered and removed his big paw from my shoulder.

'Don't worry about me,' he chortled. 'Always fancied a bit of brown fanny meself.' He winked at me, grotesquely.

My left fist swung back of its own accord and then forwards as I on-drove through his midriff. He doubled up and fell to his knees.

'You bastard,' he gargled the word, half choking on some noxious fluid that had risen from his gorge. 'You fucking shit. Robin'll have you for this. He fucking will.'

I left Kidleigh in a heap. I admit I was pleased with myself. It was something I'd been owing Kidleigh since that first day. But I was also concerned. What was Lakshmi doing prowling round the hotel? How could she take such a risk? It was totally unnecessary. And with a creep like Kidleigh lounging about the risk was that much greater.

I sauntered down the stairs and through the lobby. In the street I paced slowly up and down waiting to hear the stutter and whine of Srini's borrowed Ford. I thought of Robin. A wave of hatred swept through me as I pictured him lecturing me for taking a swing at his fast-bowling prodigy. I would tell him just what I thought of him and his Grand Prix Cricket. He'd be reading about it in the papers soon enough.

Srini pulled up next to me and I stepped into the car. He was in a good mood, over-excited perhaps at the prospect of the pantomime we were about to witness. He told me he had already dropped copies of all his documents concerning CCI, Nararyan and the Bank at *The Banner* offices.

'But your friend Srinkkanth was nowhere on the premises.'

'No,' I said. 'I couldn't find Lakshmi either.'

'I look forward to the headlines,' Srini purred like an old tom cat contemplating a bowl of milk. 'I have waited a long time for this.'

The city was dark and almost deserted. Lights burned in windows, in little shops and stalls, in improvised tents and shelters. Momentary lamplight cast a yellow glow on passing faces. It was as mild and pleasant now as it had been hot and uncomfortable in the afternoon. We parked at the rendezvous and waited for Siva in silence. It was a desolate spot, opposite a tea stall where men huddled under a tattered burlap awning supported by crooked wooden poles. From nowhere a shiny BMW pulled up next to us. Siva, in sunglasses, broad-brimmed white sunhat and dark blazer, nodded to us from the driver's seat. The small part of his face that was visible seemed eerily empty.

'It is arranged,' Srini said through his window. 'We shall proceed.'

We formed an absurd convoy, driving through the narrow empty streets, the battered old Ford held together by wire and rivets followed by the sleek, mint-condition BMW. I felt sure we would be stopped, but luckily our destination was near. We parked behind the diminutive pavilion, a white wooden shack with a green roof and weather vane like Father Time at Lord's.

The cricket ground stood in the shadow of Shrapley's factory. Its tall chimney loomed over us. Every one of the dozens of windows puncturing the brick wall was shattered. Heaps of tangled rusting metal formed a barricade in front of an iron gate. There were no lights anywhere. As we stepped from the car men came out of the night to surround us.

Srini spoke to them in low tones. Siva glided through with regal hauteur. The men seemed in awe of him and kept their distance. We were escorted inside the shack.

The room was lit by a single lamp hanging from the ceiling around which a flock of moths fluttered. Stacks of wispy printed paper filled one corner.

This was strike headquarters – an unlikely place, a cricket pavilion; yet perhaps not so unlikely after all. I remembered what

I'd been told when I first arrived in Madras: the Indian people had taken the English game and made it their own.

Siva sat alone in a corner, back erect, eyes unswerving. I took a position on a wooden bench, away from the light. Srini murmured to workers, some dressed in lungis, some in trousers, both with a variety of shirts, T-shirts, and kurtas. A few women in saris came and went among them. Their poverty was palpable, but they were strong, determined-looking people. I wasn't afraid of them, mysteriously alien as they were, but I was afraid nonetheless. My heedless bravery of an hour ago had evaporated. Would this be the end of D. T. Stott, left-hand bat, erstwhile county cricketer, in an industrial slum in Madras, murdered in a police charge on a workers' stronghold? I felt I had come frighteningly far since stepping off the coach with Robin and Paul and Ernie and the rest. I struggled to keep my stomach from leaping out of my mouth. In the warm evening air, I was chill with fear.

Outside there were car engines turning over, doors slamming, voices. In the room everyone went quiet. An argument started somewhere in the darkness. Insults were exchanged. For a moment I thought my worst fears were coming true. But no. The argument died away. With a flurry of lathis a troop of policemen burst into the dimly lit shack. Mohan strode briskly after them, followed by two more policemen, dragging between them the nearly limp body of Sartar, the young goonda. He wore a terrified look, and two dark swollen eyes above a heavy nose caked with blood.

They threw him on the pile of papers in the corner. The men in the room stiffened and held their arms away from their sides as if preparing for a fight. Srini walked straight up to Mohan, who commanded the centre of the room with lathi in hand and a ferocious glare.

'Inspector, Inspector,' Srini urged gently, 'we have an agreement. There is no need for this.'

Mohan drew himself up and tried to stare the old man down. When this proved impossible, he snarled viciously in Tamil, making a very different sound from the genial one he made when speaking English. Then he saw Siva sitting like a waxwork in the corner and a smile crossed his face. The betel-stained gums looked vermilion in the yellow light.

'Ah, we are honoured,' he said. 'Yes, honoured indeed.'

The policemen stood over the wounded Sartar, who squatted

on his haunches and wept silently. The workers took up strategic points near windows and door and kept sullen, suspicious eyes on the movements of the police. These people were natural enemies, that was clear. There had already been clashes between them and scores remained to be settled. I only hoped it wouldn't happen tonight.

Here on their home ground the workers seemed the more confident of the two parties. The police tried to hide their nerves by standing rigidly to attention. Perhaps they were wondering what latest turn in an obsessive pursuit of baksheesh and political power had led their superior to this godforsaken rendezvous in the middle of the night.

Sartar quivered in the pile of paper, strike leaflets printed on the cheapest second-hand scraps available. His injured foot was wrapped in dirty rags, a formless, pudgy piece of flesh protruding where there should have been a toe.

Mohan pulled up a chair and sat close to Siva. They exchanged a few quiet sentences in Tamil. Then Mohan signalled for his men to bring the captive goonda forwards. In one swift movement they picked him off the ground and deposited him at Siva's feet.

Srini backed away. It was time for Siva's performance. I watched from the other side of the room.

Siva put his long arm round Sartar's shoulders and the young man bowed his head and tears fell. The cricketer whispered soothingly in his ear. He repeated his mild feathery assurances over and over before finally, gently cudgelling a response from the boy. At last the goonda spoke, at first haltingly, then hysterically, in an incomprehensible flow of words.

Siva scolded him. Mohan, clearly intrigued, bent his head and pulled his moustache. The goonda slapped the floor several times as if swearing an oath, and each time Siva stroked his head and quietly reassured him.

Suddenly the boy pointed a finger at me and let forth a stream of vituperation. I shivered. No one else turned to me. All eyes were on the young man confessing himself in the presence of his master.

Now Siva and Mohan exchanged words in low voices while the little goonda sat on the floor, breathing heavily, but dry-eyed at last. The Inspector and the cricketer took on the air of men of affairs discussing a business transaction.

By turn they were polite, cagey, contrary, accommodating.

Outside there was movement, sounds of feet in the dust, murmurings. The workers relaxed, shifting in their places, and the policemen followed suit.

Again Siva addressed Sartar and seemed to be urging him, patiently, deftly, towards some unknown end. Sartar spoke more clearly now, indeed he spoke at some length, turning first from Siva to Mohan and then back again. By the flickering lamp I could see his bruised eyes watering, now more from physical abuse than hysterical fear. Several times he repeated a short phrase to Siva, as if reciting a prayer. Siva placed a strong hand lightly on his head and ruffled his hair, which was sticky with jailhouse dirt and blood.

Mohan stood up and signalled again to his subordinates. As quickly as they had arrived, they now departed, dragging Sartar between them. He had gone limp and might have passed out. His bad foot bumped over the old, uneven floorboards. No one took any notice.

Siva, on his feet and looking more vigorous than he had all day, extended his hand to Mohan, who for a moment seemed taken aback by the gesture, then grasped it eagerly. They spoke now in English and I could hear a little of what they said.

'It is the only way.'

'Best for the Party.'

'Best for the people.'

Though I couldn't make out the details, the tone was unmistakeable. It was a tone I had heard often among the powerful in India, a complacent tone that tonight made my blood boil, and for a while vanquished all fears. 'Best for the people.' The phrase rang in my head. Best for the strong workers guarding the famous cricketer? For the multitudes at Chepauk?

Now Mohan produced an envelope from his pocket and handed it to Siva who stuffed it inside his blazer. It might have been an invitation to dinner.

Is this it? I wondered. Property exchanged and promises made? What did it mean? Where did it leave all these people?

Mohan turned and found Srini in his way. The old man, slightly stooped, wiry, sleeves still buttoned down over wrists like an old-fashioned cricketer, smiled cheekily at the thick-set, elegantly tailored policeman. Mohan tried to reassert an authority temporarily held in abeyance by looking past the old man and catching my eye.

'Mr Stott,' he said, stepping past his adversary, and holding out a hand for me to shake, 'I believe your role in this has come to an end. That is good. You are too involved for a foreigner. Go home to England. I will look for your name in the averages.'

I put my hands on my hips and ignored his proffered palm. 'My cricket is finished,' I said. 'But I like India. I might stay around for a bit.'

Mohan bowed stiffly and led the remainder of his men out of the dark pavilion. The last policeman backed out through the doorway, lathi raised across chest, scanning the heavily built workers, who remained stock-still in their posts.

No one moved. We listened to the sounds outside. There was no talk. After what seemed an eternity we heard one engine starting up, then another and another. As if making a point of their power and speed, the cars revved up and screeched off. Then they were gone and it was silent again. We all relaxed.

Siva went round the room and thanked each man in turn, shaking hands or touching them on the shoulder. They received his thanks with respectful gestures. Eyes were lowered. Heads waggled. But I wondered just how far their faith in the great Tamil champion would now extend. To me at that moment they seemed people of bottomless scepticism. This, I was convinced, would stand them in good stead.

I went outside with Srini, who had grown quiet, thoughtful. Small groups of hard, poor, serious-looking people sat round little fires, burning scraps of wood and dried dung cakes which gave off an acrid odour. They talked and argued among themselves, unaware of or indifferent to the white man and the celebrity in their midst. Had they been here all along, sitting in the darkness, seeing but unseen?

Siva approached me. Two old comrades from county cricket confronted each other in this impoverished hole, surrounded by barricades and anonymous, angry people. His eyes met mine and issued a silent appeal.

'I cannot say what I owe you, David,' he began.

'What did he say?' I interrupted him coldly. 'Sartar, your young thug. Why did he shout at me like that?'

'He thought it was you who had informed on him, told the police where he was.'

I shook my head.

'I explained it was not you. It was Narayan. Mohan confirmed it.'

'But why did he hit me?'

Siva sighed. 'Don't you see? He didn't know what he was being used for. Narayan had cut him off, deliberately left him dangling, waiting to use him to destroy me.' There was long-standing outrage in the last phrase. 'Sartar couldn't get through to me. He was desperate. He saw you arrive at the gates that afternoon. He saw everyone else wait outside and you alone come in. He saw that you had access where he had none. He waited for you to come out again. He thought you would carry his message. But you spurned him. You insulted him. He thought you were pretending not to understand him. He followed you with that journalist woman. He saw you go into that expensive restaurant. He is very highly strung. I have known him for years. He felt abandoned, betrayed. He hit you because it was the only way he could get his message through. It might have worked, but Narayan sprung the trap too soon.'

So even Sartar had wanted to use me as a messenger man. He was the only one I had refused.

'It is one of those things. But it may have its uses yet. Your name in the paper will now mean something to people here. Your story will carry weight. It is good.'

'For who?'

He searched my face for some sign of reconciliation. I was determined to offer none. Hesitantly, in a childish whisper, he asked, 'You will make sure the story is in the papers? As we agreed?'

'I'll do what I said I'd do,' I replied frostily, though even then I could feel all the years we'd shared welling up inside me and nearly breaking the reserve I was struggling to maintain.

He stepped forwards, arms spread, and tried to embrace me. I was stiff, unyielding, indifferent. My head twisted away. He stepped back, defeated.

'You will see me tomorrow,' he said unemotionally, and walked back to his BMW.

Srini came up to me and touched my arm.

'You have done well,' he said gently. 'Come. I will take you to your hotel. Tomorrow will be an interesting day.'

CHAPTER TWENTY-TWO

It was now past midnight. The streets were quiet. Lorryloads of police flashed by in the dark. I glimpsed young officers asleep, heads lolling against rifle butts. For the first time that day the air was positively cool. It refreshed me and held back the tide of sleep rising in my head. Srini stopped in front of the hotel.

'Go. Sleep. You deserve it.'

'What about you?' I asked. 'Don't you ever get tired?'

He chuckled. 'I am always tired. It does not seem to matter at my age.'

'My god, I have to play cricket tomorrow,' I groaned. 'I can't bear it.'

'But you must,' he said. 'They must continue to think you are nothing but an Englishman and a county cricketer.'

'I am an Englishman and a county cricketer.'

'I had almost forgotten,' he smiled.

I entered the hotel and returned to my kind. I passed the dozing desk clerk, his face soft in babylike sleep, and thought how simple was my last assignment: I had to be myself and stay where I was. Yet this now seemed a peculiarly difficult task.

Then I remembered one last errand. I had to talk to Gopal. I had to explain. But I had no number for him. I decided it would keep till morning.

Lost in thought, and looking forward to the bed upstairs (even Dougie's snoring wouldn't keep me awake tonight), I wandered through the lobby. The arm seemed to come out of nowhere. Bodiless, detached in space, it gripped the back of my neck and with a powerful squeeze sent a shudder of pain down my spine. It threw my face against the iron grille of the malfunctioning lift. Cheap gilt paint flaked off against my battered teeth. A ragged cut opened inside my mouth.

'It's time we had a few words, Stott.'

It was Robin. His strength was tremendous. It made me feel a weakling, a child. I tried to turn my face to him, but he shoved me with a single decisive thrust back into the grille. The bruise on my forehead felt like it would burst with pain. There was more chipped paint, more blood in the mouth.

'I'd invite you to my room,' he said, holding my head rigid against the lift cage, 'but your girlfriend made such a bloody mess of it and the damned peon hasn't cleaned it properly. Besides, Kidleigh's been sick since you poked him in the gut and the place smells like an Indian sewer.'

For a moment I thought he was going to bang my head into pulp against the iron bars. He was fifteen years older than me, but I doubted if I could hold my own against him. Suddenly he released me. The steel in his muscles that had transmitted itself through my bones was gone. Shakily I turned to face him. Robin, polished, self-contained, carefully groomed as ever, gazed at me with cold eyes. He had given me a taste, no more, of the violence within him. It was enough. I obeyed his command and followed him to the empty restaurant.

We sat opposite each other at the table we had shared that first night with Roy Cuthbert. The same boy, perched on his stool, waited in attendance. Robin ordered him out of the room. He too obeyed without demur. My tongue flicked the inside of my lip and tasted blood. Robin sat in silence, wanting me to feel I was now at his disposal.

'You really are a bastard,' I said.

He did not rise to it. The violent genie had been put back in its bottle. He had left me in no doubt it could be summoned whenever its owner pleased.

An alarm sounded in my throbbing head.

'Where's Lakshmi?'

'Where are the papers she stole?'

I recognised the look on his face. It was the one he had worn as he waited over the stumps, poised for the run-out, watching my fast throw come in from extra cover.

Papers? Something in me said: Tread carefully, give nothing away, wait for him . . .

'I have already exercised a considerable restraining influence on my friends,' he said, with a great display of patience wearing thin. 'I think some appreciation on your part would be in order, but I have ceased to expect anything from you – anything but disloyalty and ingratitude.'

'Where's Lakshmi?' I demanded, ignoring the quick course on ethics.

'Somewhere safe.'

'If you . . . if anything happens to her . . .'

'You, David, are in no position to make threats.' Again the calm frozen exterior, and underneath, just visible through the surface ice, the violent mammoth. 'Your Indian lady will remain unharmed if the papers are returned.'

I tried to think fast.

'And if the papers are not,' Robin continued, 'there are no guarantees of anything. You will regret your disloyalty to your fellow cricketers, of that I can assure you.'

'This would be a joke if it wasn't so bloody awful,' I groaned.

Robin smiled his thin, superior smile. 'It is no joke, David. You have been playing with things you can't even begin to understand. I don't know what this woman has been telling you. I suspect she belongs to some crank extremist group. At home you would have seen through her and her friends right away. You've been seduced, old boy, seduced by India. You're not the first white man befuddled by the place. You are a renegade. You are nothing.'

He shook his head at the sight of such a pathetic specimen. I looked back at him across the table and he might as well have come from another planet. He seemed utterly remote and alien. Yet that mighty hand had swooped down from its faraway orbit and had a piece of my life in its grasp.

'What's happened to her?'

'Nothing,' he said as if it was a thing of little consequence. 'Yet.'

I sank back in my chair, knocked breathless for a moment. I was dimly aware that I still possessed an advantage. If I hadn't I knew I wouldn't be sitting here now, and I'd have suffered a lot more than a freshly bruised face.

'The papers will be returned,' Robin said. 'There will be no copies made. No release to the press. There will be silence on your part and hers and anyone else to whom you've told your dirty little stories.'

'And if that's not possible?'

He shook his head. What a stupid fellow he thought me!

'For a start the girl will vanish. You know yourself how easily these things can be managed out here. You have met Inspector Mohan. You know what can be arranged.'

'Tomorrow,' I said flatly, finally. 'You'll get the papers tomorrow. But if a hair on her head is touched, I won't care what happens to me or anyone else. You understand?'

I wiped my mouth with my sleeve. It came away red with blood.

Robin relaxed.

'You know your friend Siva is finished in any case.'

'And you're not?'

His eyebrows leapt up, then settled again in an impervious straight line. 'I'm not finished, David. I have many lands yet to conquer. But Siva's little stunt will fail. It will be his swansong.'

'His people may not agree.'

'His people!' Robin laughed, a laugh without breath, deep inside his hollow chest, where it bounced and echoed drily. 'They are nothing but a shadow – a shadow cast by a few important men. Haven't you learned that yet? They are the spectators beyond the boundary. It's what happens in the middle that counts.'

'It's all a game to you.' Robin was fading before me, retreating into the haze of middle distance, while I stayed rigid in my seat, blood oozing from my inner lip, the lump on my head pounding with a life of its own.

'Not a game, David, not at all.' He was toying with me now, indulging himself in the sheer weight and feel of the fish thrashing helplessly on the end of his line. 'Cricket has never been a game to me. You've never understood that. You floated for years in the stagnant backwaters of county cricket, moving with the tide. I gave you a chance to escape from all that. Perhaps you might have even made a few runs next year. People would have said, Stott isn't such a bad player after all. We never thought he had it in him.'

'I never wanted what you wanted from cricket. Maybe that was my problem. Funny though, it just doesn't bother me any more. No, not a bit.'

I rose slowly. He made no move to stop me. He was quite confident now that he would get what he wanted. His eyes stayed on my as my hand went up to explore my damaged face.

'You will have the papers with you tomorrow morning at Chepauk. Someone will contact you.'

'It's an exchange,' I reminded him. 'I see Lakshmi first, then you get the papers.'

'It will all be arranged.'

His calmness made my blood run cold. I left the room before a gnawing fear wiped out the last of my advantage.

Back in my room the lights were out, and rather than disturb Dougie I left them that way. Nonetheless, he turned in his his sleep, started, and woke up.

'Davey?' his voice was hoarse.

'Yeah. Didn't mean to wake you.'

The lights went on.

'Jesus Christ!' he said, viewing me with alarm. 'Now what's happened?'

'Robin pushed me into the lift cage downstairs.'

'Because of what you did to Kidleigh?'

'Who told you about that?'

'Kidleigh, when I checked up on him after we got back from that bloody swimming pool. He said you belted him in the gut.'

'I did.'

'You must have had a reason.'

'I did.'

'Well, it didn't help his diarrhoea any. Lad's been shitting blood all night.'

'Good.'

'I don't suppose you know who turned this room upside down this afternoon? And if you do, I don't suppose you'd consider telling me about it?'

For the first time I noticed the room. It had been tidied up, but everything was in a different place. And the mirror was cracked. When Dougie had returned that evening he'd found sheets, pillows, clothes, suitcases in a heap on the floor. The staff had cleaned it up but given no explanation.

'And nothing's missing?'

'Not that I can find.'

Robin's cronies had searched the room, but they hadn't found the precious papers, whatever they were. Dougie sat up in bed.

'Did the chap downstairs give you the message?'

'What message?'

'Jesus Christ, this hotel couldn't pass for a YMCA at home. Some reporter – said he knew you. Very excited he was. I told him you weren't giving interviews.'

'What did he want?'

'Wants to speak to you. Left a number somewhere.'

Dougie rummaged through the blue airmail stationery on the table next to the bed. Then, lifting the frayed Alistair Maclean novel which he was reading for, I think, the third time, he found it. I tore the scrap of paper from his hand. There was a number, but no name.

'Gopal,' I said, 'it must be him.'

'Something like that.' He stood up and confronted me in his undershorts. 'It's time you told me what this is all about. Why did you hit the kid? The truth, mind!'

'Do I need a reason to hit Kidleigh? Does anyone need a reason to hit Kidleigh?'

I went towards the door. Dougie pointedly picked up his book and started to read. I owed him an explanation. I owed him something. It would just have to wait.

I padded down the hall as softly as I could, stopping at each corner to listen for the sound of other voices, other feet. Downstairs the restaurant was empty. I woke the sleeping desk clerk and asked if Mr Barnett was still around. No, he told me wearily, Mr Barnett had gone to his room. I asked for the telephone, which he provided with a grumpy servility. He'd had his fill of English cricketers.

I dialled the number and prayed Gopal's voice would answer the ring. It did. He'd been waiting by the phone for hours. His words came out in rapid, sten-gun bursts.

'I told her. I told her not to do it. Stott, she is impossible. She was determined. I could not stop it. Believe me.'

I had no trouble believing him.

Lakshmi had told him what she knew and swore him to secrecy. He had gone with her to the hotel, just to keep an eye on her, but was soon drawn into her ruse. While she investigated upstairs, he had engaged the desk clerk and other staff downstairs.

'I said I was doing an article on the private habits of touring English cricketers. They are convinced you are all mad.'

The locks on the hotel doors, he assured me, were useless – more to reassure guests than deter thieves. Then Gopal had seen Kidleigh emerge from the restaurant and make his way upstairs.

'We thought everyone was out. You told her they would all be with Narayan.'

Making an excuse to the bewildered staff, Gopal had followed Kidleigh at a distance. He had come upon the two of them in the hall and hid himself in the laundry closet.

'At first I thought he was trying to chat her up. They both looked so calm.'

Then Kidleigh had grabbed her, twisted her arm behind her back, and propelled her head first into his room.

'She didn't scream. She didn't call for help. She is extraordinary.'

Kidleigh had bolted the door from the outside with a padlock he took out of his pocket. (I remembered the padlock; someone had warned him nothing was safe in India.) He'd passed by the laundry closet on the way downstairs. Gopal had then run out and called to Lakshmi through the door.

'She said she was all right. Really she did. And she sounded so . . . indifferent. She passed the papers under the door. There was a big gap. What could I do?'

Then he'd calmed himself and walked downstairs, passing Kidleigh on the way.

'He didn't even look at me. To him I think Indians all look the same.'

'Robin wants them back. We've got to get them back. I've made a deal.' I went on breathlessly, listening all the time for a footstep at the door, a sigh, a cough, betraying a listening spy.

'They are incredible! I would not have believed it, if I hadn't seen the papers myself.'

'I would.'

Gopal had already shown them to his editor – it was too sensitive a matter for him to deal with on his own – and along with the information Srini had sent about CCI there was more than enough material to sink the luxury liner Grand Prix Cricket with all hands on board – notably Captain Robin Barnett, Roy Cuthbert, and V.P. Narayan.

'The names!' Gopal exclaimed. 'The names!' He hurriedly listed them. Test stars from all countries and a big helping of popular county faithfuls. I realised just how far Robin and Cuthbert had got, and that my own recruitment had probably been an afterthought.

'You can't print it now. They've got Lakshmi.'

But what did that mean? 'They' had Lakshmi? I didn't know where she was or who was holding her or what they'd done to her. My imagination worked overtime: image followed horrific image. I thought unthinkable things. Gopal shared my fears.

'It is too late,' his voice shook. 'I cannot stop it now. Too many people know. Maybe I can delay it.'

'How long?'

Gopal paused. He was making his calculations, and I was making mine.

'The afternoon edition,' he said. 'Maybe two o'clock before it would reach the streets. But rumours, you know. Once a story is circulating . . .'

Robin's man would contact me the next morning. I could still make the trade.

'You must get them to me – early, as soon as possible.'

Gopal sighed. 'Yes, yes, I will try. But it is not so easy. You shouldn't have promised . . .'

'What choice did I have?' Unwisely, I raised my voice.

'I know,' he said sombrely. 'I will try. But they are in the editor's vault and he may not see it the way we do.'

'Just you damn well get them.'

'You know, David, these papers, this story, it will come out sooner or later. All of it. It is right,' he said gently.

'I know,' I whined.

'Lakshmi would be the first to insist on it.'

'I know that too.'

Neither of us said goodbye. The conversation had reached its end because we were both up against the limits of what we could do or say. We simply placed the receivers down quietly, and that was it.

I stood still and listened. There was nothing but the silence of the hotel full of sleeping cricketers, and the sounds of the Madras night: the blast of a car horn, the lowing of a cow, and an insistent rhythmic wailing in the distance.

I passed the desk clerk, who said nothing, having no doubt decided that of all the strange cricketers I was the strangest. I climbed the stairs feeling the weight of each footstep on the threadbare carpet. I was still wary of being caught out, caught out like Lakshmi who had believed the hotel was empty because I had told her it was.

At the top of the stairs I actually stopped and cursed her, in a whisper, through clenched teeth. Why had she done such a mad thing? She had said I was in too deep and the only way out was to go in deeper still. How true was that now? How deep did you have to go? And how far back was it to the surface?

Dougie was wide awake. Alistair Maclean was back in his place on the table. I sat down wearily on the edge of my bed and lowered my head into my hands.

'It can't be that bad, son.'

I tried to answer, but my voice caught in my throat. To my own surprise, a sob came out.

I felt a hand on my shoulders, Dougie's hand this time, not at all like Robin's, and I looked up. The old fellow looked even unhappier than I felt, and even more at a loss for words.

'There'll be a story in the papers tomorrow,' I said. 'You won't like it. You won't like it at all.'

Sleep was impossible, despite the late hour, and I felt I needed another ally. I told Dougie as much of it as I could keep straight in my head. I lost the thread of the story more than once, and no matter how I tried there were parts that Dougie couldn't or wouldn't understand.

'But why did Siva . . .?'

'Then how come Cuthbert . . .?'

'But I thought Siva and Narayan . . .?'

'Kidnapped! That girl?'

'Robin! Kidleigh! The bastard!'

Dougie was shocked. For all his experience in the game, for all his wanderings up and down the country in search of talent to mould, he was utterly naive. He knew so little of the world.

'There's no loyalty in some people. No decency. No respect.'

The South African connection meant nothing to him. As far as he was concerned, it was just another place to play cricket. What outraged him was the attack on tradition, on the authorities, on cricket itself, as he saw it. It confirmed his every prejudice about Robin Barnett and his hatred of the man was at last given full rein.

'Why, he's nought but a pimp for this newspaper fellow. Men like him have made a packet out of the game and they've no right to go mucking about with it.'

I told him to calm down. My own heart was beating fast enough. I reminded him of Lakshmi. Just mentioning her gave me a spasm of fear. It was as if I were dangling over a precipice and the best I could do was not to look down.

'So it's serious between you and this Indian girl?'

I laughed weakly. 'Maybe. But not the way you might think.'

I urged Dougie to go about his preparations tomorrow as usual.

'Just be there and ready when I need you.'

'No fear of that, lad,' he assured me.

Dougie was soon dozing tranquilly. I marvelled at him, a man gifted with the ability to sleep at will. I lay down in darkness and drifted from thought to thought. Among them was the worst: I had finally figured it out, I had all the pieces of the puzzle, but it was just too late. Just too late.

CHAPTER TWENTY-THREE

I woke with my inner lip swollen and blood caked on my gums. My forehead, once again, was painful to touch. I felt washed out. I might have slept, but I hadn't rested.

At breakfast the other players were sullen. The day at Narayan's had done nothing for their spirits.

'Water in the pool was warm,' said Donald.

'And there was a funny smell to it,' said Geoff.

'He,' said Paul, pointing to Robin, who sat alone with his paper, 'and that Narayan spent the whole day by themselves. Chatting away they were.'

Kidleigh had failed to emerge.

'Cor, you could smell the stink right down the corridor,' Ernie grimaced.

Robin announced his intention to take Kidleigh's place at the crease this morning. He expected a full day's batting from us. We needed a good total to bowl at tomorrow.

'And for god's sake don't panic when you see the leg-spinner. Watch the flight of the ball and play it on its merits.'

No one looked up. No one said a word I could see minds churning in silence, some determined to slog the ball out of sheer spite. I kept my eyes on Robin, but he avoided my stare. He sat down again with his paper, blithely indifferent to his players' mounting hostility.

'How about that date, then, DTS?' Ernie ribbed me with a big grin.

'Yeah, how about it?' the others chimed in gleefully. They seized on the chance for some good-natured piss-taking, a relief from the sour atmosphere.

I laughed and looked down shyly. It was easier than making up a lie and it seemed to satisfy them.

'You know you look worse than ever,' Paul observed, eyeing my forehead and swollen mouth.

'Prettier than you, I reckon,' Ernie quipped, and got the first proper laugh of the day.

The press was full of Siva. It was a strange sensation to sit on the air-conditioned coach and read about the 'disappearance', knowing all the while that the great cricketer was at this moment preparing what he undoubtedly intended to be a triumphant return. Party leaders in Madras demanded 'police action'. From Delhi came expressions of dismay. Siva, it was said, was a 'national treasure'. If the local powers had managed to misplace him it was just further proof of their inability to govern and the inevitability of President's Rule. More 'mob leaders' had been arrested. The continuing lock-out at Shrapley's factory, where all the trouble had started, was barely mentioned.

Even through the coach's tinted windows the signs of tension were plain. Police in force brandished riot shields at every intersection, bus stop and open space. Madras was hectically, frantically busy. Mount Road was awash with cars, rickshas, bicycles, lorries, horse-drawn tongas, bullock carts, and in and amongst them people on foot – women carrying huge loads, children dancing and skipping in the traffic, old men limping, beggars, holy men, traders, road workers.

Kushwant cursed his usual curses. He despised these Southerners, with their impenetrable language, their inedible food, their impossible climate. The leafleters were out again. Agile young people moved from car to car in the creeping traffic stuffing paper through open windows, leaping on and off buses, shouting and chanting incessantly. This time they ignored us. Perhaps they had read the name of the Bank on the side of the coach.

At the ground a long chain of police, at least two deep right around, encircled the stadium. They were all armed with lathis and riot shields. Every hundred yards or so a little knot would form around an open-backed lorry stocked with guns, rifles, tear gas and god knows what else. Spectators were searched as they filed through the gates. Long queues formed at each entrance, making the scene even more chaotic than usual. Fierce arguments and angry twisted faces disfigured the queues. Stinging insults flew through the air with the betel juice and phlegm.

We were again ushered through the corridor of green uniforms. The players set about their customary preparations. Paul Walker smoked a cigarette slowly, deliberately, then strapped on his pads. Robin combed and recombed his thinning hair, then checked and rechecked his kit. He cleaned the studs on his boots. He removed the rubber grip from the bat handle then unwound and tightly rewound the black twine and replaced the grip. With a flourish he pulled his dark blue county cap down firmly and snapped the brim crisply above his eyes.

The score was forty for one. With Kidleigh absent, in effect, forty for two. Robin marked his guard with toe pointed like a dancer's. The ground was packed and the crowd vocal. Many were on their feet throughout, cheering the players and booing the cops on the boundary. The cauldron was bubbling. The Indian cricketers, keen to see the fall of an early wicket, crowded the batsmen and stalked in swiftly, silently as the bowler bowled. The spectators bayed at every ball. The police turned round and round in their places. It was hot, but we all knew it would get much hotter as the sun rose in the pale immense sky, boring in on us from the Bay of Bengal.

My tour-mates retreated to the safety of the dressing room and a game of cards. I stood on the balcony. Below me sat Narayan. I saw his little bald patch nestling like an egg amidst thick, oily hair. Next to him sat Cuthbert, red nose peeking out from under a comically shrunken sunhat. They sat in comfort, two lords enthroned. It was that damned complacency again, the conviction that one simply cannot be touched by the things that touch other people, and one doesn't let on if one is. Chepauk was their place, their pleasure ground, or so they thought. Narayan acknowledged friends with a wave and a cheerful smile, carefully ignoring the humming, buzzing, swirling turbulence rippling through the crowd beyond the members' enclosure.

Robin cover drove the opening bowler, then steered him wide of gully for four. The applause was generous enough. He took two steps down the wicket, lightly tapped a suspicious piece of turf, then returned to the crease and assumed his picture-perfect stance: economical, erect, statuesque.

I could watch no more. I joined my colleagues inside. Dougie busied himself with odd little tasks, oiling bats and sharpening studs. He insisted on examining and then deftly bandaging a miniscule blister on Geoff Robinson's big toe. He was nervous, but somehow revitalised. Perhaps it was the sense of danger. Perhaps it was just the prospect of seeing Robin Barnett get his come-uppance.

I paced the dressing room. Where the hell was Gopal? This was no time to be late. I needed those papers. Lakshmi needed those papers. What if Robin's people made contact and I still didn't have them?

'Either sit still or go for a walk, DTS, you're driving me bonkers,' Ernie said.

I collapsed in the nearest chair as if shot.

'You've put Ernie off his rummy,' said Donald.

'Lord knows what you were up to last night,' Ernie boomed, studying his hand as if it held the mysteries of the universe.

In cricket, time is elastic. Some days, the sessions roll past each other in the blink of an eye. Wickets fall, runs are scored, the match seems to race towards a conclusion no matter how hard one side or the other tries to inhibit it. Other days, nothing happens. One ball follows another in an endless recurring cycle. Time opens up, as in sleep, and you hover in it weightlessly. This morning it was going too fast and not fast enough. Ahead of me was a deadline. *The Banner* would be on the streets by two o'clock. Time, one way or another, would have run out.

There was no sign, either, of Mohan or Siva. When and how would the police move against Narayan? Would Mohan keep his word? Would he play tricks and deceive us? An utterly untrustworthy man, everyone said so. Why had we accepted his assurances? How could we be so naive?

Lakshmi had taught me at least one lesson: never underestimate the brutality of the would-be masters of India. I thought of the bright, beautiful, pugnacious journalist who had picked me up that first afternoon in San Thomé. How cool she had been in Mohan's office! How fierce on the beach afterwards!

'We're different' she had said.

A wicket fell. There was a savage, delighted, vindictive roar. I looked out over the balcony. Robin was still there, prodding the pitch. Paul Walker was on his way back to the pavilion, leaving behind a set of stumps in some disarray. Below, Cuthbert and Narayan joined in polite applause for the dismissed batsman, who hurried past them with a surprising spring in his step.

By now Chaughiri was on and causing problems with every ball. The turn was slow, but more than enough to discomfort the batsmen. Occasionally he surprised everyone, including the keeper, with a faster one that bounced and straightened. In no time at all the next wicket fell and another batsman joined Robin at the wicket. It was sixty-eight for three, plus the bedridden Kidleigh. Robin was unperturbed. He was in his element, occupying the crease as if it was the last redoubt. He played Chaughiri with care and began to shield the other batsmen from him. He used his feet fluently and smothered the spin with an angled bat. Once in a while he would step back and dab the ball down to third man. Even the phlegmatic Chaughiri applauded.

I was once more on my feet and pacing. I circled the dressing room again and again. The others noticed, but by now strange behaviour was the least they expected from me. To my horror the lunch interval arrived and there was still no word from Gopal. We were ninety-five for four, with Robin forty-eight not out. Dougie made me sit down with the others. The heat inside was now almost as bad as out in the middle. Robin showered, towelled off vigorously, then sat in shorts and vest and nursed a cup of herbal tea, silently planning the next phase of his batting campaign.

'Never seen such a well-disguised googly,' Dougie observed to no one in particular. 'Impossible to pick, I'd say.'

Robin looked up. 'Not impossible. You need to concentrate. You need to study. There are signs, if you watch closely enough.'

Paul Walker's head swivelled from his half-eaten sandwich. 'Well, don't keep it a bloody secret,' he said.

'It's not as easy as that,' Robin retorted calmly. 'It takes a little time.'

Paul's mask of laconic indifference slipped and for a moment I thought he would leap on Robin and crack his skull. Dougie feared it as well, and intervened by offering another round of juice to the players.

Play resumed after lunch. The heat was at its worst. Even in the dressing room we soaked through our shirts. I thought: What if they've bought off Mohan? What if Gopal came with the papers and it was already too late? What if Robin's people decided they didn't need the papers after all? Why was I being left here to sweat and worry? What new plot was being hatched to deny me the relief I had earned?

Out in the middle Robin played a maiden over from Chaughiri. Bowler and batsman ignored each other, absorbed as they were in their own calculations. A thin layer of haze seemed to rise off the pitch. Above it the strong sunlight quivered in streams of intense heat. The cry of an appeal soared up from somewhere near the wicket. After a tantalising pause, there was an explosive roar of triumph from the crowd. Ernie Fairbanks was out, to Chaughiri, playing for a googly that never turned.

'It's you next, son.' Dougie almost apologised for it. He helped me sort out pads, box, gloves, sweat-bands. I went through the routine, familiar from ten summers on the county circuit, in a trance.

'Don't worry, lad,' Dougie whispered as he fiddled with a strap. 'Don't worry. Don't worry.'

It was all he could say, and it was said more to keep his own nerves intact than to build up my flagging courage.

Suddenly I was sure she was dead. Gopal already knew, and that was why he hadn't brought me the papers. Her body had been washed up on that beautiful beach, pale and stiff. I would be told the news after stumps. I was gripped by a dull horror. I slumped in a chair inside the balcony and stared out over the vast grey-green circle of Chepauk with its writhing human garland. The noise of the crowd was louder than before, but I couldn't focus on it. I was like a radio receiver that had lost its tuner. I couldn't get the signals straight. Out on the field a ball was delivered. It turned sharply, beat the batsman, and skidded into the wicket-keeper's gloves. Were the people pleased? Were they happy, or were they livid with anger? Was it cricket out there, or something else entirely?

There was a knock on the dressing room door. Dougie answered it. Hushed words were exchanged. Dougie called to me. Without looking at the other players (though I was conscious they were looking at me), I rose and walked to the door.

It was Nararyan, accompanied by two broad-shouldered men in brightly printed flower-patterned shirts and pressed synthetic trousers. All three glistened with sweat. No word was spoken. I looked at Narayan, who looked back at me in disgust, then turned on his heels and began walking away. The two big men stood in place until I moved to follow Narayan down the hall. It was awkward moving in my pads, but too late to go back and change them.

Silently we descended the stairway that leads to the members' seats. The familiar route was disrupted by a sudden left turn that admitted us to a strange series of lightless, sweltering corridors. Only a muted surging sound, as of the sea at a great distance at night, proved that the match was still going on, Chaughiri was bowling, and Robin was sticking out a long leg in a forward defensive push.

Narayan stopped and faced me. The two men behind came up

on either side and also stopped. I looked around. We were in a room with rakes, rough coir bags stuffed with dry brown grass cuttings, and soggy squares of green turf mashed in a pile. A thin slat of sunlight penetrated from above a painted wooden door on the far side of the room. The ceiling was cold concrete and it dripped green condensation. We heard an agitated rumbling, like a herd of cattle trampling over a bridge in panic.

'Now you will hand over our papers,' Narayan said, with no trace of his usual bumptious politeness. In the weird half-light he looked pallid, olive-green, cadaverous.

Next to me I smelled the two slick speechless goondas and felt their breathing. The noise from above grew more insistent. The cattle were stampeding.

'No one sees any papers until I see Lakshmi,' I said. I was surprised how rational and confident it sounded. I hadn't thought what I was going to do. Bluffing was never my strong point, but I had no alternative.

'It is also possible for you to disappear, Mr Stott,' said Narayan, feverish but controlled. 'A South African agent operating in India can disappear and no one will shed a tear, certainly not the papers or the police. You were trying to recruit cricketers for a pirate tour. Worse, you were trying to recruit Siva Ramachandran. No one would be surprised if harm was to come to such a person in Madras.'

'Where is she?' I demanded. How harsh my voice sounded in that horrific little hole somewhere in the bowels of the great cricket ground. 'Threaten all you like. I heard it all from Robin last night. You want your bloody papers? You want all your bloody papers?' I paused and looked him directly in his jaundiced eyes. 'You want the copies too?'

Narayan thought for a moment. Shadows ran across the horizontal beam of light causing a strobe-like ripple in the dark storage room. I suddenly became absurdly self-conscious of my batting pads. Were they a pathetic tip-off to those earnest men of politics that after all they were dealing with nothing more than a mere cricketer?

But the mere cricketer's bluff worked, to his own surprise. Narayan spoke briefly and one of the two big men promptly vanished from my side.

'We will wait.'

The rumble overhead was now a thundering roar. There were

successive reports, like gunshots, followed immediately by tremendous crunching echoes. Maybe it was my imagination. I thought I felt the great concrete stadium shudder. The three of us – Narayan, his goonda, and I – waited in the little room, sweating, listening.

'David!'

She was pushed in front of me, her arm twisted behind her back by the big goonda. Her clothes were filthy. Her face was smudged. Both eyes were shadowed with bruises. There was a red graze on her chin. Her hair was tangled and glued to her forehead and cheeks.

'Lakshmi!'

'The papers!' Narayan shouted. He was near hysteria.

'Stuff your papers.'

I swung a padded leg and hard-toed cricket boot at the ankle of the goonda holding Lakshmi. He screamed and released her. Before he could stick out fat arm to restrain her, she had thrown herself at Narayan. His portly figure crashed backward against the painted door which wobbled for a moment on rusty hinges, then fell outwards into the light.

Sunshine streamed through and blinded us all. Lakshmi took my hand and together we trampled over Narayan and ran into the open.

We were on the pitch at the far end of the ground. Our eyes adjusted and we found ourselves in the midst of chaos. The crowd in the stands had erupted.

There were large gaps in the boundary fence. Young men grabbed broken shards of concrete and twisted metal spikes torn from the fence and hurled them at the police. Incessant, ruthless, deafening chanting came from all around. In one corner police fought a pitched battle with spectators who pelted them with bottles, sticks, tin cans, and a seemingly limitless supply of oranges and tangerines. Rolled up newspapers were used as truncheons against lathis. All around faces wore dispossessed looks of inflamed outrage. Tear gas wafted across the ground. It stung my eyes and burned the inside of my nose and throat.

In the centre of the pitch, surrounded by an army of lathi-carrying police, the Indian players huddled, with Robin lost somewhere amongst them.

Five young spectators ran past us, followed by a posse of charging police. Lakshmi pulled me in the opposite direction, towards the pavilion. I looked back and saw Narayan and his two goondas pursuing us over what had been, till recently, the long-leg boundary. Fruit littered the outfield. The crowd remaining in the stands taunted the police. A great wave of anger spread over the ground and lapped against the concrete walls.

A group of spectators charged on to the field and were met by a wedge-shaped detachment from the praetorian guard surrounding the players in the middle. They collided directly in front of us. As the lathis cracked with a sickening slap, Narayan and his men came up behind us. One of them made a grab for Lakshmi. A policeman, seeing me in my whites and pads and no doubt wondering how I had strayed from the wicket, swooped in to protect us. He raised his lathi high and to his right and brought it down and across Narayan's temple with the perfect power of a hook for six. The banker collapsed, blood trickling over his face. Meanwhile the enraged spectators swarmed over us and the two goondas were swallowed up in the fighting.

Lakshmi and I ran and ran. It must have been an odd sight, an English cricketer and an Indian woman fleeing hand in hand through a riot-torn Chepauk. The police dragged off spectator after spectator – young and old, women and men – through the gates near the pavilion. Blood ran down shirts, saris, lungis. The pavilion itself was guarded by a police cordon, but the members pent up there seemed as overwrought as anyone. They argued and shouted and cursed the police, the mob, each other. With no questions the police let us through. We must have looked, despite everything, as if we belonged. As we dashed up the steps a fist fight broke out among the members and the police stood by helpless, confused, not knowing which way to look, or who to attack.

I picked up a newspaper lying on the steps smudged and wrinkled but still readable.

MADRAS BANKER IN SOUTH AFRICAN PLOT

It was the boldest type I'd ever seen in *The Banner*.

Dougie's face broke into a broad grin when he saw us. Paul, Geoff, Ernie and the others gaped. Lakshmi and I stood panting, quaking, our eyes red and running with tear gas.

'Why don't you ask the young lady to sit down, DTS?' said Paul in his flattest sardonic drawl.

Donald produced a chair and with studied good manners

offered it to Lakshmi. She hesitated, bewildered: was this safety, at last, in a cricketers' dressing room?

'It's all right, love,' Ernie said. 'We won't eat you.'

I spread *The Banner* out on the table. Everyone read. In the first paragraph were the names Narayan, Coromandel Coast Investments, Roy Cuthbert and Robin Barnett. South African perfidy, Indian collaborators, stooge cricketers. They know how to write this kind of thing in India (they've had the practice) and they hadn't muffed the chance.

'An abortive cricket coup,' *The Banner* predicted.

Paul Walker laughed. The others just wondered.

Dougie tended Lakshmi. He told her not to worry. He asked about her aches and pains. He applied an ice pack to a bruised elbow. He even helped her wash her face and hands. He treated her the way he treated us. Somehow it seemed different applied to a woman.

The story in the paper had been the spark, that was clear. But now I saw home-made banners in the crowd with various slogans. One read in English: 'No Siva No Cricket!'

The acrid bite of tear gas lingered in the air. The players coughed and cried.

'Cold water,' Dougie said. 'It cuts the irritation.'

I wondered how he knew that.

Chepauk had resolved its conflicts into a series of concentric circles. In the centre were Robin and the Indian players and umpires. Ringing them was a battalion of police who, having managed to clear the field of protesting spectators, now appeared uncertain how to deal with the third, outer ring: the thousands standing on the inclined terraces and shouting themselves hoarse. The police could not, dared not clear the stands. The crowd could not, dared not trespass further on the playing field. The tumult rose like a whirlpool over Chepauk and for a moment it threatened to suck everyone – spectators, players, police – into the heavens and despatch us somewhere to the east in the Bay of Bengal.

A howl echoed from the far end. I couldn't make out what it was. The noise swelled and reached an ecstatic climax. It was as if all the English wickets had fallen at once. He held his arms aloft, straight and motionless. Surrounded by a small troop of armed police he turned first one way then another, acknowledging the cheers. From all across the ground people reached out to him.

Siva the prodigal was back. Not at the members' end, but at the popular end. Vindicated. Triumphant.

'Well I'll be fucked,' said Ernie, staring out across the bright stormy scene. 'I'll be completely fucked.'

The scene changed. It wasn't exactly calm or quiet, but the tension seeped out, like air through a small puncture. The crowd's fury abated.

Eventually people resumed their seats. The banners were no longer held aloft in anger but in celebration. Along with the several hundred arrested and dragged from the ground, I imagined Narayan, condemned to at least a few hours in Mohan's cells before he was bailed out by a flunkey. There was no sign of the red nose and white sunhat of Roy Cuthbert.

Cautiously the police dispersed around the boundary. A freshening breeze blew away the tear gas. Siva remained standing at the far end. His gestures appealed for a return to calm, a return to order, a return to cricket.

Yes, we played cricket. The crowd wanted it. The police wanted it. Who were we to refuse?

Half an hour later I went in to bat. I left Lakshmi in the care and protection of my fellow players. She seemed to be enjoying the situation. She'd spent the night locked up with a guard in one of the old changing rooms under the stands.

'The rats kept their distance, thank god. Even the human ones.'

When I joined Robin he was undefeated on fifty-nine. Throughout the riot and Siva's near miraculous return, he had remained in the middle. When play resumed he had somehow managed to recover his concentration, though for overs he was strokeless and scoreless, as though his whole being had gone on the defensive.

He refused to acknowledge me as I walked out and took my guard. He patted the turf in a world of his own. Chaughiri bowled. The ball hovered for a timeless moment. I played forward and was struck on the pad. The ball rolled to short-leg.

There were scattered appeals from the crowd, but most were silent. The peace was fragile. No one wanted to threaten it for an extremely dodgy lbw. The next one pitched on middle stump, I played back, it bounced like a tennis ball and turned wide of the leg.

That was the end of the over. Robin strolled down the pitch. I met him in the middle.

'Hail the conquering hero,' Robin muttered. 'I told you it was a cheap theatrical stunt, that vanishing act.' He blazed, eyes clear and white in the taut brown face.

'It's finished, Robin,' I said.

'How do you make that?'

'It's in *The Banner* – Grand Prix Cricket, CCI, the lot. You and your South African friends.'

He froze. The paper reached everywhere in this city but the middle of its celebrated cricket pitch.

'Narayan will deny it. I will deny it,' he breathed.

'Narayan will be arrested. Probably has been already,' I smiled at the thought. 'Mohan has evidence that he ordered the umpire's murder.'

'You'll never see that woman alive again,' he hissed at me.

'She's in the dressing room now. The lads are looking after her.'

He didn't bat an eyelid. Slowly he withdrew and returned to his crease. I looked up at the balcony. Dougie gave me a wave and a smile.

Robin faced up to the off-spinner at the other end. He drove the first ball straight past me. Or rather, straight at me. I hopped over it as it rocketed to the boundary. Suddenly hungry for runs, he pushed the next for a single. I took guard at the far end. The bowler was getting turn, but not a lot. His flight was easier to read than Chaughiri's. I played forward defensive strokes to three balls in succession – the careworn, boring forward prod that has brought the county game into such disrepute. I didn't mind. I was looking. I was waiting for something. I wanted to be on the front foot when it came.

The last ball was in the right spot. My backlift was perfect. I drove it as hard and straight as I could. It smashed the stumps at the far end, missing Robin's knee by inches. There was no hop from him. He stood in place and glared at me down the pitch.

Chaughiri took the ball. Robin waited in total stillness. Four jerky steps and the arm whizzed over, launching the ball like a satellite in orbit. Robin let it strike the bat and killed the spin. Chaughiri came in again – a high-flighted delivery that again struck the pad and rolled harmlessly away. The next one he tried to turn behind, but square leg cut it off. Robin paced the crease like a caged animal. The crowd, sensing his frustration, began to barrack him. He was utterly alone.

Chaughiri bowled. The same four paces. The same high flight. Robin stretched far down the pitch and played a violent stroke off the front foot. The bat flowed with terrific power directly at me and finished high above the batsman's head. But the ball, a perfectly concealed googly, sneaked between bat and pad and knocked both bails into the air.

Staring icily ahead Robin strode from the wicket. I watched his erect carriage disappear into the members' enclosure. It was the last I ever saw of him.

POSTSCRIPT

I can't remember the rest of the innings, just the noise of the jubilant crowd celebrating Chaughiri's conquest of Robin Barnett. I recall skying a catch to the wicket-keeper and feeling nothing but relief.

Lakshmi was waiting in the dressing room when I returned. Soaked in sweat, I embraced her. It felt so good to feel her body alive that it didn't seem to matter any more that it wasn't mine. The players laughed and Paul Walker gave a languid clap.

Robin vanished. A week later he turned up in England, but refused to comment on any of the stories then appearing daily on television and in the papers.

Chaos reigned in Madras. We managed to finish our match under the captaincy of Ernie Fairbanks. The papers called it 'an honourable draw'.

Lakshmi wrote a long story detailing the background to Grand Prix Cricket and Coromandel Coast Investments, but leaving out certain well-known names. Brilliant stuff, run front page by *The Banner* and syndicated throughout India. She was none too pleased, however, with the English press, who used her material but omitted any mention of its original source.

Lakshmi had been reluctant to spare Siva in her articles but Srini insisted; it was part of our deal. The incriminating documents, of course, were now in Siva's possession, thanks to Mohan. But Siva was only too well aware that there were other documents and, more dangerous than that, other people, who knew what he had done and how far he had gone to cover it up, even though in the end it had been short of murder. When we explained the deal we'd made with Siva and Mohan, Lakshmi once again taxed me with naivety.

'It is all very well for you. You are leaving. But what about Srini? Mohan hates him already. As long as he is out there, Siva will feel nervous. And you know what nerves can do to a man in his position.'

Srini dismissed the notion with a laugh. How long did anyone have a right to live anyway? But I sent one last note to Siva, reminding him there was always one person who knew the whole story, and however far away I might be I would find a way, if the need arose, to come back to Madras and reveal all. I didn't get an answer to that. I didn't need one.

I think it was Mohan who said to me that information was power. I had thought he was trying to pull the wool over my eyes, but experience has since taught me otherwise. With what Mohan himself now knew, or had guessed, he too had acquired yet more power, and from Lakshmi's letters to me (I tear open the aerogrammes so excitedly I sometimes have to sellotape them back together) I have learned that he and Siva appear to have struck up a good 'working' relationship. 'The police and their friends in high places need Siva,' Lakshmi explained. 'They would never blow the whistle on such a useful figure.'

I guess the whole thing was really a draw. It was like the match itself: there just weren't enough overs left to complete it. But like all draws, it gave me a chance to learn something about the form and fitness of the opposition.

Poor Gopal. By the time he'd arrived with the papers the police had sealed the ground and he had spent several anxious hours frantically circling the stadium. We dined together, Lakshmi, Srini, Gopal and I, on my last night in Madras, and sang each others' praises. Srini and Gopal got into a long argument about the nature of the Party, which Gopal insisted was still the lesser of two evils. I spent a lot of time staring at Lakshmi, who had covered her bruises with make-up and looked more ravishing than ever.

Narayan was indicted for the murder of the umpire and forced to post an enormous bail. The incident was given sensational publicity and the banker was disgraced, but he never actually stood trial. 'A 'technicality' forced the government to drop the charges. Sartar was not so lucky. Somewhere in India he is serving an endless prison sentence.

Siva announced his retirement from Test cricket the day after his momentous reappearance. He explained that he had required a period of private meditation before taking such an important decision. At the same time he declared his candidacy for the State Legislative Assembly. He emerged as a new strong man in the Party, and eventually won his election.

The workers at Shrapley's factory were allowed back to work, their wage-cut rescinded. Lakshmi felt this was as much due to Shrapley's own keen political instinct as to Siva's influence. Not long after, some of the militants were beaten up and several have now gone missing. There has been a strike at another factory, more disturbances in the streets, and this time the State Ministry, with Siva among its leaders, is openly talking of bringing in the army.

Robin has taken up residence in South Africa, where he plays in the Currie Cup and scores masses of runs. Apparently he is a popular figure there. Roy Cuthbert emerged from the whole episode unscathed. His newspapers have recently imported a young South African tennis prodigy to play at Wimbledon under British colours.

I ended up with a contract after all. Robin's old county, looking for an experienced middle order batsman to shore up the side after their captain's departure, offered me a job. Dougie's recommendation clinched it. They were impressed, I was told, by my 'exemplary loyalty'.

In her most recent letter Lakshmi writes that she plans to visit England this summer. Not, of course, to watch me graft for runs at Worcester or Weston-Super-Mare, but to follow up some leads Srini gave her on South African links with the English cricket establishment. I can't wait to see her.